"Take Your Pick,"

he offered. "The couch, or the bed in the other room." He rose and Malou was pierced by a stab of regret.

"I'm fine here," Malou answered, no longer wanting the separation she had caused.

"Good choice." He reached for a thick log and settled it expertly on the fire, then tucked the quilt up around Malou's shoulders. "There, that ought to keep you through the night. Need anything else?"

"Just you," Malou whispered, but it was too late, for Cam was already out of earshot.

TORY CATES
undertook a career in journalism that has taken her to the Southwest many times. Tory is a professional photographer as well as an avid cross-country skier.

Dear Reader:

Romance readers have been enthusiastic about Silhouette Special Editions for years. And that's not by accident: Special Editions were the first of their kind and continue to feature realistic stories with heightened romantic tension.

The longer stories, sophisticated style, greater sensual detail and variety that made Special Editions popular are the same elements that will make you want to read book after book.

We hope that you enjoy this Special Edition today, and will enjoy many more.

The Editors at Silhouette Books

TORY CATES
Different Dreams

Silhouette Special Edition
Published by Silhouette Books New York
America's Publisher of Contemporary Romance

Silhouette Books by Tory Cates

Handful of Sky (SE #65)
Where Aspens Quake (SE #125)
Cloud Waltzer (SE #196)
Different Dreams (SE #236)

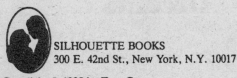

SILHOUETTE BOOKS
300 E. 42nd St., New York, N.Y. 10017

Copyright © 1985 by Tory Cates

Distributed by Pocket Books

ISBN: 0-373-09236-9

First Silhouette Books printing May, 1985

10 9 8 7 6 5 4 3 2 1

Map by Ray Lundgren

America's Publisher of Contemporary Romance

Printed in the U.S.A.

To my brother, John,
the model for all my
boldly creative entrepreneurs.

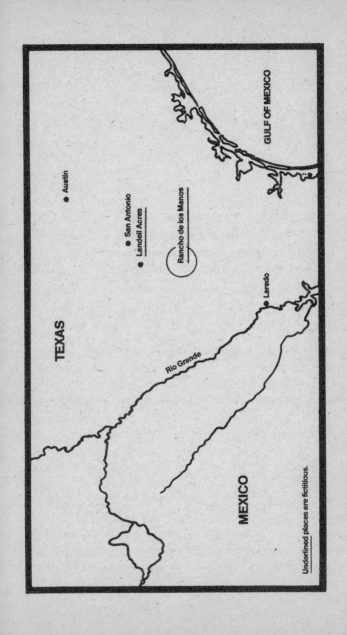

Chapter One

The April breeze was laden with the fresh green scent of mesquite buds just beginning to blossom. It riffled gently through Malou Sanders's wispy, wheat-colored hair, a color that was repeated in her khaki shirt and shorts. She breathed in the moist air, knowing that the Texas sun, still just a scarlet crack of dawn along the far horizon, would sear every bit of softness out of the air before long. Spring in this sunbaked land so close to where the sweltering borders of Mexico and the U.S. rubbed together was little more than a crack in time. By May, just a week away, the brief season would be well on its way to becoming memory.

Sitting down on a large flat rock within the grassy, fenced-in enclosure, Malou tucked up her legs—extravagantly long for her height and already tanned to a rich coppery color—and lifted the binoculars hanging by a strap around her neck to scan the two hundred acres spreading out before her.

Her eyes burned slightly from lack of sleep. She blinked them and focused on her search. In an unconscious gesture of nervousness, she nibbled at her bottom lip, exposing teeth that were strong and white but ever so slightly crooked. Malou had never been bothered enough by the tiny imperfection to correct it.

"Where are you, Jezebel?" she whispered to herself as she strained to see beyond the stands of prickly pear and mesquite that blocked her view.

Her gaze slid over sleeping forms that, from a distance, appeared to be slightly fuzzy, tawny gray boulders. They weren't. The furry clumps were monkeys, Japanese macaque monkeys to be precise. To Malou Sanders, resident manager of the South Texas Primate Research Center, known locally as El Rancho de los Monos—the Monkey Ranch—they were much more. Besides being the focus of her life's work, each and every one of them was a clear and distinct individual complete with a unique face, name, family history, and personality. And one was missing. That was her first worry. Her second worry also had a name, though no face. The name was Mr. Cameron Landell, and he was a far more serious source of concern.

When, at long last, Malou had been able to chase that ominous name from her thoughts and fallen asleep last night, there had been 313 members in the troop. If her calculations were correct, there should be 314 monkeys this morning. She swiveled around searching for the newest troop member to be born in this strange land so far from their ancestral home in Japan. She hadn't worried this much about the other births, but Jezebel was different. Since

Jezebel herself had been abandoned by her mother as an infant, there was no telling what the flighty creature might do after delivering her first baby.

"Where are you, you little bubble brain?" Malou muttered to herself; like all the monkeys, in Malou's eyes Jezebel had a very pronounced personality. She reminded Malou of a cross between the scatterbrained comedienne Gracie Allen and a simian Huck Finn, always looking for adventure and never wanting to grow up.

While Malou was studying the sleeping macaques' watermelon pink faces, suddenly, as if a switch had been thrown, they all came to life at once. As many times as she'd witnessed the awakening, it never failed to thrill Malou. For the moment she forgot her anxiety about the newborn and her even more pressing preoccupation with this Cameron Landell person who suddenly loomed so large in her life. Being present at the instant when the complex drama that was macaque life began anew with the rising of the sun was Malou's reward for the long years she'd spent in lecture halls and labs. Her reward for the absorption in her field that had left her few outside interests and a social life that extended no further than her colleagues and her family. For Malou—when the sun was rising, at least—it was enough.

Elbows propped on brown knees, binoculars pressed to her face, Malou became lost in the quickening pace of activity. A streak of gray fuzzed across the prairie, followed hotly by three more streaks as a quartet of young monkeys, "juveniles" in primatology terms, chased one another across the dusty earth. New mothers with infants snuggled to their bellies awoke to suckle their babies. Sumo, the troop's alpha male, its leader, stretched with a lordly yawn. His powerful squat body and combative nature gave clues to the origin of his name. A small harem of the highest-ranking females began to groom him, combing carefully through his thick fur. He remained imperiously detached throughout the process.

Lower-ranking females and their offspring occupied spots farther away from the center of the troop. Farther still, the troop's cast-outs, the peripheral males, perched in scrubby mesquite trees along the fence enclosing the compound. Malou chuckled. It was so much like small-town human society, with the mayor and his cronies living at the center of town and the less affluent and prestigious fanning out from there.

It was all so complicated, she marveled, yet so orderly. So structured, yet so unpredictable. She pulled out her field notebook and jotted down some notes on the interactions she was observing.

As she continued watching, Malou saw that she wasn't the only one observing the troop. Kojiwa, at well over thirty the oldest monkey in the troop, sat in the shade of a cactus, keeping an eye on the troop he had once led. The old curmudgeon held a special place in Malou's heart, for he was one of the few males who could be counted on to intervene in a fight in behalf of a weaker combatant. He was also the only male she'd ever seen care for an abandoned infant. That infant had been the errant Jezebel.

Just as Malou was reflecting on the unique relationship between Kojiwa and his adopted daughter, Jezebel, the capered out of the backcountry bush, rushing forward to greet her guardian. Malou winced. Jezebel was alone and clearly no longer pregnant. All Malou's worst fears were confirmed. Knowing no better, Jezebel had abandoned the baby she'd borne during the night, just as her own mother had abandoned her.

Before Malou could begin searching for the baby, a distant, mechanical hum intruded to remind her of far greater worries.

Just as he promised! Malou fumed, remembering the telegram she'd received yesterday. Undoubtedly, Landell would have called had the phone been working. But the phone was just one of a dozen problems she'd had to postpone solving ever since Mr. Stallings had died two weeks earlier. The telegram had said Landell would arrive bright and early. It was certainly early, but for Malou, the morning had now become considerably less bright.

She trained her binoculars on the plume of dust rising along the dirt road that led up to the compound, and she groaned softly. Of course he *would* drive a Mercedes 380SL. It fit the land developer's image to a T. She was sure Cameron Landell would live up to all her worst fears of what a soulless, money-grubbing Texas wheeler-dealer was like. He was of a type and from a world that usually would never concern her. But, because of Mr. Stallings's death, their worlds had collided: Cameron Landell was the new owner of El Rancho de Los Monos. Malou couldn't concern herself anymore with Jezebel's baby; she had the whole troop's survival to worry about now.

The claret-colored Mercedes stopped alongside the portable building that served as both research station and home for Malou and for Ernie Pierce, the researcher-in-residence temporarily living at the ranch. Malou didn't make a move. She kept her binoculars trained on the Mercedes and waited for her first glimpse of her adversary.

Cameron Landell stepped out and, in one split second, shot Malou's preconceptions all to hell. Where she'd expected a paunchy middle-ager, Cameron Landell looked to be the kind of man that, even when he did reach middle-age, would never let his age show. He had the tight, spare build of a prizefighter or a dancer, an aggressive modern dancer. And instead of the polyester leisure suit she would have predicted, Landell was wearing loose-fitting trousers belted at the waist and a cotton shirt with the sleeves rolled up. A felt fedora shielding his eyes from the sun gave Landell the look of a forties land surveyor.

Malou shifted her focus and zoomed in on his face. She needed clues and needed them fast. She needed to know everything she could about this man. Again, the face surprised her. She'd figured that a man responsible for turning that much natural, unspoiled land into ticky-tacky tract housing would have a much different face. A bland face that never registered any second thoughts, any qualms, any deeper consideration than, will it make money?

But Cameron Landell's face wasn't like that. More than the thickly lashed dark eyes and full mouth, Malou noticed the edgy wariness that animated it. His eyes searched the landscape with a predatory intensity. Malou had the impression that everything Cameron Landell saw registered. That nothing escaped his notice. It was a most unnerving first impression.

His appraisal completed, Landell moved to the front door of the research station. His walk was brisk, much faster than the loping gaits of most Texans she'd known in the ten years since her father, a physics professor, had moved the family from Chicago to Austin to teach at the university there. Landell's was a tough, muscular walk that again brought to Malou's mind the aggressive motions of a modern dancer. Cameron Landell walked like a man in a hurry. Even on a spring morning in the middle of nowhere with the day barely begun.

Malou couldn't hear the sound of his knock against the door of the distant research station, but she could tell from the force Landell put into it that it was loud. Several minutes passed while he stood bouncing slightly from foot to foot like a tennis player waiting to receive a match-point serve. Finally Ernie opened the door.

Her fellow researcher looked as if he too had had a hard night—hair tousled, eyes swollen, shirt buttoned crooked. Of course, Malou reminded herself, Ernie *always* looked as if he'd had a hard night. He was doing some study on visual acuity, comparing the vision of caged versus free-ranging macaques. Malou could never remember the precise subject. Just that it involved running tedious but harmless tests on animals in his lab. Her interest lay strictly with uncaged animals, with the fascinating behavior rituals that bound the troop together. Blinking into the morning sun that sliced across the land, myopic Ernie, blind without his glasses, pointed a vague finger in the general direction of the enclosure. With a brisk wave of both thanks and dismissal, Cameron Landell left Ernie, who was still speaking, and headed toward the enclosure.

Malou sighed and rested the binoculars on her chest. The signs were not good. Not good at all. She'd searched Cameron Landell for signs of vulnerability, softness, a crack in that stern facade. She hadn't found any. Her hands went icy in the south Texas heat. So much depended on this meeting. On her. She had to do whatever was necessary to charm, cajole, intimidate, and/or educate Cameron Landell into keeping the troop together. She stood, pulled herself up to her full five foot four and a half inches, and marched to the front gate. She tried reviving her sagging confidence by reminding herself that she was a competent adult of twenty-seven, a highly trained professional, and a scientist who, at a very early age, had already won several major awards in her field.

Cameron Landell reached the gate before she did. He leaned against it with a loose-jointed ease as he waited on the other side for her. Waited and watched. Malou suddenly became very conscious of her walk and of the length of brown leg her khaki shorts displayed. She even noticed, for the first time ever, how the binoculars pressed against her breasts, rising and falling with each step she took. Landell clearly noticed too, soaking in that detail just as he seemed to absorb every other detail around him. She felt his eyes on her, appraising her as if she were a prime piece of real estate he was interested in acquiring—acquiring and despoiling.

In that same instant, Malou realized something else: She was coming to him. Just like the female monkeys who came to Sumo to offer their services, she had put herself in a subordinate position by being the one to come to Landell. She was certain the same pattern held in human society. Landell probably would have made her come to his office in San Antonio if he hadn't wanted to inspect the property himself. No, Landell was the sort that somehow always turned others into subordinates, always made them come to him.

And that, Malou realized, anger sparking within her, was precisely what he had succeeded in doing to her. He'd managed to make that damned gate he was leaning on into his office for the moment, and to turn her into a humble supplicant coming to him. Well, she hadn't studied the behavior of lower primates for this long without picking up a few tricks of her own. Such as overfamiliarity. She'd observed the way low-status troop members always deferred to Sumo, cringing and cowering and fleeing any contact with the head honcho. Malou was determined to win back the ground she'd inadvertently lost—there would be no cringing or cowering.

"Cam," she called out casually, "I'd forgotten when you said you were coming." She could see by the slight flutter of those thickly fringed, espresso brown eyes that she'd momentarily nonplussed him with her nonchalant greeting. She followed up her advantage by coming to the side of the gate where he waited and thrusting her hand out boldly. "I assume you are Cameron Landell, proud new proprietor of El Rancho de los Monos. As you've no doubt guessed, I'm Malou Sanders, resident manager."

"You're right on the first count." His voice was as clipped and staccato as his walk had been. Betraying origins Eastern and urban, it was a far cry from the good-old-boy Texas drawl she'd anticipated. "As far as being proud goes, that remains to be seen." He took her hand in his. An ironic smile flirted around his lips.

Remembering Sumo's model, Malou brought her free hand over to rest on top of Landell's clasped hand. She patted it lightly in a condescending way, touching him with the easy familiarity that Sumo would use with an underling. "Hope you didn't have *too* much trouble finding the way out," she said, implying that he had experienced difficulties.

"Not really," he answered, still holding her hand, his words edged with mocking irony. "Once you leave San

Antonio, it's pretty easy. You just head south. If you end up in Mexico, you know you've gone too far.'' The edge softened and he smiled. Still holding her hand, he now held her eyes as well.

''And you're clearly not a man who ever goes too far,'' Malou shot back, freeing her hand and her gaze. She'd wanted Landell to be the one to withdraw first, but the feel of his hand, strong and warm against her own, was far too disconcerting; if there was one thing she absolutely could not afford to be at this moment, it was disconcerted.

''Oh, clearly. Never,'' Landell agreed. But the quirk of his eyebrows told Malou that just the opposite was true. Dangerously true. ''And now, Mylou? Milieu? What in the devil is your name?''

''Muh-lou,'' she sounded out the name that no one ever got right the first time. ''It's short for Mary Louise.'' Malou reflexively bit her lip. She shouldn't have told him that. Shouldn't tell the enemy anything more than what was absolutely necessary—name, rank, and serial number.

''Well, Mary Louise . . .''

She knew she shouldn't have told him. She hated her real name. So prissy, so refined, so everything she never wanted to be.

''Malou,'' he corrected himself, catching her look of distaste. ''If you're through trying to one-up me, why don't you tell me the history of this, this *monkey* ranch.''

Malou winced. Landell had seen through her power play so easily. Even more unsettling, though, was his condescending tone when he'd said the word ''monkey.'' It told Malou all she had to know about the contempt in which he held the animals she'd chosen to devote her life to studying.

In any other situation, facing a man as commanding and

as attractive as Cameron Landell, Malou would have withdrawn. She would have retreated, forsaking the human apes she found so bewildering for the company of the lower primates she was more comfortable with. But she couldn't run away now. For once she stayed. She had to.

"One-up? What could you be talking about, Cam?" she asked, dragging out her words with the barest hint of the Southern accent she'd never actually acquired. She would *not* be disconcerted.

Landell smiled, a pirate's grin that said he would be willing to play along—up to a point.

"Step inside your 'monkey' ranch," Malou said, holding open the gate so that he could pass inside. "I'll give you the deluxe tour complete with a history of the troop, and I'll try not to get too esoteric."

"Oh, spare me no epoch-making detail," Landell teased.

Malou smiled tightly at his mockery and launched into the history she'd recited dozens of times for visitors from around the world. This performance, she knew, was the most crucial she would ever give.

"The troop's ancestral home is high atop Mount Arashiyama, Storm Mountain, outside of Kyoto, Japan. For centuries the monkeys lived wild there, feeding on persimmons, chestnuts, and berries, enduring the snow and rain from the indigo clouds that gave the mountain its name. Their breed is often called 'snow monkeys' because they are the only primate other than man able to live in such a cold climate."

Malou glanced over at Landell, attempting to gauge his reaction. It was impossible. He wasn't reacting, he was absorbing—both her words and the animals they described. He watched as a monkey with an infant clinging to her belly bent a mesquite branch down to her mouth and stripped off the tiny leaves.

Malou kept on. "These macaques are the 'see no evil, hear no evil, do no evil' monkeys. The Japanese call them 'little old men of the forest.' They are beloved in their native land and appear in many Japanese fairy tales, where they have a reputation for wiliness."

"I'll bear that in mind," Landell commented, "and not be taken in by any wily macaques."

That was far from the moral Malou had intended to be drawn.

"Now, much as I'm enjoying all this, I have a closing I need to get back for, and if I miss it I'll be out several thousand in earnest money. That would make for a fairly pricey natural history lesson. So, if you have no objection, could we move on to the part of this story that concerns me?"

Malou was so irritated that she had to look away to hide the fumes she felt were pouring off of her. Her glance fell on old Kojiwa and his adopted daughter, Jezebel, lounging in the shade of a leafy mesquite. *This is for you*, she thought, bringing herself under control. She was a model of composure when she turned back to face Cameron Landell.

"Of course," she demurred sweetly, picking up the thread of her narrative again. "In 1947, the Japanese institutionalized their affectionate regard for the snow monkeys by declaring them national treasures."

"Sort of like sacred cows in India, eh?"

The analogy was completely off base, but Malou bit her tongue and continued. "Well, they *were* protected, and the entire mountain was turned into a monkey sanctuary.

Primatologists laid out rations of wheat and apples to coax the animals down out of hiding so they could study them.''

"Hmmphf.''

Malou ignored Landell's derisive snort and went on. Whether Cameron Landell realized it or not, what she had to say was important; and whether he was interested or not, he would hear it.

"Anyway, the monkeys were close enough that researchers could study them, but their social patterns, which caging would have destroyed, were intact. That was so important.''

Unconsciously, the urgency that Malou felt leaked into her words. "That's how they learned how vital kinship is in the macaque world and how it's the basis for each member's status in the troop.'' Malou's excitement about the area that was the subject of her life's work came through, enlivening what she said.

She stopped short when she glanced over and found Cameron Landell staring, no longer at the monkeys capering past, but at her. Staring very hard and very long. She stared straight back. Landell was the first to break off. "It all sounds like monkey heaven back there in the Land of the Rising Sun. So why did the beasts end up here where there is not only no snow, but damned precious little water in *any* form?''

"You're quite right,'' she began again. "It was heaven until the late sixties. Then, with all the provisioning and protection, the population of the Storm Mountain troop exploded and split into two groups. The alpha male stayed with the old troop and they drove the new group off, keeping it away from the rations at the food station. The hungry monkeys of the new troop were led by that old fellow over there.''

Malou pointed to Kojiwa. Abruptly, as if he didn't like being talked about by the meddling humans, Kojiwa turned his pink rump to them and took off, bounding stiffly on all fours across the field.

"With old Kojiwa in the lead, the new troop left Storm Mountain and started raiding gardens in Kyoto. Worse than that, though, the raiding band took to sleeping in the rafters of the Buddhist temples."

"Ho-ho," Landell signaled his comprehension, "and the national treasures became a public nuisance. I can imagine that monkey manure in the temples was not a popular decorating idea with the Japanese people."

His conclusion was annoyingly accurate.

"Not popular at all. There were a lot of suggestions about how to deal with the renegades." Malou tried to keep her voice light, but inwardly she shuddered as she said, "One small faction of primatologists felt that the offending monkeys would make ideal candidates for the . . ." She stumbled over the words. "The dissection table. Primatologists around the world rose up to protest such an immoral waste." Her voice rose with the ongoing urgency of her story. It was a tale whose end had still not been told.

"Not too hard to guess which faction you agreed with, is it?"

"These monkeys, with all that's known about them and their family histories, are invaluable for behavioral research."

The quirk of Landell's eyebrow made Malou aware that she'd turned her last few sentences into an impassioned plea. Her voice was neutrally calm when she began again.

"A worldwide search was conducted to find a new home for the displaced monkeys of Storm Mountain. When the Japanese primatologists called Professor Everitt of the anthro department at the university, he called Mr. Stallings. In addition to being a rancher and a big landowner, Stallings was known to be an animal lover.

"Professor Everitt made Stallings the oddest proposition of the old man's life: If he would fence in a couple hundred acres of his land, he would become the owner of a monkey troop. In return for provisioning the monkeys, once the troop was established, Mr. Stallings could sell any surplus animals he wanted to for lab studies."

"But there never were any 'surplus' animals, were there?" Landell asked with his usual irritating accuracy. He pointed toward the troop poking around for breakfast. "I mean, every one of those stumpy creatures out there is some vital link in the great monkey society you've got going here. Stallings never made a dime on the deal, did he?"

"He stopped caring about that," Malou blurted out, aware too late that she'd tipped her hand. But it *was* too late. Besides, it was the truth and she was tired of tap-dancing around it. "He found out that there are more important things to care about than making money. That the monkeys, keeping them alive and together, was the most crucial thing."

"Most crucial to you," Landell amended.

"Mr. Stallings believed in what we're doing," Malou protested. "Besides, keeping the monkeys wasn't that expensive. My salary is paid by a grant from the National Science Foundation, and Mr. Stallings had money anyway."

" 'Had' is right," Landell shot back. "I didn't know it,

but by the time I met him, his money was either all gone or going fast. There had been a couple of oil wells that ended up spouting dust and a few other bad business investments. When he came to me for a loan on a wildcat well up north, he used his south Texas holdings, including Los Monos, as collateral. That well was a duster too. Mr. Stallings died broke and I ended up with a monkey ranch on my hands.''

Landell stopped and stared down at Malou. ''There's one other thing you should probably know. Stallings went bust trying to protect these monkeys you esteem so highly. Maybe the day-to-day costs of maintaining them don't seem high to you, but there are a few hidden expenses you've no doubt overlooked. Like keeping a couple hundred acres of land fallow. Not using them to raise beef or citrus or anything else that's going to pay you back for the use of that land while taxes are eating you alive. Now *that*, I guarantee you, is not cheap.''

Landell pivoted around, sighting along the fence lines winging out in either direction. ''All this fence. Not cheap. And that pond.'' He pointed to the pond that had been dug into the brown earth for the monkeys to use as their swimming pool, cooling off during the scorching days. Even now, two youngsters were splashing happily. ''Not cheap to keep water pumping through that.''

He continued his survey, looking now at the research station. ''Having those buildings and that road put in. Stringing power lines all the way out here. Putting in a septic tank, a well. Phones. None of it was cheap.''

Malou was caught off-guard. Like a four-year-old child, she'd entered this world and accepted it without question. The range cubes she fed the monkeys once a day during the driest part of the summer were the only expenses she'd seriously considered.

"Never thought about any of it, did you?"

Malou nodded agreement—the truth was too obviously written on her face to attempt a lie.

"Didn't think so. Your type never does."

"My 'type'?"

"Okay, those of your 'socio-economic status.' Those of you from the creamy top of the middle class. Correct me if I'm mistaken."

Malou didn't. Child of the suburbs, her father a university professor and mother a pharmacist, she couldn't. Indulged, an only child, she *had* existed all her life at that creamy top. "Well," she shot back, stung again by the acuity of his perceptions, "correct *me* if I'm wrong, but judging from your car, clothes, and speech, you haven't exactly led a life of deprivation."

"You're wrong," he stated flatly. The only elaboration he offered was, "Cars, clothes, even speech can be acquired if you want them badly enough." Abruptly he changed the subject. "What would one of"—he pointed to the group of monkeys hovering nearby—"your little buddies sell for?"

"As a laboratory animal?" Malou choked out the words. If she hadn't been sure Landell could find his answer in five minutes without her help, she would have refused to answer. But he could. "Fifteen hundred dollars."

He nodded. "Fifteen hundred. Not a spectacular return, but enough to balance off some of Stallings's debt."

"You can't be thinking what I'm afraid you are," Malou said, her very worst nightmare about the troop's future coming to life—the nightmare that all the families would be torn apart and the monkeys sold to labs.

"What? That I might be so unspeakably callous as to want to make back a fraction of the money I've already lost? Yes, believe it or not, that's what I want to do."

Malou turned away, unable to face him with the look of sick shock on her face.

"Though it's absolutely none of your business," Landell informed her, "I'll tell you anyway. I got beat on this deal. Beat bad. Stallings, wonderful humanitarian and friend to monkeys everywhere that he might have been, skinned me on the loan I made to him. He represented Los Monos as a going concern, turning a healthy profit every year. He made off with roughly five times what this place could ever conceivably be worth, sunk it into that duster, then died and left me holding the bag."

"How very discourteous of him." The ice in Malou's voice fairly cracked in the heat.

"So the pretense of cordiality shatters," Landell observed. "And all because I'm not willing to fill in for Stallings as troop benefactor to the tune of a few hundred thousand a year so you can play Jane Goodall or Dian Fossey down here."

Malou was stunned and angered to hear the names of her two childhood heroines on Landell's lips. Stunned that he even knew of the existence of the two women who had rewritten the book on primate study, and angered that he used their names with such cynical contempt. "Those two scientists have added immeasurably to our knowledge of primate behavior." Malou couldn't help the note of prim outrage that tightened her voice. If she'd given in to her true emotions, she would have wept right there in front of this odious Cameron Landell. "If I can make even the smallest fraction of the contributions they have, I'd be delighted to 'play' them for the rest of my life."

"You'd better start thinking about doing it on another stage," Landell told her. "Because I've made all the contribution to monkey study I intend to. This whole fiasco has blown up at just about the worst time imaginable. I needed Stallings to pay back that loan with hard cash and healthy interest so that I could cover my own debts. Not that I expect you to care, but I have two very short weeks before my banker expects me to start paying off the largest note he ever allowed me to put my hands on."

Malou looked away, unwilling to face Landell or the troubles he was telling her of. She had enough of her own.

He took his hat off and slapped it against his thigh in a gesture of annoyance. "Prepare to start dismantling this operation, Ms. Sanders. I'm selling out to the highest bidder who comes along, and if that happens to be a laboratory, so be it."

Malou bit down hard on the inside of her mouth. She would not cry. Not now. She had to think. To do something. To stop him. A chaotic jumble of ideas churned through her mind. She blurted out the first one she could articulate.

"I won't let you do it," she threatened. "I have friends, reporters. If you try sacrificing the troop to your greed, I'll plaster the paper with stories about you slaughtering innocent animals, wasting a priceless research resource."

"So, you plan on adding monkey murderer to my list of credits. A bold threat, Malou, and not a particularly wise one. You've got a lot to learn about the delicate art of negotiation. For starters, it doesn't flourish among heavy-handed threats. I think I've seen enough. I'll be in touch with you about closing the place down and shipping the animals off. If you really care about them, you'd be wise to hunt up a few new homes that are to your liking.''

He strode off without a goodbye. His clipped gait now seemed almost forcefully brutal, but it was herself that Malou derided. She *had* been heavy-handed, and now it was too late to know what might have happened if she had been more reasonable, more open to compromise. The Mercedes had faded to a blood red drop against an immense, sun-bleached background by the time Malou slumped down to sit on a rock.

Several juveniles cautiously approached her. Soon they were scrambling over the rock she sat on, touching her hair and clothes. As usual, though, it was her binoculars that fascinated them most. They were forever entranced by anything shiny and metallic. Anything that glinted in the sun. She felt a tiny furred paw hesitantly reach up and touch the salty tear shimmering on her cheek.

Malou smiled wanly at the little face lifted up to hers, just a figure-eight of deep pink inside a furry ruff. There was so much she'd never be able to make them understand, so much she never wanted them to *have* to understand. A glimpse of Jezebel crouching down to slurp a drink out of the pond reminded Malou that she still had to find the flighty monkey's baby and see if she could prod Jezebel into taking up her maternal duties. With a great heaviness weighing her down, Malou stood and set off to scout the back country where Jezebel might have borne her infant.

Before she'd taken two leaden steps, Malou sighted Kojiwa returning to the troop. At first, Malou couldn't believe what she was seeing. That dark spot on his chest, that couldn't be . . . Malou grabbed for her binoculars. It was! A tiny newborn with the characteristic chocolate brown fur of the macaque infant was clinging weakly to the old fellow. He'd found the baby that the ditzy Jezebel had abandoned.

Kojiwa delivered the baby to Jezebel, transferring the infant to his mother's chest, where it began to suck greedily. In the instant that the baby faced toward her, all Malou could register were two huge eyes staring helplessly out at a new and scary world. She christened the baby Peter Lorre and entered the name into her census book.

Malou's joy at the baby's discovery was short-lived, however. She wondered darkly about what, precisely, the infant had been saved for.

Chapter Two

Cameron Landell was thirty miles outside of San Antonio before he stopped seething long enough to glance down at the speedometer and register the fact that he'd been speeding. He eased his foot off the accelerator and tried to remember the last time he'd been so provoked. Anger was a luxury he almost never allowed himself. It was a self-indulgent emotion that clouded perceptions and dimmed judgments. He could not afford to let his business judgments be either clouded or dimmed.

He'd let that happen once and look what it had gotten him. A monkey ranch, of all the bad jokes. And now, today, he'd finally gotten to the punch line—Malou Sanders. For the hundredth time, Cameron berated himself for letting the old man bamboozle him. Undoubtedly, he snorted to himself, Stallings had acted out of all the same self-righteous impulses that guided the infuriating Malou

Sanders. For a fraction of a second, a memory of wheat gold hair dancing in the sunlight frisked across his mind. Cameron chased it away, tension gripping him even tighter around the neck and shoulders.

He glanced at his watch and relaxed a bit. His anger-quickened pace would put him into San Antonio in plenty of time for the closing. He even had a few spare minutes to drive by Landell Acres. He turned off on the loop that circled the sprawling city and headed west. A few exits later he got off and pointed the Mercedes in the direction of his new development. At this point it was only row upon row of stick-figure houses, the bare bones of their frames outlining the structures they would become. The car moved slowly along dusty strips of future roads. Cameron couldn't bother with a full inspection. He checked in with his foreman, Virgil Yates.

"Yessir, Mr. Landell, the Public Works inspector's already been by, checked out all the new utility cuts and approved every one of 'em."

"Good work, Virgil. Keep on it. And mind those trees we marked," he cautioned his foreman, indicating the live oak trees with strips of orange plastic tied around their trunks. Roads serpentined around them.

"Count on it. We won't so much as scrape the bark on any of them big boys."

As Cameron headed out, a station wagon pulled up at the entrance to the development and two women and a man emerged. From the back of the car they unloaded signs that read, "Save the Golden-cheeked Warbler" and "Stop Landell Acres!!!" Cameron sighed at the familiar sight of the protesters. Odd that they'd never once bothered to come by and discuss the plight of their beloved golden-cheeked warblers with him. Just like that woman and her monkeys, all of them had jumped at the most melodramatic solution—trying to stir up public outrage rather than the less flamboyant, but usually more effective, method of private negotiation.

Minutes later, Cameron was back on the loop heading for his appointment. A deep, strangling tension grabbed him as he contemplated the upcoming meeting. He *had* to close on that piece of land along I-35 he was selling. He hated to do it. He knew for a fact that if he could have held on to it for a few more months, it would have appreciated in value faster than the price of an umbrella on Noah's Ark.

That had been his strategy. Then Stallings had come along and he'd been fool enough to make the old man a short-term loan without bothering to check out the collateral he was offering. Never in a million years would he have guessed that Stallings, noted throughout south Texas for his honesty, would deadbeat on the loan. But he sure as hell had, leaving Cameron with what was euphemistically known as a "cash-flow imbalance." He was strapped. If he didn't raise the cash today to pay off the interest on the note on Landell Acres, he stood to lose everything.

If Stallings had paid off on time, he could have held on to the I-35 property *and* continued with Landell Acres. But all that had changed. Now, rather than an appreciating piece of property he owned a godforsaken *monkey ranch!* Worst of all was knowing that even if he did manage to sell off the property today, it would only be a holding action. The real battle would be to get enough together to pay off that note coming due at the end of May. Desperation was a bad—no, Cameron amended his thinking—it was the *worst* position from which to bargain.

Cameron began fuming again. Not only at his own stupidity in having been duped into a bad deal, but at that woman's incredible gall, threatening to call the press on him if he did something so outrageous as attempt to recoup a fraction of his losses. As he pulled into the reserved parking space outside of his office, two images of Malou sprang unbidden into his thoughts.

The first was of that plump lower lip she'd insisted upon nibbling away at. He wondered how it would taste. And the second was of those impossibly long brown legs. How would they feel wrapped about his own?

Cameron slammed the claret-colored door and stormed into his office. This was going to be one hell of a day.

"What'd the slimewad say?" Ernie asked eagerly the instant Malou walked through the door of the research station.

Though Malou had taken a long walk through the compound trying to steady herself, her voice still trembled when she relayed the verdict. "He wants to sell them. All of them."

"All of them?" Ernie repeated incredulously.

Malou nodded.

"Jeez, I could tell the guy was a hard charger, but Attila the Hun?"

"I told him I'd get press coverage. That the world would know what he was up to."

Ernie nodded thoughtfully. "How'd he take that threat?"

"Not well. Not well at all. There's something dangerous about Cameron Landell. Something very unsettling."

Ernie paused and studied Malou. He had his glasses on now. They were thick and made his eyes shrink away to two tiny raisins behind them. "Pretty ruthless guy, huh?" he finally asked eagerly. "Wouldn't hesitate to stoop to anything that would accomplish his ends?"

"Well . . ." Malou hesitated. For some reason she couldn't bring herself to agree with Ernie's blanket indictment. The coldly objective, scientifically trained part of her brain wouldn't allow it. That part of her had sensed in Cameron Landell something far different from the cutthroat entrepreneur she wanted to believe he was. Not only that, but if she let herself think about it long enough, she feared she would begin to doubt that the danger she'd sensed pouring off of Cameron Landell had anything at all to do with the monkeys. Still, Ernie was watching her anxiously, eager for her to agree to his assessment. She obliged him. "He might," she agreed tentatively.

"I knew it the minute I set eyes on him," Ernie elaborated dramatically. "I said, here is one bad hombre who only cares about money and not at all about how he gets it."

"I'm not sure I'd go that far," Malou equivocated.

"You wouldn't? You heard about his latest development? His exalted Landell Acres?" Ernie asked snidely. "He put it right smack in the middle of the nesting grounds of Texas's only native bird."

"That's true," Malou allowed, "but it was inevitable that someone would build there. The city's already pushed out to the edge of that area." Malou couldn't believe that she was actually defending Cameron Landell.

"And Landell is pushing it a few steps closer to the edge," Ernie concluded, slipping into the white lab coat he always wore when he worked. He clucked his tongue against the back of his teeth and headed to the back of the building and his air-conditioned lab.

Malou shook her head. This had been a thoroughly perplexing and bewildering day, and it had only begun. Though fascinated by the labyrinthine complications of macaque society, she had never been able to deal with the frustrating intricacies of human interaction. Her usual reaction to them was to escape, which is precisely what she did. She grabbed the tennis hat she wore to protect her from the south Texas sun, her notebook, and a jug of water and headed back out to the compound.

Far down the fence line, she spotted the stocky figure of Jorge Maldonado, Stallings's Mexican foreman. A lifetime of hard physical labor had left the foreman knotted with muscles and as weathered as the stump of an oak tree. He wore a *campesino*-style wide-brimmed straw hat with a small ball dangling off the back that jerked up and down as he worked on a tear in the fence. His horse, a beautiful chestnut bay, was tethered nearby.

Though Jorge's English was limited, he had managed from Malou's first day at the ranch to communicate to her his distaste for *los monos,* the monkeys. He was hewn from the Mexican cowboy *vaquero* tradition that dictated that the only animal a true man ever had any truck with was the horse. Jorge considered her and her monkeys a galling nuisance. Reluctantly, Malou walked over to him.

''*Buenos días,*'' she hailed him.

Jorge turned away from his labor and glared at her. That was the extent of the cordiality she had ever seen Jorge extend to anyone other than Mr. Stallings, to whom the menacing foreman had been slavishly devoted.

Fishing through her entirely inadequate Spanish vocabulary, Malou, putting her fist to the side of her face, tried to communicate that the phone was still not working. *"Teléfono, no funciona,"* she tried. *"Cuándo reparar?"* Though she knew she was butchering the language, apparently Jorge understood that she was asking when the phone would be repaired, for he began shaking his head in a vigorous negative.

"No repair. New *jefe* say no repair."

Thank you, Mr. Cameron Landell, Malou thought wearily. From the deep frown furrowing Jorge's face, it was clear that the foreman had shifted his loyalties to the "new *jefe*," the new boss, who now owned Stallings's property. He turned his thickly muscled back to her. Malou, turning up her palms in resignation to the language and emotional barriers between her and Jorge, went on into the enclosure.

Dozens of crouched monkeys were quiet as they concentrated on foraging enough edible plant matter from the stingy earth to sustain life. With an expertise born of painful practice, they stripped spines from cactus pads and picked the tender shoots out from the middle of saber-sharp yucca plants. For Malou it was a miracle. Few primatologists ten years ago had seriously believed that the 150 monkeys who'd been transplanted from the serenely cool Storm Mountain could survive on a patch of south Texas brushland where summer sun could broil the land with 130-degree heat.

She tried to imagine what old Kojiwa must have thought when he'd been unloaded ten years ago in his new home. He might have landed on the moon for all the resemblance the desolate landscape bore to the piney mountain refuge where he'd grown up. Where respectful tourists had made the long uphill trudge to the mountaintop feeding station simply to see him and his troopmates silhouetted against the Kyoto skyline and to offer selected tidbits of rice cake, nuts, and pickled vegetable. Where, long ago, the fearless samurai warriors had brought their mistresses so that they too might enjoy the snow-muffled tranquility of Storm Mountain and, if they were lucky enough and patient enough, catch a fleeting glimpse of the "old men of the forest."

Then to find himself brutally thrust into a world of heat, dust, and strange predators must have been an incomprehensible ordeal for the old one. Malou had heard the history of the relocation many times. For the first few weeks, the troop had been able to do little more than lie panting in the sparse shade offered by scattered spiked plants. Death had been an ever-present companion in those first terrible weeks. Kojiwa had watched five members of his own family, the Miwata clan, die horrible deaths. Two had died after eating the bright berries of the coyotillo bush. Bobcats, rattlesnakes, and drought claimed the other three as well as a dozen more from the other five families that composed the troop.

Gradually they'd learned how to get past the stinging spines of the cactus to the surprisingly palatable food beneath, and to seek relief from the battering heat in the water of the pond. They not only survived, they thrived, doubling their number in ten years. In short, they astonished the doubters with their incredible adaptability.

Malou's reverie was interrupted by soft sucking sounds. A new mother, Tulip, who had borne her first infant, Mesquite, several weeks earlier, was already starting to teach the cocoa brown bundle to walk. Placing Mesquite gently on the ground, she backed away, then made sucking sounds to encourage her offspring to try toddling to her. The baby, however, wasn't able to manage even one step before a cluster of adult females, mostly Mesquite's aunts, gathered around wanting to hold and play with the infant. At that point Tulip, with the protectiveness characteristic of macaque mothers, rushed forward and snatched her son up, the walking lesson over for the day.

The chastened monkeys, led by Tulip's sister, Tawny, backed away for a moment as Tulip hugged the baby to her breast. One by one, though, they cautiously approached their sister and began grooming her. Soon Tulip, exhausted by her vigilance of the past weeks, was lulled into a slumberous state by the feel of Tawny's expert hands combing softly through her fur. As soon as Tulip's head lolled onto her shoulder and her lilac eyelids fluttered shut, the other aunts stealthily crept forward, reached out curious hands, and surreptitiously stroked the baby at their sister's breast.

Malou jotted down the details of the aunts' strategy. Any other day she would have been vastly amused by their caginess, but there wasn't much that could make her smile today. After making her notes, Malou picked up her binoculars again. Far away from the central area where the majority of macaques clustered, she spotted Jezebel.

Malou adjusted the focus and zeroed in more closely on the new mother to see if she still had her baby, Peter Lorre, with her. Thank God, she did.

Jezebel had never formed the alliances that other adult females had built among themselves. Instead, she'd always preferred to traipse after the peripheral males, the troop's outriders. Males other than the troop leader and a few subleaders were only tolerated by the troop until they reached puberty, at around five years of age. After that age, they were banished to the edges of the compound. Here they served as the troop's early warning system. With no mother to link her into the female's social structure, Jezebel had gravitated toward the other troop outcasts. Her search for male companionship had earned Jezebel the name given to her by some long-gone resident manager. Now, even with a baby, Jezebel was still tagging along after the lone males who perched in the branches of tall trees far from the heart of the troop they'd been exiled from.

Along with all the other impossible wishes she had been making since Cameron Landell had pulled off in a cloud of dust, Malou wished that the errant Jezebel were just a bit more like the overprotective mother, Tulip. Jezebel's baby dangled from her belly by only the scrawniest fistful of fur as Jezebel clambered up a tree in search of a playmate. Malou's heart stopped when, eight feet off the ground, the weak infant lost its grip and fell to the grassy earth.

"That's it," Malou sighed. She tried to keep all human intervention in the troop to an absolute minimum, but she couldn't stand by any longer while Jezebel neglected her baby. She was halfway to the fallen baby when she noticed a furred form ambling stiffly in the same direction.

It was Kojiwa. Jezebel scrambled down the tree, ever eager to interact with her adopted father. Kojiwa picked up the infant and examined it closely, expressing great interest in little Peter Lorre, who stared up at him with the huge dark pools of his eyes. Like a spoiled child who wants only the toy that another child has, Jezebel soon snatched her son away from Kojiwa and began suckling it. The baby fed hungrily. As if he were satisfied that his mission had been accomplished, Kojiwa returned to his spot in the shade and kept up his watch over the troop he had once led.

That crisis resolved and her energy flagging, Malou went back to the research station. She trudged through the next several days. Unable to sleep well and barely able to eat, she seemed to have already entered a period of mourning for the monkeys that Cameron Landell planned to sell off.

Only Ernie kept her from complete despair. Oddly, the lower her spirits plunged, the higher Ernie's rose. He carried on with his experiments, even whistling as he went. Malou figured he must be one of those rare humans who thrived on adversity.

During the long, sleepless nights, Malou would imagine herself presenting all manner of irresistibly persuasive schemes to Cameron Landell for keeping Los Monos open. These imaginary presentations always had the same conclusion, though—Cameron Landell sneering at her naiveté.

Even worse than the imagined one-sided debates were the moments when Malou did manage to drift off. Inevitably then the dream would return. She would be staked down in the middle of a barren plain. The day would be overcast, the light diffuse. For no reason that she could discern, Malou could feel her heart pounding with terror. Then suddenly, bursting out of the foggy distance, would come a claret-colored chariot drawn by a white horse the size of a Clydesdale. Strain as she might, Malou could neither break free nor even see who drove the chariot that was thundering toward her.

It was upon her in a flash. Just as the mighty horse's hooves seemed poised to trample her to death, they dissolved as if made of snowflakes. Then the rest of the horse and the chariot dissolved and, in the way of dreams, she was no longer staked down on a foggy plain, but was lying, naked and warm, upon a bower of pillows looking into a pair of thickly lashed eyes brown as espresso coffee.

It was too dark to see the rest of his face, but Malou was no longer straining to do so. She was submitting gladly to the delights being wrought upon her yearning body by heaven-guided hands and tongue. They caressed her in ways beyond her imagining, anticipating what would give her the most sublime pleasure and providing it. It was all so wonderfully weightless, so superbly tantalizing. Malou surrendered her will to the stranger moving over her with such a skilled grace that it was more like a dance than lovemaking. A tireless, always surprising modern dance. That association invariably jolted Malou out of her dream.

In the troubled moments between sleeping and waking, she realized that her dream lover had been Cameron Landell. Worse than that, she realized that she still hungered for him, for his hands, his lips, to finish what her imagination had started. By the time she was fully awake, Malou could succeed in banishing such despicable thoughts and concentrate again on how truly odious Cameron Landell was.

It was at the tail end of just such a disturbing dream, five days after her first meeting with the man who had inspired all this psychic turmoil, that Malou dragged herself out of bed shortly after dawn. There was no use in trying to court sleep that would not return. She dressed in a clean pair of khaki shorts and a cream-colored jersey top. As she tiptoed outside, she could hear Ernie snoring away happily down the hall. She glanced at the phone, glad that it was broken. There would be bad news coming soon. News that Landell had found labs eager to buy experimental animals that came complete with nearly four decades of genealogical records. She had expected it to arrive already and preferred to receive that news by telegram rather than hear it directly from Cameron Landell.

She hurried outside, anxious to check on Jezebel and the infant, Peter Lorre. With Kojiwa's constant prodding, Jezebel had assumed enough of her maternal duties to keep her baby alive, but little else. She didn't spend any time cuddling the child or encouraging it to discover which of the bits of food that fell from her mouth were edible. She didn't do any of the things that the other mothers did that would help their babies survive and grow into accepted members of the troop. Malou prayed that the infant was a male because, with Jezebel as a mother, any female child she bore would be doomed, as Jezebel herself had been, to a life as an outcast trailing after the peripheral males for company.

The troop was still sleeping. That was good. Malou scrutinized the sleepers, from the pale pink faces of the infants clutched by their mothers to the almost scarlet faces of the old-timers. Malou didn't become alarmed until, on her second visual roll call, she still hadn't spotted Jezebel but had noticed Kojiwa awake and clearly distracted. He too was searching the troop and having just as little luck as Malou was.

"You fleabrain," Malou whispered to herself, convinced that Jezebel must have left the safety of the troop to sleep off at the edge of the enclosure with the peripheral males. Traversing the boundary of the two-hundred-acre compound was no Sunday stroll, but Malou knew she'd have to do it if she wanted to put her mind at rest about Jezebel and her baby.

She didn't have far to go before she found Jezebel. Approaching from a distance, Malou wondered what the silly creature was doing lying there in the high grass. And why she was ignoring the pitiful whimperings of her baby huddled next to her.

A pulse of urgency suddenly beat through Malou. She dropped her field notebook and ran. Her binoculars pounded against her as she ran faster. She reached the fallen monkey and dropped to her knees. Jezebel's amber eyes were open, staring blankly. Malou fumbled for her wrist and fought to find a pulse beating through the animal's body. There was none. Malou gently laid poor Jezebel's paw down upon the earth.

Peter Lorre snuggled against his mother's side, trying to rouse her. Malou picked up the baby, cradling him against her. He was a female, Malou could see that clearly now. The newly orphaned baby clung to her soft jersey top, burrowing in its folds for a teat to suckle.

The infant's futile, wordless plea for life was what finally undid Malou, what broke through her shock and unraveled the tight skein of control she'd wound within herself. All of it—the sleepless nights, the missed meals, the broken dreams—returned to haunt her, bringing the tears with it.

With the same feeling of an unreal shift from one scene to another, totally different and unexpected one that had marked her dreams of the past five nights, Malou felt herself being lifted from the ground. Still sheltering Jezebel's baby in her arms and still sobbing uncontrollably, Malou looked up into a face bare inches from her own. For the first few seconds, all that registered were a pair of espresso brown eyes. They reflected back every fiber of the pain she felt.

Stronger at that moment than even her dislike of the man whose arms encircled her was Malou's overriding need to be comforted. She collapsed her head against Cameron's shoulder and wept out the grief in her heart.

"I'm sorry, Malou. I'm really, really sorry," Cameron whispered soothingly. The feel of the two bodies in his arms—Malou's warm and supple against his own and convulsing with grief, and then this minuscule monkey clinging to his chest and trying to burrow into his shirt—was almost more than he could bear.

The monkey baby looked up at Cameron and searched his face for an answer, an explanation. Those eyes. Its tiny face seemed consumed by nothing but two huge pools of bewilderment. Tears and pain—Cameron could not deal with them. His own pain, certainly—he'd *had* to learn how to deal with that, to save it up and use it to drive himself. But someone else's pain, someone else's tears . . . Cameron was defenseless. He ached inside for both the suffering creatures he carried in his arms.

"It's okay," he whispered into the golden cap of hair, breathing in the intoxicating scent of clean pink scalp and sun-warmed hair. The baby-fine strands felt like the softest of down against his cheek. He turned his head ever so slightly and the silken mass caressed his lips. Malou, her sobs subsiding, turned her face to him. It was as filled with puzzlement as the little monkey's had been. Her eyes sparkled with tears in the morning sunshine. As he stared into that questioning face, the tears receded, but the sparkle and the questions remained.

A stab of regret plunged through him. How could he have ever been fooled that first day by her games of one-upmanship? She might, as some rudimentary research had revealed, be a world-respected scientist, but she was a child where these damned monkeys were concerned. A child whom he had inadvertently wounded very badly.

"It'll be all right," Cameron soothed again. "We'll try to work something out." He would have promised anything to wipe those terrible questions away. But still that look of slightly dazzled wonder remained. Then, in a motion so nearly indetectable that Cameron almost missed it, she moved toward him. For a second, he was sure he'd imagined that slight inclination in his direction, thought he'd brought it into being through the sheer power of wishful thinking. He'd gone several steps before his mind reconfirmed the evidence and produced the stupefying verdict—she wants me to kiss her.

Terrified lest he'd grossly misinterpreted her look and gesture and that he'd unloose the snarling wildcat who'd threatened the other day to tar him in the press, he stopped and leaned tentatively forward, one half of his being anticipating the feel of those deliciously swollen lips beneath his own, the other already wincing from the sting of a slap.

It was all happening with the same inevitability as in her dream, Malou realized, with the one difference that, this time, she had started it. This and a dozen other thoughts darted through her mind as Cameron stopped, bent his head down to bring his lips a scant few inches from hers, then halted, almost as if he were deliberately tantalizing her. Malou's lips parted as her pulse and breathing accelerated. She inhaled his warm, sweet breath and pleaded silently for his lips to continue their journey downward. His eyes, so hard and cutting five days before, were clouded and soft now with questions.

The questions were banished as Cameron held his lips above Malou's. They hovered there stealing breath, antagonism, and all sense from Malou. This kiss she hadn't yet tasted, that she could almost feel, was already more devastating than any she had ever received.

Like a plant drawn to sunlight, Malou lifted her lips up to meet his.

Cameron's heart lurched within him as he felt Malou shift within his arms. After that, no power on earth could have halted the descent of his lips, could have stilled him until he had known the feel and taste of those lips.

Held secure in his arms, the kiss had the same weightless quality as in her dream. His lips seemed to suck all her secrets from her. They seemed to touch her in a thousand delirious places at once, but in fact, they only touched her lips and that one virgin spot within her soul that no man, no matter how ardent, had ever gained access to before. And Cameron Landell had reached it with one gentle, almost chaste kiss.

For a long moment after their lips had parted they stared into one another's eyes trying to figure out what had happened and why on earth it had happened to them in, of all places, the middle of a monkey ranch.

"I'd kiss you properly if I weren't scared of crushing junior here."

Malou laughed her first real laugh in five days as her hand went to pat the frail monkey clinging to Cameron's shirt. The tiny creature was glancing from him to her, trying to figure out the strange human ritual he'd just witnessed.

"I can walk now," Malou said.

With her feet firmly planted on the earth, she removed the monkey from Cameron's shirtfront and let the baby attach herself to her shoulder. Suddenly Malou began to doubt the wisdom of her command to be placed on her feet. She swayed forward and was caught within the steadying bonds of Cameron's arms. She leaned gratefully against his chest. His great, strong heart pounded against her ear, her pulse beating back with the same impassioned rhythm.

The sun beat down on her back, warming her just as Cameron's body warmed hers. Off in the distance, three young monkeys scampered across the prairie, chasing each other in an endless game of tag. They seemed very far away.

"I could get to like holding women with monkeys on their shoulders. What's the little nipper's name?"

Malou was disconcerted by Cameron's jocular tone. The kiss that had so undone her had obviously not had any measurable effect on him. She pulled away from his embrace and felt for the baby's featherlight weight on her shoulder. With an effort, she steadied her breathing and answered in an even voice, attempting to match his joking lightness.

"I named him Peter Lorre for the big eyes, but it turned out I'd overlooked some other vital equipment and he is a she. So I suppose I'll have to come up with another name."

"Why not simply Lorre?" Cameron suggested, reaching out for the newly christened baby. Lorre went to him with an eagerness that surprised Malou, wrapping her tiny arms around Cameron's wrist. Cameron held Lorre up and grinned into the little monkey's face.

Malou told herself that, objectively, she had known men technically more handsome than Cameron Landell, but she had never known another who made her feel as if her insides were a sandbar dissolving beneath the course of some current, a current that flowed out of a place within her, a current that she hadn't suspected and certainly couldn't control. She didn't like any of this. Not the feeling of being out of control, not the inexplicable yearning that had made her lean toward Cameron for that one mistake of a kiss, not the awkward, adolescent discomfort that was gnawing at her now. She didn't know what to say, to do.

Abruptly she turned away from Cameron and strode back toward the research station. Escape, that was the one solution that never failed her. She'd learned early that tangling in the morass of human complications was something that she was simply not suited to handle. How could she have forgotten that essential fact long enough for Cameron's lips to find hers, to find that one unguarded spot within her that no man before had ever found?

"Mary Louise, you want to slow down a minute and tell me what's happening?"

Cameron easily kept pace with her blistering stride. Cursing herself for ever revealing her full name, Malou kept right on striding.

"Okay then, let me guess. One, this is the first leg of a new Olympic event—speed-walking with small monkey perched on your shoulder. Two, I've offended you. Now which is it?"

Malou stopped and pivoted toward Cameron. What on earth did women say to men in this kind of situation? She wished she had a clue. Under no circumstances, deep instinct told her, must Cameron Landell learn of the devastating effect he had upon her.

"Offended?" she asked as if unfamiliar with the meaning of the word. "How could you have offended me?" Good, she liked that. She'd struck exactly the right note of casual indifference. Or had she? Why then was Cameron grinning?

Fortunately, she was saved from pondering that mystery by Ernie bolting out of the research station and calling to them, "Why do you have the baby?" The rays of the sun caught his thick glasses and turned them into two silver orbs blocking out his eyes.

Malou closed the distance between them. "Jezebel," she said softly, her grief welling up within her again as she pronounced the name, "she's dead."

"Dead," Ernie echoed dully, his eyes still unreadable behind his glasses.

Malou placed a comforting hand on Ernie's shoulder. Jezebel had been one of the three or four monkeys he'd worked with most closely.

"Any idea what caused it?"

Malou shook her head no.

"Guess I'd better bring her into the lab and find out. Where did you find her?"

Malou described the spot where she'd left Jezebel, and Ernie set off. Inside the research station, with Cameron watching her every move, she mixed up a batch of infant formula and poured it into a tiny bottle. Lorre resisted the rubber nipple until enough of the formula had trickled between her lips to convince her that the stuff was edible; then she put every ounce of her fragile being into sucking out the nourishment she needed.

"Such a gigantic will to live for such a tiny creature," Cameron said, as Lorre drained the miniature bottle with a loud slurping noise.

Malou debated within herself whether or not to press her advantage. She decided to take the risk. "Yes," she answered. "Wouldn't it be a shame to subvert that will?"

Cameron caught her eye and arched a brow in her direction to indicate that her meaning had not been lost on him. "I promised you that I'd try to work something out."

Malou smiled.

With the furry baby cradled in her arms, its lids fluttering closed sleepily, Cameron reflected on what an odd sort of madonna she made. She was so at peace, so serene and happily in her element with monkeys and so prickly and unpredictable with humans. At least with him. Cameron wondered why. More important, he wondered why he cared so blasted much. She placed the monkey gently onto a nest of terry cloth towels that she transferred into a clean cage along with a softly ticking alarm clock.

"That'll make her think she's lying next to her mother's heart," Malou explained. For a few quiet seconds, they watched the baby sleep.

"I wonder what monkeys dream about," Cameron asked.

"Storm Mountain," Malou guessed, but had no chance to theorize further because Ernie burst in carrying a dried piece of a shrubby bush with a few bright berries still attached.

"Look what I found not ten yards from where Jezebel was lying."

"Coyotillo," Cameron identified the plant.

"Not a bad botanical analysis for a businessman," Ernie said, eyeing Cameron sharply.

"The stuff's a plague to livestock," Cameron elaborated. "The berries are deadly poison. Costs me a fortune to keep it off property where I run cattle."

"Unless I'm seriously mistaken, this is what killed Jezebel," Ernie went on.

"But how?" Malou asked. "We've been over every acre inside the enclosure, wiping the weed out. Not only that, but the monkeys learned long ago not to eat that plant."

Ernie shrugged, turning the bit of brush over in his hand. "Beats me, but here's the evidence. What's odd is, look here." He indicated the broken end of the branch. "This is how I found it. Obviously ripped off the plant."

"What's so odd about that?" Cameron questioned.

"That's something you wouldn't know about," Ernie answered in what Malou felt was an unnecessarily snide tone. "Macaques rarely uproot plants. They feed on the sprouts, buds, and berries and leave the plant itself intact."

"No, I wasn't aware of that," Cameron admitted.

"I didn't think you would be."

There was a peculiar intensity in Ernie's comment. It infected Malou with unhealthy suspicions that rankled beneath the surface. She was certain that she had not left any coyotillo plants within the enclosure.

Ernie was strafing Cameron now with unconcealed dislike. Cameron was returning the hostility in full measure.

His eyes had hardened again until they reflected nothing but frozen glints of steely determination.

Malou was astonished by the change. Or had Cameron merely reverted to his true nature?

Behind her, in a voice so soft that only she could hear it, Lorre whimpered in her sleep.

Chapter Three

Watching Ernie and Cameron glare at one another made Malou acutely uncomfortable. If they were macaques, she thought, fur would have flown or the dominant male would have chased off his underling by now. Such tension could never be supported in the wild.

"If you need me, I'll be in the lab." Ernie broke first, stomping away and slamming the door behind him. Cameron had prevailed. *Dominance does not mean right,* Malou reminded herself. She was certain that Cameron Landell had not gotten to where he was in his world by making a habit of backing down. Or of being overburdened with scruples.

In the silence that followed, Lorre's whimpers seemed to grow louder. Huddled tightly against the clean towel, her parchment-thin eyelids twitched as she followed the course of a nightmare.

"There must be a storm on Storm Mountain," Cameron commented. Malou was surprised that he'd remembered her references to the monkey's ancestral home. She warned herself that she would do well to keep in mind the fact that Cameron Landell didn't miss much and that he forgot even less. As the bad dream receded, Lorre's whimperings subsided and she relaxed.

"Your friend certainly had a burr up his . . . under his saddle," Cameron continued.

"He *was* pretty upset," Malou replied noncommittally. "I think it's understandable." She recognized in her own voice the arid, detached quality it took on when she was attempting to be scientific, objective. Cameron noticed it too.

"*Highly* understandable," he repeated. "Listen, I don't know what the options are here for keeping the troop intact, and you sure didn't present any viable ones at our first meeting. Want to give it another shot?"

It took Malou all of five seconds to drop her suspicions and her pose of scientific detachment. "You mean it? You really want to hear my ideas for keeping the troop together?"

Her breathless eagerness caused the hint of a smile to flicker across Cameron's lips. "Something like that, yes. You are still interested, I presume."

Malou had to take a moment to collect herself. But only a moment, for all the wild schemes she'd conjured up in the long sleepless hours of the past five nights bubbled close to the surface. "Grants," she blurted out. "Given the unique family records we have on the troop, there's no reason why we shouldn't be able to get all kinds of grants for genetic studies. Then there's the whole incredible topic of the troop's adaptation. From piney, snowy mountains to cactus prairie. That's at least a dozen studies right there. And all the social interaction, the dominance structure. We're only just beginning to understand that. Then there's—"

"Whoa. Hold on there," Cameron broke into her pell-mell inventory of possibilities. "With grants, you're talking foundations, bureaucracies. It would be months, years, before agencies like that could come up with funding. We're going to need a few speedier solutions than that. Something on the order of three weeks, when my note falls due at the end of May."

"Oh," Malou said, her enthusiasm draining away.

"Look, don't go all glum and wimpy on me. If we're going to work together on this, there's one thing you need to know—Landell Acres takes precedence over everything." He fixed her with a gaze of deadly intensity. "It's *the* project I've been working toward my whole life. Before this, I've only been developing land. For the first time, I'll be building on it as well. The stakes are high. In this particular case, they're a bit too high. Do you understand?"

Malou nodded weakly.

"Good, because no man, and *certainly* no monkey, is going to stand in the way of my completing Landell Acres."

"We might be able to get some kind of an emergency award if we let the foundations know what the situation is."

"Go to it. Get on the phone and start calling around."

Malou was already lunging for the receiver when she remembered one significant detail. "It's broken."

"Right. No problem, I was on my way up to the ranch house. I haven't had time to check it out yet. You can make your calls from up there."

Malou looked around her. The baby—she'd have to stay for the baby. No, Ernie could certainly mix up formula as well as she could. Observation notes? Clearly the survival of the troop was more important than a few hours of missed notes. No, she really had no excuse for not going with Cameron Landell. No excuse other than fear of being alone with him. She scratched out a quick note to Ernie giving him Lorre's feeding schedule and explaining where she'd gone. "Let's hit the road," she said, taping the note to a spot where Ernie was sure not to miss it—the front of the refrigerator.

The interior of the Mercedes was all rosewood, with pewter leather seats that felt like a kid glove against the bare backs of Malou's legs. She drank in its deep, rich smell as the barely perceptible hum of the finely tuned engine sent smooth vibrations purring through her. After so many months of no-frills living at the research station punctuated by dusty, jarring jeep trips into Laredo for supplies, she sank gratefully into this moment of luxury. The main road leading to the ranch house was lined with wildflowers— bluebonnets, Indian paintbrushes, wild daisies. It was a riot of unending color.

Cameron scrutinized the passing landscape. Slowing down, he arched his torso slightly forward so that he could jam a hand into his jeans pocket. Malou was not unaware of the play of strongly developed muscles beneath Cameron's shirt and trousers as he wriggled a hand into his pocket and brought forth a crudely drawn map. "I got directions over the phone from Stallings's foreman, Jorge, and since his English is about as bad as my Spanish, I'm not terribly confident of this map I drew. You've never been to the ranch house, I take it."

"No. Mr. Stallings was very jealous of his privacy. He never invited any of the researchers to his home."

"This must be it," Cameron said, matching the scrawled lines on the crumpled paper to a road ahead. They turned off on an asphalt road that curved beneath a rusted wrought-iron arch. At the crown of the arch was a tipped-over S representing Stallings's Lazy S brand. "This ranch house had better really be something," Cameron grumbled as they moved out of sight of the highway. "It would have to be the Southfork to make Stallings's property worth even a third of what he claimed."

The road dipped down through a low water crossing. A thin trickle of water ran across it. "Bet that's hell when it rains," Cameron noted disapprovingly.

Malou barely glanced at it or noticed when the paving ended. She was spellbound by the beauty of the property. An infinity of tender spring green stretched out all around her, wrapping the land in the promise of new life that sprang forth like a miracle each year to defy the harsh surroundings. With the trained eye of an ethologist, she caught glimpses of animal life that most people would have missed. Of startled deer peering through the foliage. Of armadillos trundling through the underbrush. Of javelinas bolting away from the sound of the oncoming car.

"It's remarkably unspoiled," she exalted.

"Yes, and even more remarkably undeveloped," Cameron groused. "I haven't seen any of the improvements, the fences, the pastureland, the buildings that Stallings told me were here."

They emerged from the jungle of green and rounded a curve. At its end sat a lovely stone house.

"It's like something out of a Grimm's fairy tale," Malou

breathed in wonder at the small structure almost buried in the dense vegetation.

"It's pretty grim all right. But the only way it's connected to a fairy tale is how Stallings portrayed it to me." Malou noticed that as he shook his head in disgust, most of it seemed to be directed against himself.

Outside the car, Malou caught the tumbling, crystal song of a canyon wren and the poignant scent of the wisteria-like purple blossoms of the mountain laurel. A creek sparkled in the distance, cutting a silver trail around the giant trunks of century-old live oaks. She touched the stone of the house and wondered what long-dead craftsman had chiseled it with such delicate precision. For her, the air was as redolent with enchantment as it was with the spicy scent of the mountain laurels.

Even Cameron could not remain totally immune to its spell. With each fragrant breath he inhaled, a bit more of the tension that coiled around him eased its grip. "Pretty," he pronounced the deliberately tepid verdict. "Not profitable, but pretty. God, if you could only put pretty in the bank, all our problems would be solved."

"But you can't," Malou sighed.

"Not unless you happen to have a highly unusual banker. In which case I'd like to meet him. Soon."

That little bit of levity was all that was needed to bring the scene's magic to life. As they approached the front door, Cameron halted her. "Uh-uh-uh," he warned, pointing to the base of the massive door, which was supported by a sturdy oak plank. "That is a threshold if I've ever seen one. Custom demands that I carry you across it."

Malou was trapped securely in his arms before she had a

chance to protest, "I'm pretty sure that custom only applies to newlyweds."

"Who wants to risk it?" he asked, pressing close to her as he leaned in to turn the knob. With a grand step, he crossed the threshold. "You know," he said, pausing on the other side, a distracted look on his face, "I can't remember another time in my entire life when I've swept a woman off her feet, and now I've done it twice in one day. What do you suppose it means?"

"That you're in training for Olympic weight lifting?" Malou hazarded.

"Cute. Criminally cute."

And, there in a stone house smack in the middle of spring, with the fragrance of mountain laurel blending with birdsong, held for the second time in *her* life within a man's strong arms, Malou *felt* cute. She didn't feel like a dedicated researcher and the winner of several prestigious awards in her field. She felt cute. Criminally cute. "We've made it across the threshold, Cameron."

Without making the slightest move to put her down, he said, "Call me Cam. It'll take so much less effort—and breath."

"All right . . . Cam. But we've still crossed the threshold."

He glanced down. "So we have." He let her slide to the floor. "You wouldn't happen to have a small monkey handy that we could perch on your shoulder? That seemed to have made wonderful things happen earlier."

"I didn't think you'd noticed." Malou turned away to hide the goofy grin spreading across her face and to tamp down the intoxicating rush of feelings bubbling through her as if a geyser of champagne had been unloosed. She forced herself to focus on the interior of the house. The living room they'd stepped into was dominated by a fireplace of fieldstone. The oak floors shone with the rich gleam of decades of polishing. Charming watercolors, botanical drawings of the local plants, hung from the thick walls. The furniture was sturdy and wood. A candlestick phone was mounted on a wall by the door leading into the kitchen, where a pump handle curled up over the sink.

"It's a place out of time," Cam said in a low voice, just beginning to take everything in. "Other than the phone, there's not a thing in here from this century."

Malou looked around from the old cast-iron pot hanging in front of the fireplace to the wooden butter churn sitting beside the sink in the sunny kitchen. "You're right," she whispered, an eerie feeling seizing hold of her.

"No TV. No air conditioning. No electric lights," he said, taking an inventory of all the artifacts of the twentieth century that were missing from the cozy dwelling.

"It's hard to believe that Mr. Stallings conducted all his business dealings from here."

"He *did* have a telephone," Cam said, picking up the old-fashioned receiver and holding it out to Malou so that she too could hear the dial tone.

"And a gramophone," Malou declared, opening up a mahogany box to reveal an old crank-type record player. A stack of thick 78 RPM records stood beside it. "'By the Light of the Moon,' 'Don't Sit Under the Apple Tree,' 'Chattanooga Choochoo.'" Malou read out the titles.

"What a strange old codger," Cam said, studying the books on a shelf. All were bound in dark leather, black and maroon, their titles lettered in gold on their spines. A complete collection of Dickens, some Robert Louis Stevenson, several slim volumes of poetry, and several more thick books on botany. Cam moved into the kitchen. "At least we won't starve," he called out. "Ample supply of canned goods. Hope you like peas, Spam, and peaches."

"My favorites," Malou answered. "Right up there with Chateaubriand and Godiva chocolates."

"And we certainly won't go thirsty," Cam announced, stepping back into the living room, a bottle in either hand. "At least the old boy had taste in what he drank. Glenlivet scotch and good Kentucky bourbon."

For a fleeting moment, with Cam framed in the doorway, beaming with pride in his discovery and absorbed with boyish curiosity, Malou wished it really could have been her threshold he'd carried her across. That this were their own little house, far from the rest of the world and all the problems pressing in on both of them. The memory of the most pressing of those problems broke the spell. "I'd better start trying to get in touch with some foundation heads." She dragged a stool up next to the kitchen door.

"Right. Work," Cam reminded himself as he put the bottles down and headed back outside. He returned with a leather attaché case and settled down on the sofa to begin reading through a stack of legal-sized documents.

Malou's first call was to her mentor at the university, Professor Everitt. He supplied her with names, numbers, and tips on the best approaches to take with the various foundation directors. He also suggested a number of renowned primatologists she could call for support and testimonials as to the value of Los Monos. She thanked him and dived into the long list she had accumulated.

Not surprisingly, most of the men and women she needed

to speak with were out. Those she did catch were treated to a sincerely impassioned plea. Impressed enough by the urgency in Malou's voice not to brush her off with a standard reply, most promised to look into the matter further.

"Don't look too much further," she ended her spiel to the director of the National Genetics Research Lab. "There's not time enough if we're going to save the troop. The new owner has only given me three weeks to come up with new funding sources."

Cam, who'd obviously been listening in, asked as she replaced the receiver, "Why do I feel like the heavy here?"

"You're not," Malou assured him, still not entirely convinced herself. "You've given me a fair chance to save them. You didn't have to do that."

Before Cam could respond, the phone rang. Malou grabbed the receiver. It was Charlotte Dunsmore returning her call. Malou was surprised to find herself addressing the founder and director of the Dunsmore Foundation.

"Yes, yes, Albert has told me all about your monkey ranch down there," the woman, who sounded to be a very jaunty seventy, interrupted when Malou started in on her set explanation of exactly what Los Monos was. It took her a second to realize that "Albert" was Professor Everitt. "Now, what's the current difficulty?"

Malou outlined the problem.

"Sounds serious," Mrs. Dunsmore said.

Malou waited for Mrs. Dunsmore to tell her to submit her application in triplicate and she would give it "every consideration." Instead, the older woman asked, "Would two thousand help out?"

Malou felt her mouth working, but no words were coming out.

"We aren't a large foundation, you realize," Mrs. Dunsmore continued, a slight annoyance at Malou's silence prickling her voice. "All we'd be able to do is help tide you over this emergency; then you'd have to find permanent support elsewhere."

"Oh, two thousand would be fantastic!" Malou was finally able to force the words out.

"Fine, I'll put a check in the mail today and we can look after the paperwork when it's convenient. You'll have to excuse me now. Polly just wheeled in the tea tray."

In the middle of Malou's effusive thanks, the line went dead.

"We got two thousand dollars!" she whooped.

Cam cocked an eyebrow in her direction. "Bravo. You've saved one and a third monkeys."

Startled by his cool response, Malou's exuberance sagged.

Cam put down the forty-page contract he was reviewing. "You still don't understand, do you? We have to have more than just enough to pay the water and feed bills for a few months. We need steady, long-term income to cover taxes, lost revenues, and, more than that, *I* need a great big lump of cold, hard cash to plunk down on my banker's desk in three weeks' time. All of which means that you'll have to find a foundation interested in purchasing not only the monkeys, but also the land along with them. Because I'll guarantee you this: I can most certainly sell that land *without* the monkeys on it."

"Forgive my naiveté," Malou said, her flashing temper

frozen into her icy tone. "My childish enthusiasm over such a pittance must be a sore trial to you."

"Don't be snippy," he commanded. "You need to know what the facts are if we're going to work together. You keep trying to make me into some kind of ogre out to crush you and your little monkey farm. That's not who I am, Malóu, or how I operate. My idea of winning is when both sides get what they want. No losers, no tears. It's not in my power to *give* you what you want unless I forfeit everything I've worked for all my life, so you'll have to work for it. Your two thousand is an encouraging sign. When you multiply it a few hundred times, we can start thinking about breaking out the champagne. Until then, if you plan on holding up your half of this joint venture, you'd better graft that phone onto your ear."

Malou turned away, smoldering. Furious at Mr. Cameron Landell and even madder at herself because he was, once again, right. Undeniably, insufferably right.

Chapter Four

M alou turned back to the old-fashioned phone. So intent was she, that Malou didn't notice when the canyon wrens fell abruptly silent or when the temperature began to plummet or when sullen gray clouds began to shroud the sun. Had she been paying attention to anything other than a series of disembodied voices, she surely would have felt in her bones the ominous stillness that fell across the land just before the first fat, angry drops of rain pelted from the sky to kick up tiny geysers of dust wherever they fell. But it was Cam, disentangling himself from the slippery tentacles of legalese in the contract he was studying, who noticed first.

"We'd better think about starting back," he said, directing Malou's attention to the downpour.

"But that was Edward Darden," she moaned, gesturing to the receiver she'd just hung up. "*The* Father of American

Primatology," she explained to Cam's blank look. "He's just gone to check on a funding report he received yesterday; then he's going to call me right back."

"Well, we certainly wouldn't want to walk out on *the* Father of American Primatology," Cam jibed.

"It'll only be a few minutes."

"With the way that rain is coming down, you'd better hope it's not much longer. Like every other kind of weather down here, rain is serious in south Texas."

"Don't worry," Malou reassured him. "I've lived through lots of rainstorms at Los Monos."

"I'm sure you have, and that's because Los Monos is on high ground. We're considerably lower here."

"Just a few more minutes," Malou pleaded.

"Take all the time you need. I'm quite comfortable here, far from the incessant jangling of phones that are always for me."

And so they waited: Cam stretched out on the couch with his contract and a ceramic mug filled with spring water and some of Mr. Stallings's fine scotch. Malou perched nervously by the phone, waiting to take up the conversation with Edward Darden, a man she'd read about in textbooks and admired since her first days in primatology. And the sky growing darker and hurling more rain with each passing minute.

By the time the phone rang, raindrops were pattering down on the tin roof with the machine-gun vigor of a team of tap dancers rehearsing for a Busby Berkeley spectacular. And all *the* Father of American Primatology had to report was that he'd been unable to locate the papers he'd gone to hunt for. But he did promise to alert everyone in the primatology community to how dire the situation was ou at Los Monos. Malou thanked him politely, hung up, jumped off her stool, and began scurrying about collecting her papers and hat.

Cam, disturbed by the sudden flurry of activity, peeked his head over the top of the couch.

"It's raining," Malou explained. "We've got to get out of here."

"Why didn't I think of that?" he asked, bundling papers back into the briefcase.

A few seconds later he was holding the door open as Malou bolted out into the cloudburst. They were both drenched by the time they reached the car. Sheets of rain made the short drive to the low water crossing into a twenty-five-minute test of navigation by instinct. Half the journey was conducted with Cam's head stuck out into the downpour, trying to ascertain whether or not they were still on the road. But the worst was yet to come, and come it did at the low water crossing. Unable to see it, Cam stopped cold mere inches away from plunging into the trickle, which had been transformed into a rushing torrent.

"Looks like this is the end of the line," Cam announced jauntily.

"Why?" Malou asked with sudden alarm.

"Why?" Cam echoed with disbelief. "Malou, there's no way we're going to make it across that."

A kind of panic swirled up from the pit of Malou's stomach at the thought of being trapped overnight with Cam. "Can't we at least try?" she asked.

Cam's brow furrowed at the suggestion. "Malou, that water's four feet deep if it's an inch. The Germans engineer good cars, but this is no amphibious vehicle. I don't intend ending up as one of those silly people you read about every year who are swept away when they try to cross a creek in a flash flood.''

"You're right. I guess I was just worried about Lorre and . . .'' Her voice and explanation trailed off weakly. In the awkward silence that followed her fib, the sound of the rain drumming on the car roof seemed to be amplified.

"Malou, you were worried about spending the night with me." Cam's voice was gentle as he stated the obvious truth.

A withering shame flushed through Malou. Was she really *that* transparent?

"You can put your mind at ease," he continued. "I'm not in the habit of compromising the honor of prim primatologists.''

"What a boon to the profession," Malou answered with a mocking gaiety, trying to disguise her abashment as Cam put the Mercedes into reverse.

Dashing back into the stone house left them drenched again by the cold rain. Cam went for his third fully clothed shower of the day by running out to the woodshed for an armload of logs. After dealing expertly with a temperamental damper, he sparked a blazing fire that restored the room, gloomy and darkened by the storm, to its former cheeriness. Malou stood before it trying to bake out the chill that had seeped into her bones.

"This will not do," Cam announced, watching her shiver. He pulled a quilt off a chair and wrapped it around her shoulders, then lit a kerosene lantern and set out to explore the rest of the house. A few minutes later he returned with several thick terry towels slung over his shoulder, dragging a steamer trunk behind him. He tossed a towel to Malou and opened the trunk. Inside was a complete wardrobe, male's and female's, circa 1935. "If you don't mind, I'll just slip into something a little bit drier." Without any further preamble, Cam stripped off his sodden shirt, used it to rub away the beads of moisture trickling down his back, and dug into the pile of clothes.

Malou was mesmerized by the display. His back, bathed in the golden light of the fire, was magnificent. It was the leanly muscled back of the modern dancer he had reminded Malou of at their first meeting. His body, spare and strong and limber, suited him and thoroughly unsettled her.

He fished out a shirt of unbleached muslin, soft and pale from many washings and dryings in the sun, and slipped it on. As it fell to just below the tops of his legs, he stood and unceremoniously unbuckled his jeans. They dropped away to reveal a dancer's long, muscled thighs and calves. His grace and ease of movement confirmed the impression. They also signaled to Malou that Cameron Landell was a man who had long ago lost any self-consciousness he might ever have had around women.

Before tugging on the dry jeans, he turned to her. "Do pardon me," he asked again. "But modesty will have to goeth before I getteth pneumonia."

"Please, carry on," Malou replied as if the sight of such a gloriously sculptured male body were one she was treated to every day. Cam, hopping from one foot to the other, quickly slipped into the slightly baggy jeans.

"All I need now is a blade of hay sticking out of my mouth," Cam said, appraising his countrified outfit. Malou silently disagreed. The soft, loose clothes flowed around his torso, emphasizing its grace and subdued power. "Now you," he commanded.

Malou shook her head. "No. Thanks. I'm fine." She bit off the words as she pulled the quilt a bit more tightly around herself. Unlike him, she had an ample supply of self-consciousness to deal with.

"Please, I've already told you that you have no reason to play the prim primatologist with me. Off with those soaking clothes." He turned back to the trunk. "Surely we can find something in here for you too. Why should I be the only one dressed like a hayseed?" He ripped into the trunk, pulling out a cotton dress. "This looks like it would do."

Malou was unable to resist the delicate garment. Even its smell was alluring. Rather than the musty odor she'd expected it to exude, the dress was fragrant with the scent of cedar from the trunk lining and the lavender and dried mountain laurel blossoms that had been packed away with the clothes. It had been hand made of a fine, powder blue cotton, its front lovingly worked with an intricate pattern of tucks and embroidery. The embroidery had all been done in ivory, so that the effect was one of understated elegance rather than contrived busyness. The skirt and long sleeves both flared out with an abundance of soft drapes.

"Go ahead, put it on. It'll be warmer than those damp things you're wearing," Cam urged. "Here, I'll hold up the blanket and you can change in absolute privacy." He took the quilt from her and held it up with his arms stretched over his head so that his view was entirely blocked. Malou hesitated for a moment.

"Hey, I'm not Hercules. I can't hold up this temple to your modesty all day."

Malou shucked off her damp shirt and shorts, relieved to have their clamminess away from her skin. She wondered if she dared remove her bra and panties as well. The warm, dry feel of the fire against her bare skin answered her question, and she stripped them off too. Standing there, naked before the flames, she became acutely aware that only a thin quilt separated her from Cameron Landell. She glanced over. The quilt rose and fell beside her with the deep, steady rhythm of his breathing. Firelight played across the cold-stiffened tips of her breasts, gilding them in gold. The tops of her thighs and the gentle curve of her stomach were also traced in the flickering light. Lost in shadow were the full underslopes of her breasts, the indentation of her navel.

A disturbing thought made itself known—she *wanted* Cam to see her. She *wanted* his gaze, for one brief moment, to travel over her breasts, her waist, her thighs. She *wanted* the quilt to fall away, and to stand naked before him. Horrified by the blatant sexuality of such impulses, Malou rubbed fiercely at herself with the towel almost as if she were mortifying her traitorous flesh, then swiftly pulled the pale blue dress on over her head. It floated over her body like a cloud grazing a mountaintop. She hurriedly buttoned the tiny carved mother-of-pearl buttons at the wrists and the back of the neck as if she could seal off the frightening desires raised by the man inches away from her.

"I'm through," she announced, feeling chastely invulnerable now, covered from her neck to below her knees.

Cam lowered the improvised curtain, and the pang of desire that had attacked him the first moment he'd seen her turned now into an undeniable ache. Silhouetted against the fire, the thin material of the dress might just as well have been a puff of smoke. He was stunned by the womanly

fullness of her breasts, the curve of her waist, the flare of
her hips where they melted into those impossible legs. His
mouth went dry, and a spasm of need twisted within him.

"Well, what do you think?" she chirped. "Are we the
Hayseed Couple of the Year?"

Cam reached out unsteadily, the quilt trembling in his
hands. "Here," he said, wrapping it around her shoulders.
"That dress can't be very warm. You don't want to catch a
chill." Malou looked up at him, puzzled. Her face sparkled
from the cleansing shower of the rain and glowed from the
heat of the fire. Her hair, usually blown dry into a straight,
elfin cut, had dried naturally into soft blond waves that
curled like petals around her face. And some diabolical
force had swollen her lips beyond even their usual tantalizing fullness.

He weighed the urgency driving at the most primitive
part of himself against the dangers of involvement. Especially with someone who had just become a sort of business
associate. Especially with someone whose honor he had
promised not to compromise. The balance tipped agoniz-
ingly toward denial.

"Dinner." He pronounced the word as if it were the
answer to the $64,000 question. "I'm starving." He turned
Malou in his arms and headed her out toward the kitchen,
grabbing the kerosene lantern as they went.

As Malou walked away from the light and heat of the fire,
she felt that she'd been cast out from both. Had Cam seen it
all in her eyes? Felt it in the staccato pound of her heart?
Had he known how much she'd wanted his kiss? His touch?
Had he known and chosen to withhold both?

Dinner was a slapdash affair pulled from the first couple

of cans that Cam opened. Neither of them had any appetite. It was certainly clear, as he barely picked at the food before him, that Cam had not been in any state even close to "starving."

He left his plate and stood for a long time at the pump, working the creaking handle until water ran clear and sweet into the earthen jug he slipped beneath the trickle. Malou followed his lead and mixed a bit of the scotch in with the crystalline water. The smooth, warming taste fit the evening perfectly. Even more welcome was the way it untangled a few knots of the tension snarling up inside her.

They took their drinks and sat in front of the fire, listening to the hypnotic drum of rainfall on the roof and to the unsettling progression of thoughts through their own minds. It was warm in front of the fire, far too warm for the quilt. Malou shrugged it off.

"You know . . . ." Their voices bumped together. Out of the long, thought-filled silence, they'd both managed to speak at once.

"Go ahead," Cam said, far too aware of the flash of color that had brightened her cheeks and the way her eyelashes had swept downward to mark those cheeks with dark crescents. And far, far too aware of the soft jut of her nipples, so clearly outlined beneath the diaphanous fabric. Christ, he felt like a teenage boy confounded and controlled by hormonal urges.

"It was nothing," she demurred. "Just wondering if you'd ever been married or any of that stuff."

"Nothing, eh?" he taunted her. "No, never been married. What about you? Ever gone in for any of 'that stuff'?"

She shook her head.

"Any serious contenders lurking about? Jealous lovers poised and ready at this very instant to storm the cabin and blast my head off in a hot-blooded crime of passion?"

Malou smiled. "No, the lovers I've had haven't been of the hot-blooded, passionate variety." She felt bold and something of a fraud even talking about her "lovers" with Cam.

"What fools they must have been."

Whose fault had that been? she wondered, thinking back over her amorous history. Always, it seemed, experimentation and curiosity had been much larger factors than desire. She'd invariably been the one to swiftly end the brief affairs, escaping before the entanglements became so damnably complicated. Never, not until Cam's kiss that morning, had she felt anything close to passion. She reached for her glass.

Cam felt his blood surge within him as her lips parted slightly, firelight playing over her moist bottom lip.

"And what of your jealous lovers?" she asked, liking the intimacy of the question, the casual ease she'd managed to imitate. "Certainly there must be more than a few of those lurking about."

"And why 'certainly'?"

"Well, because . . ." How had he managed to turn her question around so that, once again, she was the one under scrutiny? She wished she were better at the dodges and feints of conversation between men and women. More practiced at coming up with saucy one-liners. Instead she had to keep resorting to the truth. "Because of your position, your money, and besides, you're no Quasimodo and don't duck the question."

"No Quasimodo, eh? Thanks for the stunning evaluation.'' Cam raked her with a mocking grin. "Hmmm, I don't know what to tell you, Malou. There have been women in my life, probably too many in my more boisterous youth, but fewer and fewer as the years go along. I suppose the turning point came a couple of years ago. I'd just finished a project and turned the developed land over to the builder. He staged this huge, gala affair and invited every San Antonio notable he thought could get him an inch in the society columns.

"I ended up with what is generally regarded as San Antonio's most beautiful woman on my arm, squiring her to the event of the year. Should have been a moment of glorious triumph, right?''

"The elements sound right,'' Malou agreed, peeved at herself for the slight twinge that shot through her at the thought of San Antonio's most beautiful woman on Cam's arm.

Cam shook his head. "At the time I was halfway through a Ludlum thriller, and the whole night all I could think about was that book and how much I'd rather be home reading. From then on I always asked myself one question before I went out. Would I rather be home reading? I was amazed at how often the answer was yes. Why are you laughing? Do you prefer swinging singles? The indefatigable stud ever ready for any action from any corner?''

"No,'' Malou countered. "I'm laughing because that's the exact question that's kept me happily at home tucked in bed many a night. I just didn't think that a man like you would ever ask it of himself.''

"Sorry to disappoint you.''

"I'm far from disappointed,'' Malou answered, noticing that, somewhere in this totally unexpected conversation, the knot in her stomach had untied itself. She no longer felt strangled by intricacies she didn't understand. Cam no longer seemed like such a menacing mystery. "So, you're a Ludlum fan. Who else do you read?"

"Name the author, I've probably tried him or her at one time. Books, they were my salvation. Everyone I grew up with was always looking for a way out. Most of the kids found it in drinking, drugs, sniffing glue, fast cars, whatever made them forget for a little while. I was lucky. I turned on early to books and nothing else afterward ever came close to that high, the ability of the printed word to put you into whatever world you chose." Cam stopped himself with a self-deprecating chuckle.

"Doesn't exactly fit my image as the ruthless developer with no social conscience or thought for anything other than that almighty bottom line, huh?"

Malou winced inwardly as he verbalized exactly what she had expected him to be. "So you hung out with a fast crowd when you were a kid."

"Fast?" Cam repeated. "Not really. Where I grew up, that was the only speed there was. You still don't have the complete picture of what the boyhood of Cameron Landell was like, do you?"

"I suppose I don't. Why don't you fill me in? How about some basic stuff like, where did you grow up?"

"I'm flattered that you can't guess."

"Flattered?" Malou echoed, liking the companionable ease that had sprung up between them.

"Yes, my part of the world is not exactly renowned for the melodiousness of its accents. Come on, try to guess."

Malou cocked her head one way, then the other, as if she

could find a clue to his place of origin if she studied his face hard enough. "I don't know, but you have a decided Mediterranean look to you."

"Swarthy, eh?"

"Well, something that would suggest you have ancestors lurking somewhere who were not unfamiliar with the taste of olive oil." That "something" Malou jestingly referred to was his eyes, which had gone meltingly soft in the firelight and were causing visions of Venice in the moonlight to disturb her thoughts.

"Now, let's see," she said sternly, corraling her thoughts, which had been wandering down gondola-patrolled canals. "I'm a scientist. I should apply a little deductive reasoning to this problem."

"You're doing pretty well so far. My maternal grandmother came right off the boat from Naples."

Pleased to have her first deduction confirmed, Malou directed, "Okay, speak a few words and I'll analyze the inflections."

"The gingham dog and the calico cat, side by side on the table they sat . . ."

"Oh, that's good," Malou broke in, delighted to hear one of her favorite childhood books being quoted. But as delightful as the quote was and as surprising as it was that Cam had it stored away, it did little to aid her inquiry. "You know, your voice is like a newscaster's. You don't particularly sound as if you belong anywhere."

A triumphant grin spread across Cam's face, lighting his features with a boyish glee.

"Now, don't gloat," Malou chided him. "Smugness does not become you at all. I know," she blurted out in a moment of inspiration. "Where else on earth do none of the people really belong where they are? Where they're all from somewhere else—California!"

Cam burst into full-throated laughter at Malou's guess. "Me?" he gasped between howls. "A beach boy?"

Malou smiled, unable to resist the contagion of his mirth. As attractive as she found him in general, he was irresistibly *likable* right now, crumpling up with good-natured amusement. "Okay, bad guess. Let me try again. Somewhere in the Midwest? Chicago?"

"Let me give you a little help . . ." Suddenly Cam's whole demeanor changed. He threw back his shoulders and pulled open a few buttons to expose more of his chest. He spread his legs so that he dominated more of the couch. His full lips dipped down into a tough-guy sneer, and then he spoke. "Dis here's more like duh way I grew up tawkin'. It ain't real preddy, but id's duh only way duh guys on duh street'll unnerstancha." His accent was nasal and unmistakable.

"The Bronx?" Malou whispered, barely able to countenance the thought.

"The same," Cam confirmed her guess. Then, as if he'd suddenly returned to his senses, he straightened up in the chair and quickly buttoned his shirt. He took a long drink, emptying his glass, then went to the kitchen for a refill.

Malou was still flabbergasted when he came back in with the bottle of scotch and topped off her glass. "You grew up in the Bronx?" she asked, still not believing it.

"Toughest part." He took a long drink and looked at her for a long, hard moment. "We didn't start off there. At least my mother didn't. She came from a wealthy family. She was the one who kept me from developing an accent.

Or taught me to switch it off when I wanted to.'' He settled back onto the couch and placed his drink on the floor beside it, where it sat ignored as Cam unfolded the latest unexpected aspect in his makeup.

''From what I can gather, my mother was fairly wild in her younger days. Resisted her family's efforts to ship her off to some nice safe Seven Sisters college and insisted on going to NYU right in the heart of New York City. Back in those days, the thing for slightly wild college girls from rich families to do was to hang out at the jazz clubs.

''That's where she met the old man.'' Cam's tone shifted dramatically with the mention of his father. It was not a positive shift. ''He played alto sax in a group of black musicians. And he was good. He still played a little now and then when I was young, and even as a kid I could tell he was good. But he lost his lip.''

Malou inclined her head toward Cam in a gesture of puzzlement.

''That's what horn players call it when they lose whatever it was that made them special on their instrument. My father lost his to drinking.''

Malou was caught by surprise by Cam's casual tone, which contrasted so starkly with what he was revealing.

''But I'm getting a little ahead of the story. Or what I've been able to piece together, anyway. Seems my rebellious mother fell in love with this sax player and married him. Her family had a fit and told her that she would be disinherited if she didn't have it annulled. Then, right into the middle of this drama came World War II. My father was drafted and ended up in a USO band touring the Pacific. For the time being, my mother went home to Connecticut and lived with her family.

"My father was sure that in time my mother's rich family would forget about disinheriting her, and her family was sure that she would forget about my father. But nobody forgot anything."

Cam stopped and looked off into the flames as if he could see his parents' sad history being played out there. Abruptly, he glanced over at Malou. "This is strange. I've hardly thought about any of this stuff for twenty years, and I've never talked about it with anyone."

"It's interesting," Malou said, her tone and the way she was leaning forward indicating much more than simple interest. It communicated that she was interested in Cam's story because she cared about him. "So what happened when your father came home?"

"Ah, when Johnny came marching home. Of course, my mother went to him. My theory is that my father was convinced my mother's family would turn loose of the purse strings and that he would finally begin living in a style to which he yearned to become accustomed. But that didn't happen. When my mother went back, her father told her she'd never see another dime of his money and he was as good as his word.

"I've seen pictures of the two of them back then. My mother always in some nicely tailored suit with a little hat perched on top of her head and some kind of a veil or something sticking up off of it, looking like she was about to embark on some grand and romantic adventure. And my father . . ." Cam paused, his voice again shifting into a tone of residual bitterness as he spoke of his father. "My father always looking like the professional tough guy in his two-tone suits with the shoulders out to here." He indicated the broadly padded contours of a zoot suit. But he was a handsome devil, and he could blow that horn in those days. So I suppose I can understand why the sheltered, romantic girl my mother was back then would fall in love with him.

"Anyway, I came along, and my father named me after my maternal grandfather, hoping that that would soften the old man up a bit. It didn't work though. Once my father realized that there wasn't going to be any money, any easy street for him, he started drinking more and playing the sax less. Then my younger brother was born and things became all too real. The romantic adventure went sour. So my mother took her college degree and found a job as a typist to keep us all fed since my father had lost any interest he might ever have had in his family.

"Through the years, though, my mother sort of tried to keep the faith alive. She was determined that, just because we lived in a tenement, she wasn't going to lose her sons to the streets. So she read to us and wouldn't let us talk like bums and made us believe that we could do anything and be anybody we wanted to be."

"She sounds like a remarkable woman," Malou said softly, feeling almost as if she were intruding on a very private reverie.

"She was that indeed. And still is."

"What's she doing now?"

"Working as a librarian in the small, very exclusive town where she grew up. I bought her a house there about ten years ago, right after I made my first big speculation deal. She played around with being the lady of leisure for a few years, making a career of going to lunch with all her old friends and reestablishing ties with what was left of her family. Then she announced she was either going to go back to work or off her rocker."

It warmed Malou to see Cam's open admiration for his mother. "What about your younger brother?"

"Joe College," Cam laughed. "I sent him to a nice, safe Midwestern college, where he got a nice, safe degree in accounting. Married. Has two kids now and is supremely happy."

"What about your father?" Malou almost didn't want to ask, but curiosity drove her.

"Disappeared. Just walked out of the apartment one day when I was—what?—ten, eleven years old. Sax case under his arm. Said he had a gig. First one he'd had in longer than I could remember. Funny how clear it all was. My mother was at the sink peeling carrots, and she looked up, stared at him for a long time, then said, 'Bye, Johnny.' That was his name. I guess kids are like dogs, more attuned to the tone of a voice than to what is actually being said. Anyway, I knew just from the way my mother said those two words that my father was leaving. Never saw him again."

Cam shrugged and looked down at his hands. Malou didn't know what to say, how to tell Cam how remarkable she thought he was having done so much with his life when he'd started with so little. But something in his expression told her that he had never thought of himself as having been deprived and would resent anyone else thinking that.

"So, what about you?" he asked jauntily, whisking away all the old memories with the ease of a man who has had practice putting such things in perspective so they will not loom any larger than they must over his life. "Any dark and sordid secrets lurking in the girlhood of Mary Louise Sanders?"

"Just that name," Malou responded. "It was my very darkest secret." Though she made the reply into a joke, she realized it wasn't far from the truth. The story of Cam's young life had entranced her with its passionate upheavals. Her own life had been so neatly contained within tidy, ivy-covered walls. Her father, the esteemed professor. Her mother, the esteemed researcher. She laughed.

"Why the chuckle?" Cam asked, a grin teasing the corners of his mouth.

"I was just thinking about how radically different the houses we grew up in must have been. Your apartment, with your mother working and two young boys being two young boys, must have been chaotic."

"Chaotic was the best we ever achieved," Cam replied with affection. "That was right after we'd cleaned up. The rest of the time it was your standard disaster area." With those words, Malou put away the pity she'd brought out for Cam, since it was clear that, whatever hard times Mrs. Landell and her sons had weathered, there had always been ample love between them.

"My house was the exact opposite. I never even realized that people hung things on their walls until I saw paintings and posters and bulletin boards in my friends' houses. My mother was fanatically anti-clutter. A place for everything and everything in its place. Or else.

"My little rebellion was to clutter up my room with various collections of things that I'd found out in the woods and fields, where I spent most of my waking hours."

"A little tomboy, eh?" Cam surmised.

"The worst," Malou confirmed with a smile. "I don't think there were more than three days running, from the time I learned to walk until I finally discovered boys at an alarmingly late age, that my knees weren't a solid mass of scabs. I was always falling down chasing after butterflies, and dropping out of trees where I was investigating an owl's nest or something.''

''Our younger years *were* radically different. The only birds I ever set eyes on were the pigeons in my friend Monty's coops.''

Malou smiled, and Cam studied her face for a moment that stretched out, taking them both into the tantalizing territory that lay beyond polite conversation. As the moment lengthened, Malou became aware again of the rain drumming on the roof of the snug stone house, of the tangy scent of mesquite burning in the fire, of the warmth of the fire itself. It was a warmth that seemed to intensify along with Cam's gaze.

Malou felt herself flush beneath its heat and her thoughts scattered. She asked inanely, ''Why don't you tell me about the pigeons?''

Her eyes strayed involuntarily to the flexing bow of his lips as they formed the answer that was so long in coming. ''Because there's something else I'd rather do.''

His desire was as palpable as the scent of the wood and the warmth of the flames. It twined around Malou with an inexorable seductiveness until she knew it as her own. Until there was no need for her question, ''What's that?''

''To kiss you again, Mary Louise Sanders.''

''I . . . ,'' she started to protest, but her words fell away into the void that seemed to have opened around them, leaving them, only the two of them in the whole world, safe and alone on an island far beyond the reach of mundane cares. In a remote corner of her mind, Malou realized that, once again, Cam had dodged her. She wasn't going to learn any more about the boyhood he had alluded to. Suddenly, though, she no longer cared.

The rain was a pelting curtain drawn tight around them, shutting off all that had gone before or would come after. Cam raised a hand haloed by golden hairs as it passed in front of the fire. He touched Malou's cheek, the barest glance of his fingertips. In some odd way, the gesture reminded Malou of the teenage monkeys, of the way they had touched her tear-streaked cheek with that same combination of gentle curiosity and wonder. The effect, Malou noticed, was profoundly different.

Like a cat leaning into a petting hand, she stretched toward the exploring touch. Cam opened his warm palm to the unimaginable softness of her cheek, sliding it from there up into her hair. Still with the barest, most electric of touches, he trailed the tips of his fingers, raking lightly with his nails, across the nape of her neck and around toward the area tingling beneath her ear. His hand stopped and spanned the fragile hollow of her collarbone. Malou's pulse leaped, pounding against Cam's palm.

"So delicate," he whispered, marveling at the finely wrought structure of bone and honey-colored skin. "Yet so strong." He was so close that Malou could feel his words as a deep bass rumble and a warm vapor against her skin. Passion coiled about Malou's lungs, demanding to make itself known, felt. She could not deny it. Struggling for the breath that seemed to have been squeezed from her, Malou's lips parted.

That nearly imperceptible parting was the signal Cam had been waiting for, searching for. Once he knew that Malou was not unaffected, the titanic pull of the attraction he felt for her surged through him with a power that he was hard pressed to keep in check. But restrain it he would. With an aching slowness, he cradled the nape of her neck in his hand and drew her to him. For a moment he lingered, his lips almost touching hers, as he savored the exquisite bouquet, freshened by the drenching rain and warmed by the fire's heat, that wafted up to him.

Malou thought he must be deliberately torturing her, keeping his lips less than a breath from her own. Yet she knew that, had he lunged at her in an overheated attack, she would have resisted. No, his coolness, his control, excited her far more than any grappling advance ever could. Within the loose but enticing coils of his passion, she was free to experience her own arousal. It came not as a pounding, grasping thing, but rather as an unraveling, a letting go. Bonds within her snapped, and knots slid apart. She felt herself untangling and all the loose ends seeking out a new union. She leaned toward Cam.

The feel of his lips obliterated all her thoughts. The ragged tear of his breath spilled over her as he took her mouth. A thrill of nervous pleasure skittered through Malou, half of her fearing, half of her yearning mightily for Cam to unleash his passion. She waited for his mouth to grind over hers, to plunder and possess it. Instead, Cam lightly played his lips over hers, teasing them even further as he flicked his tongue over their waiting ripeness. The light stab of his tongue drove her ever further into a pounding readiness.

He pressed her back against the wide bed of the age-softened leather couch. As he paused above her, the dancing flames bronzed his features. They flickered over the tousled mat of his dark curls. Twin blazes leaped in the impenetrable darkness of his eyes. His lips found the hollows of her throat. Tendrils of electric pleasure spiraled out from the touch of his mouth. The spiral widened as the warmth of his kiss moved down, drawn ineluctably to the gentle swell of her breasts.

The tissue-thin cotton of the dress was more provocation than protection; it heightened rather than hid the bounty beneath, just as it heightened Malou's pleasure in Cam's discovery as he brought the tips of her breasts to vibrant life. She was aching for him by the time his mouth returned to hers. The intensity of her need was a frightening surprise. For Malou, who had chosen the society of monkeys over men, that need was new and dangerous. Every atom of her being seemed to be rising up to reach out for completion, for a joining with the man beside her. A shimmer of panic passed through her as she felt control slipping away from her.

"Cam, I . . . ," she gasped, betraying too much of the tumult raging within her. "We should stop."

Cam looked at her with fond amusement, as if her words were a provocative tease like the thin material of the dress he'd found for her. No woman had ever before felt so instantly right in his arms. He couldn't believe that Malou wasn't in the thrall of the force that now possessed him. He moved to reclaim her mouth and felt her stiffen in his arms.

"You mean it, don't you?" he asked, still not believing she could be serious.

"Yes." Malou struggled for a grip on her rampaging emotions. "It's not a good idea. Everything's happening so fast."

"Malou, darling, I can make it happen as slow as you are able to endure."

Malou's mouth went dry at the blatant sexual promise. She knew right down to her toenails that Cameron Landell could make good on that promise.

"No, Cam," she began, her mind wheeling for excuses. But they weren't needed. Cam was already opening a gulf between them as he backed away. The fire had died away. When the warmth of his skin left hers, a slight chill crept through the flimsy dress.

"You're right," Cam announced, all signs of arousal now scrubbed from his brisk voice. "You've got too much to gain here and I've got far too much to lose. The balance between us is all skewed. We wouldn't want to start off our association with one of us taking advantage of the other."

"That's not what I meant," Malou protested, but the flames that had danced only moments before in Cam's eyes had already died.

"Nonetheless, that's what it would have come to." He rose and Malou was pierced by a pang of regret. She wanted to take back her words, her fears, her caution. But the moment had passed. "Take your pick," he offered in a jarringly chipper voice. "The couch, or the bed in the other room."

"I'm fine here," Malou answered, no longer wanting the separation she had caused.

"Good choice. I had a look at that bed earlier, and it appears that Stallings slept on pinecones." He reached for a thick log and settled it expertly on the fire, then tucked the quilt up around Malou's shoulders. "There, that ought to keep you through the night. Need anything else?"

"Just you," Malou whispered, but it was too late, for Cam was already out of earshot, striding out of the room.

It's for the best, she told herself, wondering if she would have succumbed if Cam had not heeded her protest. But he had, she reminded herself, forcing her lids shut to seek inwardly for the sleep that would be a long time in coming.

Beyond the pool of light cast by the fire, Cam stopped and watched, marveling at how controlled Malou was. Only seconds after breaking off one of the most heated embraces of his life, she could calmly drift off to sleep while his heart was still thudding like a kettledrum. God, he couldn't deny it though, watching her lids flutter down on those sun-blessed cheeks. He wanted her. Badly. He issued himself a stern warning that in the future he would never again let *his* control come so close to slipping away.

Then each of them on their separate beds, in their separate darknesses, listened for several long, solitary hours to the rain pecking at the roof of the small stone house they shared.

Chapter Five

Even before she opened her eyes, Malou knew that she had not slept long enough. She burrowed farther underneath the quilt to escape the pounding sound that was dragging her toward consciousness. The creak of footsteps padding across the old wooden floor brought her fully awake. Her senses awoke before her mind did. They were alive with a pulsing awareness of Cam's nearness even before Malou had time to completely recollect where she was and who was with her.

The door scraped open behind her. Shielded by the high back of the couch, she listened, seeking to learn the identity of the insistent early-morning visitor knocking at the door.

"*Buenos días,* Señor Landell."

Jorge Maldonado.

Malou was surprised to hear such respect and deference

in Jorge's usually curt voice. Obviously, he had brought the Mexican *peón*'s fear of the almighty *patrón* with him when he crossed the Rio Grande. She was even more surprised though to hear his voice, in any tone, at such an early hour.

"Todo es—"

"You'll have to try English, Jorge," Cam whispered.

Haltingly, Jorge began again. "Everything is done as you ordered."

The statement came out with an oddly formal finality. Before Malou had time to puzzle over its meaning, Jorge was asking, "But, why do you sleep here? I came only by luck. Why do you not sleep at the ranch house?"

Malou was jarred by the question and strained for Cam's answer. It was a whisper even lower than the one he'd been using.

"We can't talk in here. Let's go out onto the porch."

The heavy oak door swung shut, cutting off any further possibility that she might pick up another scrap of conversation. Malou quickly slithered out from beneath the quilt and into her clothes, which had dried by the fire, then went to the front window farthest from the door. Cam was wearing only the jeans he had found last night. A bit too large, they rode low on his hips. Hard juts of bone protruded on either side of his flat stomach. He was gesturing decisively, his hand pointed and chopping like an ax. Jorge was nodding deferentially. Then the Mexican hired hand pointed into the distance, his brown finger snaking through the air. Malou followed it into a day sparkling with the rain's cleansing.

Finally, Cam nodded a couple of times, then shook Jorge's hand and patted him on the back. Jorge's stunned, then pleased reaction was the only part of the exchange that

Malou understood. He was quite clearly honored and delighted by the simple gesture. Malou backed quickly away from the window when Cam turned to come back in.

"Sorry we woke you. How did you sleep?"

"Not bad," Malou lied, forcing her gaze away from the rugged contours of his chest, his stomach. He seemed so cheerily unaffected, she would have to make an effort to appear equally unperturbed, both by the events of last night and by the peculiar encounter she'd just witnessed.

"Apparently we made things unnecessarily rough on ourselves. According to Jorge, this isn't the main ranch house at all. We turned off too soon. This"—he circled his hand around to take in the stone house—"is just some shrine Stallings maintained to his wife for the past half a century. She died giving birth to their first child here close to fifty years ago, and Stallings just closed the place up and moved. Not long after that he made his first big oil strike and built a new house, the house he wished he could have built for his wife. Anyway, he never remarried and kept this old place just as it was, with everything maintained and in working order."

The story both saddened and uplifted Malou. She fingered the old quilt, knowing a bit now about the woman who had pieced it together and about the man who had never stopped loving her.

"Want to have a look at what we were originally aiming for?" Cam asked. "The telephone connection's probably better there."

"Sure," Malou agreed hesitantly. Something was not right. She knew prudence would dictate that she leave immediately and cut off any further involvement with Cameron Landell. But two factors propelled her back into the claret-colored Mercedes: her concern for the troop of monkeys she was trying to save and sheer, unshakable curiosity. Curiosity about Jorge's cryptic words and about Cam and what he was up to out here.

The drive that had been such an arduous ordeal in the rain was a matter of minutes in the sun-sparkled day. Though she hadn't thought it possible, the surrounding country was even lovelier than it had been the day before. A terrible feeling of missed opportunity, of a paradise lost, swept through Malou as they bumped off the rutted road back onto the smoothly paved highway. She wondered what she should have, *could* have, done differently. She glanced over at Cam. He drove with one hand draped casually at the apex of the steering wheel. His free arm rested on the open window. His gaze was intent as he looked out with a keen eye over the ranch he now owned. His concentration on the passing countryside was so total that Malou felt free for the moment to scrutinize Cam. The longer she looked, the more lost she felt. At the instant she saw Cam turning toward her, she quickly cut her glance away, out to the awakening spring.

The landscape was a muddled green blur, however, for Malou was still seeing Cam's sun-etched profile in her mind. It galled her to notice that her pulse was fluttering and that her stomach felt as if she were looking over a thousand-foot drop. It piqued her even more to have to admit to herself that her motivation for coming with Cam was not simply concern for the troop. Curiosity *was* a factor, but not of the sort she'd originally thought. Deep in her heart of hearts, she was forced to own up to the fact that she was curious about what might or might not develop between her and Cameron Landell. And there he was, she

thought with a final stab of irritation, sitting over there with
no thought on his mind other than the value of the latest
chunk of land to come into his possession. She seamed her
mouth into a tight line as the car surged forward with a
sudden burst of speed.

Cam had felt her gaze on him as he'd stared out at the
land he owned. He'd been attempting to force himself to
take the all-consuming interest in it that he usually took in
his property. But instead of carefully evaluating the parcel
in front of him, his mind saw only torturing images of the
woman beside him gilded in firelight and dressed in a nearly
transparent cotton dress. But what really tortured him was
wondering what might have happened if he had pushed past
her resistance last night. Pushed just the tiniest bit.

He had known she was watching him. Was he imagining
it, or did her gaze actually feel warm against his skin? For
as long as he could stand it, he continued looking out the
windshield; then, ever so slowly, he turned toward her. She
had instantly jerked away to glare out the window. Cam had
chided himself for letting his imagination—and, he had to
admit it, his hopes—get the better of him. He had felt her
frostiness, seen it in her posture and in the hard line of her
mouth. Her interest lay strictly with those infernal monkeys
she wanted him to sponsor a retirement community for. As
if he could outrun his quashed hopes, Cam had jammed his
foot against the accelerator and the car had leaped forward.
The drive was grimly silent for the next couple of miles
until they approached the real entrance to Stallings's ranch.

"Now this is more like it." The sight cheered Cam a bit.
The front gate was a massive structure built of enormous,
smooth river-bottom rocks. They passed beneath it into a
world of neatly mowed and fenced pastures full of sleek

quarter horses feeding in the shade of enormous live oaks. The road twisted back past a water tank seemingly large enough for a small town, then over a sturdy bridge. On the far side of the creek were endless miles of plowed field. They turned up a gentle rise that led to the main house, situated at its peak. It looked like a cross between Tara and a feudal baron's fortress, with thick stone walls fronted by graceful, sweeping porches. Malou immediately envisioned a lawn party being held on the thick grass in the shade of the oaks.

"Maybe Mr. Stallings wasn't such a liar after all," Malou suggested.

Cam's mind had turned back fully to evaluating the extent and value of the developments on the property. They did indeed seem pretty much as Stallings had represented them. Outside of the monkey ranch. "It's a solid piece of property," he allowed. "But the fact remains that I never wanted to own it. I never intended to even have to see this place, much less work it. All I wanted the Lazy S to be was collateral. Now I'm stuck with having to dispose of it as quickly as I can. And, since the market in this area is depressed right now, I stand to lose a bundle. I just hope I can make enough to cover the note on Landell Acres, or I'll lose that too."

"The house is lovely, though," Malou added, beginning to genuinely understand the calamitous position Stallings had put Cam in.

"Yes," Cam admitted without enthusiasm, "the house is lovely." He parked the car. "Let's go see if this lovely house has two phone lines so both of us can get to work."

The interior was as baronial as the exterior had promised it would be. The entrance hall was two stories high. Thick exposed beams ran across the ceiling. Furnishings obviously selected by a decorator were clustered in groupings. One such grouping sat around the fireplace, which extended up the two-story wall. A second-story hallway overhung the magnificent room, opening onto the upstairs bedrooms. Though it was all quite splendid, the outsized scale of the place intimidated Malou a bit and made the warm humanness of the small stone house seem all the more inviting.

"Lord, all the families in the building I grew up in could fit in this place," Cam said, pivoting around. Malou liked him for the comment, for the undramatic way he acknowledged his background. Her curiosity about Cam flared anew. How could she be so drawn to a man she was so suspicious of?

"It is fairly immense," she agreed.

"Immense? It's a bleeping castle." He dumped his attaché case on the leather couch fronting the fireplace and stared off into the dining room with its twenty-four-place table. "I wonder if Stallings was happy here. For all its grandeur, I don't get a sense of a life having been lived here, at least not a happy one."

"Maybe he never got over losing his wife."

Cam nodded. "I can understand that." He seemed to be speaking to himself as he continued staring out past the dining room. "I can understand a love that would consume a life." He caught himself and, returning his thoughts and words to the present, laughed as if disowning what he'd just said. "Of course, I'm speaking hypothetically here. The loves I've known would barely consume a lunchtime."

Though Malou smiled and even helped gloss over his comment with a crack of her own—"I've had a few that would have been hard pressed to stretch over a coffee break''—she knew that Cam had spoken from his heart. Knowing that he did have the capacity to care so deeply made Malou regret all the more the moment between them that had passed forever.

"Well, shall we scout out a human-sized room and get to work?" he asked with what struck Malou as a forced briskness.

She followed him through the dining room out into the kitchen, where a little round Mexican woman, her silver-streaked black hair pulled back into a braid, looked up in shock at their appearance.

"You must be Jorge's wife," Cam said to her startled brown face. "I'm Cameron Landell." The look of shock did not abate until Cam tried a Spanish translation. All the worry lines changed course then, and her face was wreathed in pleasure. She smiled, revealing several teeth outlined in gold.

"I thought you didn't speak Spanish," Malou hissed.

"I don't," Cam answered under his breath, still smiling at Señora Maldonado. "That was my patented Tex-Mex hodgepodge."

"Seems to have done the trick."

The woman put away her gold-rimmed smile and began rattling away in Spanish. Cam put up his hand for her to slow down and she obliged. He interjected a few words, then placed a friendly hand on her shoulder. *"Muchas gracias*, Señora Maldonado." The woman beamed again in response.

Malou thought that if Cam were as skillful in dealing with all his employees as he'd been with the Maldonados, he must certainly have a contented and loyal force behind him. Cam set off again.

"What was that all about?" she asked as they turned down a wide corridor.

"She was apologizing for not having something ready to eat and promised that lunch would be early and dinner special. You are staying, of course."

"Cam, I should be getting back to the station. Ernie will start to wonder what's happened to me."

Cam pressed his lips together. "I can't for the life of me understand what Ernie's opinion could mean to you one way or the other."

"I have to work with him, Cam. He may not be the most scintillating human, but up at Los Monos, he's the only human for miles."

"I guess he just hasn't worked very hard to endear himself to me. I resent his insinuations."

"Primatologists aren't famous for their social skills," Malou admitted. "It's one of the reasons we do what we do instead of running for elected office."

Cam stopped and looked at her thoughtfully.

Afraid that she'd exposed too much about herself in explaining Ernie, Malou moved briskly away toward the office at the end of the hall. "This must have been where Mr. Stallings worked," she said brightly as they entered the room. It was by far the homiest room in the house.

"The rest of the place was probably just for show," Cam observed, picking up a gold-framed photo that showed a young and handsome Mr. Stallings with a shy, willowy woman by his side. "But this was the old man's lair." A large partner's desk sat in the middle of the room with a console phone on each side. "No worries about phone lines," Cam said, pulling out a comfortably upholstered swivel chair and seating himself at the smaller half of the desk. He gestured toward what had obviously been Stall-ings's chair. "Be my guest."

Malou, feeling like a child playing in her father's office, seated herself in the high-backed chair. A cozy intimacy wrapped the two of them together as they sat facing one another across the double-sided desk. A window behind Malou let in streams of morning light that played across Cam's dark hair, lighting it up with highlights of red as he bent his head over the pile of contracts he pulled from his case. Malou had to forcibly prod herself into action as she turned back to the phone and picked up where she'd left off yesterday, working her way down the list of foundations and other possible grantors. Soon they were both absorbed in their tasks, each one conducting their phone business without self-consciousness.

The low-slanting morning sunlight had long since climbed away from the office's east window when Señora Maldonado timidly knocked on the frame of the open door to tell them that lunch was ready.

It was a light, tasty, and swift affair of quesadillas— cheese wrapped in grilled tortillas—and a glutton's array of fruit from the bountiful Rio Grande Valley. And then they were back at work.

The afternoon sun was already beginning to cut into the west window when Malou paused long enough to realize that the day had been amazingly productive and that Cam had been responsible. She had caught his sense of urgency as he machine-gunned his way through stacks of papers and a volley of concise calls. It was no longer any mystery to her why Cameron Landell had risen so far, so fast. The man was indefatigable. And so handsome. Her appraisal was sabotaged by that observation. By the thick fringe of lashes shadowing his hard-planed cheeks. By the seductive intensity that wrapped his features in an aura of contained energy. She marveled at how, even sitting at a desk, Cam exuded a sense of motion only barely leashed.

Cam glanced up and caught Malou watching him. Amusement at her embarrassment crept over his face for a few seconds before he turned back to his work. Trying not to sound as flustered as she felt, Malou made her next call.

Her voice had been honed to a rasp by the time Señora Maldonado appeared to shyly announce dinner.

Two places were set at the end of the banquet-length table. They swam in a pool of candlelight. A crystal bowl of red hibiscus complemented the sprightly colors of the Mexican place settings gaily painted with birds. A carafe of white wine cast an amber gleam across the white linen tablecloth.

Cam held Malou's chair out for her with a courtly flourish that added a light note to the gesture. He exchanged a few words with Señora Maldonado, who had appeared with a cart laden with domed serving trays, then excused herself.

"I told her we could manage ourselves if she wanted to take the rest of the evening off," Cam explained as he lifted the lid from a steaming tray. Prawns grilled in butter lay curled up against one another in a succulent pink line. Cam transferred several to Malou's plate, then added rice pilaf and marinated vegetables.

"Señora Maldonado mentioned that Stallings had sent her to a cooking school in Mexico to be trained. They certainly did a superb job," he concluded, finishing off a prawn.

"Mmm," Malou murmured, her thoughts elsewhere. They'd been drawn again into that dangerous zone that had Cameron Landell at its center. A cooking school in Mexico was the last thing on her mind as candlelight glanced across Cam's buttery lower lip.

"Turn up any promising prospects?"

It took Malou a second to process the words formed by those mesmerizing lips. "Oh. Prospects. Yes, actually I did. Won't know anything firm though for a week or two, which is breakneck speed for foundations."

"Ah, bureaucracy. If I added a hundred people to my organization, I'd cut efficiency by over half."

"What did you major in at school? Business administration?"

"That question," Cam answered, his eyes gleaming, "is based upon the false assumption that I majored in anything at all. No, I got my degree in hard work, with special courses in being in the right place at the right time. Land development is a game people are either born with an instinct for or not. It's not something you can pick up at school. Motivation helps. Real, bone-deep drive. That, I'd acquired by the time I was old enough to ride a bike. Not that I ever had one growing up."

"Never had a bike?"

"No bike. No degree. What kind of Martian am I?" Cam asked with a slightly bitter laugh.

"That wasn't what I meant. It's just that, for me, a bike was my salvation. My way to get out of my house."

Cam's mildly affronted expression softened. "Yours wasn't a happy childhood?"

"It wasn't unhappy. Just sort of . . ." Malou searched

for a word to describe her airless, controlled upbringing.
"Claustrophobic?" she tried, hoping Cam would understand.

"And so you grew up reading about Dian Fossey and
Jane Goodall and dreaming of escaping to the African
savannah."

"Pretty much," Malou said with a chuckle. Cam's
perceptiveness bridged the gap that had opened up between
them. It gave her the courage to voice her own insight.
"And you grew up dreaming of escaping to the world I was
running from."

Cam's laugh floated easily on the candle-warmed air. "I
guess it was inevitable, then, that our escape routes would
intersect."

"Oh, predestined, I'm sure," Malou quipped back,
enjoying the ease that was enfolding them again. She tried
to remember exactly why she'd been suspicious of Cam, but
all the reasons suddenly seemed very distant and dusty with
age.

"Shall we take our coffee out by the pool?" he asked,
grabbing the pot off the warmer. Malou gathered up cups
and saucers. As they left, Cam paused to snatch a bottle of
Kahlua off the sideboard.

The evening was the silken deliverance of spring's
promise. The air caressed Malou with vapors of a thousand
flowers. Malou closed her eyes and drank them all in. "A
person could get tipsy just breathing on a night like this."

Cam relieved her of her burden, placing the cups and
saucers on a small table between two chaise longues, then
stood close beside her. "It is intoxicating."

His voice was a growl that vibrated through Malou,
striking chords buried within her deepest center. She looked

up, and their gazes met with the same inevitability that had brought their lives colliding together. Malou felt herself teetering, a sensation that called to mind Cam's shattering words about the imbalance between them. "You have too much to gain and I have too much to lose." That was still true.

She dragged her eyes from his. "Oh, coffee," she announced inanely, darting away toward the pot. "Can't let it get cold." She settled herself into a chaise, the giddy shrillness of her words still echoing tinnily.

Cam watched her bolt away from him like a frightened fawn and felt the nick of regret again, knowing he had caused her skittishness. He knew that, from a business standpoint, his entire involvement here was one long series of mistakes. The loan to Stallings had been a mistake, his promise to allow Malou time to save the troop had been a mistake, but he was committing the biggest mistake of all by being here with her tonight and feeling what he was feeling. Good sense demanded that he offer to take her back to Los Monos immediately and stop flirting with the danger that he was allowing to lick away at his control.

Yes, Cam told himself as he went to the other chaise and stretched out on it. They would finish their coffee, and then he absolutely must return her to the research station. He had far too much to lose in this situation.

"Cream or sugar or just a shot of Kahlua?" Malou asked.

"Just the Kahlua."

She held the cup out to him. Her hair, silver in the moonlight, had curled again in the humidity into those elfin petals, Cam noted with an inward groan as he took the cup. Their hands touched beneath the saucer. It was only for an instant, but no more time was needed for Cam to learn again the velvet touch of her skin, its maddening effect upon him. His heart felt like a wild creature uncaged. He drank the coffee hoping it would steady him, would stop the infernal, adolescent pounding of his pulse. He breathed in the coffee vapors wanting the smell to drive away her scent.

"Oh, look, a shooting star," Malou said, and he looked over.

She was a slender curve of tawny ivory against the midnight blue of the chaise cushions. Before Cam had time to censor the image, he imagined her nude, imagined the feel of the full, high breasts thrusting up beneath her blouse. In direct defiance of all his most prudent wishes, he felt his body responding. This was madness, Cam knew. He had to do something.

"The sky is *that* way." Malou pointed to the spot where the shooting star had long since charted the fiery course of its destruction. He was looking at her as if he too felt the same churning desire that she was attempting to suppress.

"Ah, right. Ummm, quite spectacular." He looked off vaguely at the stationary stars glittering above them. "How about a swim?" He jumped up with a rush of heartiness that convinced Malou she must have been mistaken. He was with her simply because he had to be. Because the mistake of his loan to Mr. Stallings had thrown them together. Period.

"No suit," she shrugged off the suggestion.

Cam strode over to a louvered wooden door and opened it. Inside were shelves of towels and an assortment of swimwear. "Take your pick," he announced, holding a maillot in one hand and a bikini in the other. "I'd heard stories that the old man had a flock of nieces and nephews.

Surely one of these will fit.'' He disappeared into a stall with the only man's suit available, a slim racer's band of blue nylon. Malou hesitated a moment, then put her coffee aside and went to change into the more modest of the two suits, the one-piece maillot.

Cam was already in the pool when she emerged. Parabolas of moonlight arced across the water around him. His wet hair fell in dark waves around his face. Malou was uncomfortably aware of how emphatically she was silhouetted in the light from the changing room. She turned and switched it off and was cloaked in a sheltering darkness. The water was just cool enough to be refreshing without jarring her nervous system.

''This was an inspiration,'' she exulted, jackknifing into a dive that took her into the cool depths. She had almost forgotten how much she loved swimming. She pushed off from the bottom and jetted to the surface with a splash.

Cam watched her frolicking like a happy otter. She was a sprite, he decided, a lovely, innocent sprite, more creature than human and more spirit than creature. She belonged in the world of animals that she loved. His reflections were scattered by a well-aimed blast of water that Malou splashed into his face.

''Why you little otter,'' Cam sputtered. Malou's answering laugh sounded as if it had come from the rosebud mouth of a mischievous water nymph. He lunged out after her and she easily evaded his clumsy pursuit. Cam whirled around, searching the inky water for the merest hint of a bubble. It seemed as if Malou had escaped forever to some mythic underwater kingdom, until Cam felt the gentlest of currents rippling against the hairs on his legs and he realized that she had swum between them!

Cam dived after her. In the watery darkness, Malou was just a tantalizing shadow as elusive as the mermaids whose siren songs had tempted ancient sailors to their deaths. She was quick and agile, as if the water were her natural element. Each time he thought he'd cornered her, she vanished. Again and again he lunged for a shadow. His lungs burning, Cam finally surrendered and popped to the surface.

"You almost had me a couple of times there." Malou was beside him. Where she had come from, Cam had no earthly idea.

"You are one slippery customer," he gasped, still trying to catch his breath. "But not slippery enough." In one fluid motion, he whirled around and trapped her in his arms.

"That's not fair," Malou protested.

"All's fair in . . ." He left the phrase uncompleted, knowing only that he had just committed his latest and possibly most fatal mistake. Now that he had her in his arms, Cam knew how wrong he'd been—Malou was no sprite, no creature of myth and innocence. She was a woman, every delectable, achingly desirable inch of her.

At the moment of contact, Malou felt the emotional current change just as surely as a riptide current changed the ocean's staid rhythms. That moment tore the mask of detachment away from them both. They came together with such an inarguable rightness that neither could pretend any longer that their joining was an impossible mismatch.

Malou felt Cam's arms lock about her waist. It was an imprisonment she had unknowingly been waiting for from the first time she'd set eyes on Cameron Landell. She struggled no more against it.

"You should always be gleaming wet in the moonlight." Cam's voice was husky with wanting, with the burden of restraint. "You look and move like a bolt of quicksilver."

"My hair probably looks like a bolt of seaweed." Malou arched backward and, without breaking the bonds his arm had forged around her, Cam let her dip her hair into the water. The motion pressed Malou against the full evidence of Cam's arousal. As she came up, her curls were sleeked back into one satiny ribbon pulling away from her face. Water ran across her face and glistened like diamonds on her eyelashes. Cam never let her regain her position.

The feel of his lips upon hers was unspeakably sweet. It was a taste that Malou had hungered for far more deeply than she'd realized. They both indulged their hunger, filling themselves with a glutton's boundless rapacity for all that can be savored by lip and tooth and tongue. Malou felt her legs losing their power to hold her and Cam sweeping them away entirely from under her. She was cradled by the water and his arms. Floating in the weightless ecstasy she had dreamed of so often, she succumbed to its hypnotic power.

Cam slid the straps of her suit down, exposing one, then the other breast with a tantalizing slowness. He cupped his hand and dipped it into the water, then let a shimmering rivulet trickle over what he had laid bare. The crowns of her breasts tautened beneath such exquisitely delicate stimulation. A breeze brought them to even fuller life, straining against the limits of his teasing attentions. Cam took her in his mouth. His tongue was warm against her breeze-cooled nipple.

Malou felt everything. The gentle rasp of his beard. His hands beneath her lifting her, bringing her even more fully into his mouth. The thrilling patterns his tongue was inscribing upon her. The warm lap of the water between her legs. She was a vessel that she thought could never hold enough pleasure, could never be filled full enough with the sensations that she'd been afraid belonged exclusively to other women. And now she knew them and wanted the knowing never to end.

Her suit was off before she could be aware of its removal. Cam stood with her floating beside his chest and stared, hypnotized by the magical assembly of curves before him. With one reverent hand he traced a path across the arch of Malou's neck, lightly raked his fingertips across a swollen breast, down the ridges of her rib cage, the inward slope of her belly, and on to the slender columns of her legs. A trail of pulsing desire followed his touch, each tantalized cell yearning fiercely for more.

With an expert hand, Cam massaged Malou's feet, then began the return trip. By the time he reached the juncture at the top of her thighs, all Malou's wanting had coiled there. His touch seemed part of her dream, as if he telepathically knew all the tiny motions and increments of pressure that fit her body most perfectly.

Malou felt herself sailing, and she was a bit startled to discover that Cam was actually moving her through the water until her head rested on the slanting edge of the pool. Cam moved the hand that had been supporting her head down until he cradled the firm swell of her hips. Then, without ever interrupting the mesmerizing massage, Cam replaced his other hand with his mouth. Sliding both hands beneath her now, he brought her even more fully to him, to raise her against the ardent ministrations of his tongue.

Malou was aware only of being leashed to Cam by bonds even stronger than those forged by his hands holding and lifting her, joining her to him in the most intimate of embraces. It took several rings before the shrill of the poolside phone broke through, and several more before she could rouse herself enough to speak.

"You'd better answer it, Cam." She sounded like someone talking in her sleep. "It'll wake the Maldonados."

Slowly, Cam's hands slipped out from under her. He looked up at her as though the interruption were causing him physical pain.

The phone continued ringing. Cam turned toward it, slashing through the water in his haste to reach the phone, to silence its damnable ringing. He scrambled up the steps and grabbed it.

"Who is it?" he barked, his voice a harsh rasp. Malou pitied the caller.

"They're doing what!" Cam demanded. Light from the house behind him silhouetted his glistening wet form. It outlined the extent of Cam's desire only barely hidden beneath the flimsy nylon swimsuit. Malou reverberated to the sight, mirroring as it did her own intense arousal.

"Have any press shown up yet?" He paused, listening for the answer to his question. "Thank God. That kind of media attention now could cripple the project. Okay, stay on it. Work with them any way you can. I'll be there as soon as I can." Still leaning over the phone, Cam hung on to the receiver after hanging up. Finally, a defeated look on his face, he glanced over toward Malou.

"There's trouble at the project." He exhaled the words on a long sigh. "A bunch of those environmental protesters have formed a human barricade around the front gate."

"And you're worried that someone with a TV camera might show up."

Cam nodded. That one weary gesture told Malou far more than she had previously known about the crushing weight of the responsibilities that consumed Cam's life. She felt around for her suit, fished it out of the dark water, and wriggled quickly into it. The evening air was cool against her wet skin as she stepped out of the pool and went to Cam. He was still hunched over the phone when she reached him and put her arms around his bowed shoulders. He reached up and covered her hand with his.

There was something even more intimate about that touch than the one of only a few moments ago. For the first time Malou felt as if she and Cam were allies, not adversaries.

"Sometimes . . ." He shuddered. "Sometimes I wonder if it's all worth it." He turned to face her, to take her fully into his arms again. The hum of passion, which had barely stilled, vibrated again between them. "Just say the word," Cam offered, "and we'll dive right back into that pool and stay there until we both sprout fins and have a whole family of little babies with webbed feet."

The barest hint of a smile played across Cam's lips. But Malou knew that at the merest gesture from her, Cam would stay. Instead she laughed warmly, knowing that her laughter was Cam's release. The smile blossomed more fully on his lips.

"You have to go," she said, stating the painfully obvious.

His lips tightened in sad acceptance of the onerous fact.

He bent down and kissed her neck, then raised his mouth to whisper in her ear, "Thanks."

"And I have to get back to Los Monos. Ernie's probably already called out the Texas Rangers to look for me."

"Ah yes, your suspicious colleague. Just give me two minutes and I'll be ready to whisk you back to him."

When Cam pulled up at the research station all the lights were off except for one in the far back lab.

"And not a Ranger in sight," Cam jibed as they stepped out. "I'm not even going to say good night," he informed her outside the station door. "Because I have every intention of continuing this night as soon as I possibly can."

"Sooner," Malou answered. A facade had been stripped away from between them, and she gloried in the freedom of acting and speaking without pretense.

Their kiss was a down payment on a treasure that they reluctantly had to deny themselves for the moment.

Malou stood outside beneath the stars, watching Cam's taillights until they were pinpoints of red heading north through the vastness of south Texas. She turned to the door and opened it. Her task for the next day, or however long it was until Cam returned to her, was to make as much time as possible disappear.

Chapter Six

*M*alou went immediately to Lorre's cage and looked in on the little orphan. She was sleeping peacefully, curled up next to the blanket with its clock heart wrapped inside and ticking away comfortingly. The little monkey's tummy was round and her face a bit fuller than it had been when Malou had first brought her in. So Ernie was being a good surrogate mother.

Malou was pleased by that, but not by the prospect of Lorre growing up caged. Still, Malou had to remind herself, she was not much worse off than she would have been with Jezebel as a mother. With no one to tie her to the troop, Lorre too would have become an outcast and lived as her mother did, always on the outskirts. Malou sighed at all the weighty injustices imposed upon such a tiny creature simply by an accident of birth, then went to search for Ernie.

She flipped on lights all the way back. She'd never seen the station in complete darkness before, and it wasn't a friendly sight. The unfamiliar darkness combined with her absence and the compelling power that Cam now exerted over her to make Malou feel almost an interloper in her own station. What had once been the core of her world now seemed very alien territory. She shook from her mind the image of herself as a burglar breaking into someone else's home.

"Ernie!" she called out, more to break the unnerving silence than to locate her co-worker. Her call echoed hollowly through the portable building. She laughed at herself, at the very idea that a *portable* building could, in any way, be menacing. Light streamed out from under the lab door. She knocked on it briskly, then, without pausing, pushed the door open a crack.

"Ernie?" she called again. There was no answer. She tried to push the door open farther, but it would not budge. Must have swollen in the rain, Malou thought as she leaned into it. Just as she was about to put her full weight against the lodged door, Ernie's face popped up directly in front of hers.

"What are you trying to do? Knock the door down?" His abrupt appearance and odd question startled Malou.

"Didn't you hear me calling you?" She camouflaged her fright behind mild annoyance.

"You know the lab is soundproofed," Ernie rebuked her.

"Oh, of course. Mind if I come in?" Her annoyance drained away, replaced now by curiosity. Why was Ernie barring the door?

"Ah, yes, as a matter of fact, I do. I'm right in the

middle of something and don't want to lose my train of thought.''

"I'm sorry. I know how that is. Sorry for disturbing you. I just wanted you to know that I was back. I'll take over Lorre's feedings now."

"Good. Fine. I'd appreciate that. Talk to you later."

"Right, later." But the door was already shut. The bolt slid into place, locking it with a click. So much for the Texas Rangers, Malou thought. It was clear that Ernie hadn't been chewing his nails about her absence. Regret flickered through her; she should have gone with Cam. To San Antonio, to the fulfillment of the evening's golden promise. In the next instant, she was chiding herself for the dangerous turn her emotions were taking. She was, first and foremost, a primatologist, and she'd better start acting like one. And, if she was forgetting how, she had Ernie to serve as a pointed reminder. Her purpose at Los Monos was research, not romance.

That admonition, though, was not enough to chase away the phantoms that tormented Malou as she lay in bed, tantalized with memories only a few hours old. When she did drift off into sleep, she moved directly from remembrances of floating with Cam between her legs, into the dream of weightless lovemaking with a Roman charioteer with espresso brown eyes.

In a clap of thunder, the charioteer disappeared and Malou jerked awake. It wasn't thunder at all, but the bang of the lab door. She heard the rattle of a key and the bolt clicking home again and wondered why on earth Ernie was locking the lab. He'd never done that before. His footsteps, though she knew he was attempting to tiptoe, made the flimsy building rattle as he made his way to his room on the other side of the station.

He probably has research notes scattered all over that he doesn't want disturbed, Malou told herself, explaining the locked lab. But it was still a good long while before she coaxed herself back to sleep. In that time, she marveled at how deeply Cam had ingrained himself: She missed him already.

Lorre's whimperings awoke her before dawn. Still in a sleepy fog, Malou pulled on a clean pair of her inevitable khaki shorts and a cotton blouse and went to the hungry infant. The baby clung contentedly to Malou as she sucked formula from the infant bottle Malou held to her mouth. The baby's eyes were just as busy as her mouth, following the pattern of Malou's mouth, nose, eyes. Holding the helpless monkey and pouring life into its tiny body, Malou stopped minding the ungodly hour and began to understand a bit of the secret joy that helped mothers survive the early years.

The sun was just rising as Malou reached the gate of the compound. The feeling of alienation that had attacked her the night before evaporated as soon as Malou was again on the same ground with her troop of monkeys from Storm Mountain. At her approach, a couple of youngsters, awake before the others, darted up to her. With their nimble fingers they immediately began plucking at her shoestrings until they had them untied.

"You scamps," Malou laughed, shooing the pair away. One ran off and picked up a fallen branch that the other immediately decided he must have, and the chase was on.

Malou sat on a boulder and watched them scoot across the open land. The rain had cleansed everything, and the mesquite trees were fresh and green in the predawn light. She pulled out her field notebook and began to check off her census list, taking a head count of who was where before they all woke up and scattered. The seemingly random arrangement of sleepers would become significant when she started analyzing her data.

First she swung her binoculars around and noted the peripheral males sleeping perched up in the windblown branches of trees at the very edge of the compound. Then she came in closer and checked out who was sleeping in a cluster around Sumo. As she shifted her binoculars away from the center, she stopped dead on the deep watermelon face of her old friend, Kojiwa. His benevolent amber eyes were wide open, and he seemed to be staring right back at Malou. His expression was one of strained patience, as if he were still waiting for Malou to explain to him where his adopted daughter and her new baby were. Or he might even still be waiting to know when they would all return to the cool, piney heights of Storm Mountain.

Malou put down her binoculars and made a few scrupulously impartial notes devoid of this maudlin anthropomorphism she was allowing herself to indulge in.

When she picked up the binoculars again, the new mother, Tulip, loped into view. She was carrying Mesquite, the infant Malou had watched her teaching to crawl the other day. Malou started making notes on the young mother's position when a sixth sense made her pick up her binoculars again. Something was not quite right about the way she was carrying her baby. Or, more exactly, the way the baby was allowing himself to be carried. Malou drew a fine focus on the pair, then tracked their movement for a few moments.

Malou let the binoculars sag on their strap as she stood and headed toward Tulip. It was clear that the baby *had* learned to crawl. Maybe just a few tottering steps, but they had been enough. Malou waited until Tulip put her baby down. The lifeless infant still clutched a few bright coyotillo berries in his little fist. She carried him back to the station.

Malou was surprised to find Ernie up and groggily pouring a cup of coffee into himself.

"Looks like another coyotillo poisoning," she informed Ernie. "I'll go out back and find a nice place for him."

"Out back" was the euphemism she'd always used for the small plot of land used as a cemetery, usually for macaques who had lived a full and happy life.

"No, wait," Ernie stopped her. "I'd better conduct an autopsy."

"Why? He's still holding some of the berries."

"Just to eliminate all the variables," Ernie countered, taking Mesquite from her.

Malou didn't argue; her mind was on more pressing matters. "We have no choice now. We've got to inspect the compound for coyotillo."

"It'll be a waste of time." Ernie put his mug of coffee down. He was now fully awake without the benefit of caffeine. "All we'd find would be one broken branch of coyotillo."

"Ernie, level with me. Cam's not here now, so you don't have to confine yourself to nasty insinuations. You think that someone, and probably Cam, is tossing coyotillo over the compound fence."

"So, he's Cam to you now, is he? Well, it doesn't matter. Yes, I think someone is trying to do away with the monkeys."

"But why?"

"Why?" Ernie echoed cryptically. "If you could get the stars out of your eyes for a minute or two, you'd be able to see that answer quite clearly."

"Listen, Ernie, where the welfare of the troop is concerned, there are no stars in my eyes." She spoke sharply, guilt and defensiveness edging her words.

"Oh no? Then you wouldn't mind telling me where you were night before last and most of last night as well."

"Since we are a team here, Ernie, I suppose you have a right to know. We were trapped in the rain. Cam mistook Stallings's original ranch house for the main house. It's on low ground and the road washed out. I'm sorry, I had no way of notifying you."

"What a crock."

Ernie's unequivocal response jarred Malou. "What do you mean? That's exactly what happened."

"You're trying to tell me that Landell didn't even know how to get to the headquarters of the ranch he now owns. Forgive me, Malou, but that strains my credulity somewhat."

Here, in the harsh light of morning, with Cam far away, Malou too was hard pressed to believe in his ignorance.

"I imagine, though, that the next day Landell was conveniently able to find his way to his lost ranch house."

"Actually, Jorge found us and showed Cam the way." Or at least that's what Malou presumed the hulking ranch hand was doing yesterday morning as he and Cam stood talking on the porch of the stone house. Of course, Cam had whisked Jorge outside so quickly that she didn't hear most of their conversation, so she couldn't really be sure. All she had heard was Jorge saying, "Everything is done as you ordered." But she wasn't about to repeat the ominous-sounding words to Ernie.

"And you believed that?" Ernie's expression left no doubt that he was still unconvinced.

Malou had no more time to allay his doubts—or hers. "Listen," she said, trying to reestablish the camaraderie that had existed between them, "I have an idea about how to pull something good out of these tragedies. I've never read about its being done before, but I was thinking, why don't we try substituting Lorre for Tulip's baby?"

"It'll never work." Ernie pronounced his opinion as if it were the final word on the subject. His high-handedness was beginning to irritate Malou a bit.

"It might very well not work, but I certainly plan on trying." Her assertiveness seemed to snap Ernie out of the fit of grouchiness that had overtaken him. "I'm sorry, Malou," he said, sounding again like the rumpled, distracted, easygoing researcher he'd always been in the past. "This whole business about the research station being shut down and the troop disbanded has really gotten to me."

Malou reached out a hand and placed it on his forearm. "That's why you've been working so hard, isn't it? You're racing the clock, trying to come up with some headline-grabbing report that will focus attention on Los Monos, aren't you?" Malou knew his motives. It was exactly what she would be doing if she weren't trying to save the troop by raising money through foundation grants.

Ernie shrugged. "Something like that," he admitted.

"Don't worry," she reassured him. "We'll keep the

troop together. I've uncovered several strong leads already and I'll be following them up. And you shouldn't be so suspicious of Landell.'' She had switched back to using Cam's last name without even thinking about it. ''He really wants to give us a chance to keep Los Monos going just the way it is.''

Ernie stood. ''I'd better be getting back to the lab.'' His clothes looked as if he'd slept in them. With a pang, Malou realized that he probably had fallen into bed exhausted last night without bothering to take them off. Now that she understood what he was attempting to do, Malou was willing to forgive him a few outbursts. They were both after the same thing.

''Ernie, don't work too hard.''

''Everyone does what they have to do,'' he said as he ambled back to the lab.

Malou carefully unlatched the cage and took Lorre out, glad now for the extra bit of weight she'd managed to put on during her confinement. She wasn't as big as Tulip's baby, but at least the difference wouldn't be as obvious.

Outside, Tulip was racing from one new mother to the next checking the babies clutching their chest fur, searching for her own lost infant. Malou rubbed her hands thoroughly over Lorre, trying to transfer as much of Mesquite's scent to the orphan as she could.

Acting on instinct, Malou hunched down and approached the group of mother monkeys grazing on a patch of prickly pears. She clutched Lorre to her as if the monkey were her own baby and went to the edge of the group. Imitating the procedure the macaques had developed themselves only weeks after coming from Japan and seeing their first cactus, she gingerly plucked off a pale green cactus pad and dropped it to the ground. Bending down, she carefully rubbed it in the earth until all the spikes had been smoothed away. Then she flipped the pad over and debarbed the other side.

She stopped short of eating the macaque delicacy. Her aim had been to ingratiate herself to the group, and she had done that. She placed the pad on the ground, laid Lorre down next to it, and backed away.

At first none of the grazers seemed to pay much attention to either baby or cactus pad. But Malou noticed the furtive side glances of amber eyes. Then, bit by bit, an adventurous monkey, Tulip's sister Tawny, edged over toward the food left behind by the hairless monkey who walked upright. Tawny poked several times at the pad, quickly withdrawing her hand after each probe. Finally, convinced that the cactus pad was exactly what it seemed to be, she snatched up the discarded treat and chomped into it.

Next, the abandoned infant claimed her attention. Malou stood back, barely breathing, remembering how interested Tawny had been in her sister's baby when Tulip was trying to teach Mesquite to crawl. Apparently, her interest in infants hadn't faded, for Tawny began stroking Lorre, then gently poking her. Malou bit her bottom lip, ready to intervene if the poking became too forceful. Finally, Tawny picked Lorre up, delighted by her new plaything. Now came the tricky part.

On the other side of the cactus patch, Tulip raised her lilac eyelids and saw her sister with a baby. Tulip knew three things: Her baby was missing. Tawny did not have a baby. Tawny had already, at least once before, tried to steal *her* baby, Mesquite.

Tulip charged over to her sister and yanked Lorre away

from her, then ran off to a secluded spot. There Tulip sniffed at the baby. Lorre burrowed in, clinging to Tulip's chest and searching for a teat. By now Tulip's were painfully full. For a second, Tulip let the baby nurse. Then, after sniffing once more, she batted the baby away.

Malou's heart sank and the lip she held between her teeth trembled. She'd tried, but her ploy hadn't worked. Ernie was right. Lorre's life would have to be lived in a cage. She stood to collect the rejected baby. Before she could reach her, however, Tawny zoomed in and snatched Lorre back. Even if Tulip wasn't interested, *she* was still enamored of her new plaything.

For a moment, Tulip watched her sister dandling the baby and warding off the other females who came to investigate the tiny newcomer. Then Tulip turned away from the imposter who had posed as her own little Mesquite, even going so far as to smell faintly like her lost baby.

Malou edged in closer, not wanting to frighten Tawny into running off with her new toy. Tawny and the chattering group of females around her backed off. Tulip's amber eyes cut back and forth to her sister and the baby and the upright ape creeping toward them.

Malou would never know how Tulip reached her decision. Did monkeys make compromises with life just as humans did? Had Tulip weighed the possibility of Mesquite's ever coming back to her and realized that he would not? That it might be better to have a baby that smelled faintly like her own, even though she was the wrong sex and a runty thing to boot, than no baby at all? Or was it simple monkey greed—an impulse not unknown to higher primates —to have that which another coveted? Whatever the motivation, with troop attention focusing on the new baby and Malou creeping in toward it, Tulip made up her mind.

In a flash of ash blond fur and bared bicuspids, she tore into the center of the group around Lorre and grabbed her baby away from Tawny. *Her* baby. For that, Malou saw with enormous relief, was precisely what Lorre had become. Lorre, nursing hungrily, was now Tulip's baby.

Malou raced back to the station to tell Ernie the good news. But he was holed up in the lab with no inclination to emerge. His only response, muttered darkly through the locked door, was, "It won't last."

"Thanks for the encouragement, Little Miss Sunshine," Malou teased him, too happy to allow his pessimism to infect her.

He answered with a dry chuckle, then, "A telegram came for you while you were out. It's on the front table."

The building reverberated under Malou's tread as she hurried back to the front table. "Edward Darden," the return address read. Malou ripped into it and read the abrupt telegramese.

Malou,

Greetings. Have come up with plan. Must speak with new owner of Los Monos. Please have him call me.

Keep fingers crossed,

Darden

Malou shuffled through a stack of papers, looking for the letter she'd gotten two weeks ago from Stallings's lawyer telling her that Cam was the new owner of Los Monos. She dug out the piece of heavy cream stationery. Just as she remembered, it had the phone number and address of Cam's development company.

She went back to pound on the locked lab door again and tell Ernie she was going up to the ranch house to call Cam.

"Think you can find your way to the right one?" Ernie's question was muffled by the closed door.

Malou was determined not to let him needle her. "Who knows? I'll set off flares if I get lost. Listen, there's a remote chance that Cam might be out on a job site and I won't be able to reach him by phone. In that case, I'll have to run into San Antonio and track him down."

"Of course, you'll 'have' to run into San Antonio." The sarcasm in Ernie's tone was unmistakable.

Malou chose to ignore it. "Any problems with the jeep when you took it into Laredo last week?"

"Malou, do you mind? I'm a researcher, not a car mechanic."

And certainly not a diplomat, Malou thought as she headed out for the jeep. The aged and abused vehicle sputtered to life with its usual cranky reluctance. A few minutes later, Malou was pulling up in front of the ranch house. Señora Maldonado let her in and she dashed off for the phone. As she very nearly could have predicted, Cam could not be reached by phone. The receptionist offered to draw Malou a map out to the job site if she would stop by the office. That appeared to be the only solution, and Malou agreed.

As Malou pointed the jeep north for the hour and a half ride, she was forced to admit that the prospect did not displease her. That Ernie's sarcasm about her "having" to drive to San Antonio had hit a nerve of truth. She vowed to devote more time to her co-worker in the future. It wasn't easy being isolated out on a remote research station with only one other human to relate to. She'd never felt the isolation much since her work and temperament involved her so much with the troop. Ernie didn't have that involvement; he worked more with individual animals. Her absence and preoccupation recently must have been hard on him.

Odd, she reflected, the months she'd spent alone on various research stations had never affected her much. She'd certainly never felt the exhilaration she did now driving into the city. But she knew it wasn't the city, the prospect of being around people, that excited her so unbearably. One singular person was causing her stomach to roller-coaster and her pulse to race. One absolutely unique man: Cameron Landell.

Just saying his name to herself made an indefinable taste appear at the back of her mouth. She had first tasted it deeply only last night and now knew it for what it was—the taste of desire. Nervousness fluttered through Malou as she faced this expedition for what *it* was—the journey of a woman rushing to meet her lover. For, after last night, there was no longer any question that Cam intended to be just that in the fullest sense of the word. And she did not intend to stop him. It was all so new. Not the physical mechanics, but the emotional upheaval. That was what was strange and a bit frightening. That was what she had sheltered herself from so successfully for so many years, away in remote stations with only monkeys to steal her heart.

Malou had to abandon all reflection as she entered the outskirts of the city and San Antonio traffic began to crowd around her. She found Loop 410 West, as the receptionist had directed, and followed it around until she hit the right exit. Cam's headquarters were in an elegantly subdued office building set back from the road in a tropically landscaped refuge. An inconspicuous sign beside the drive quietly announced Landell Development.

"You must be Malou Sanders," chirped the receptionist, an older woman with a ready smile, as Malou walked in. "You're in luck. Cam's back from the job site. He didn't know when you'd arrive, so he kept a racquetball appointment. You're to go right over and disturb him."

"Is the court far from here?"

"Only if you consider a short walk down that hall far," the receptionist answered, pointing to her left.

Malou took the hall she indicated, wondering how on earth Cam had been able to fit a racquetball court into what appeared to be a fairly small complex. The answer turned out to be not "on earth" but under it. At the end of the hall, Malou found herself staring over a railing into the pit of a racquetball court dug into the ground.

Cam was center court below. A bandanna headband caught the sweat that poured from his brow even in the air-conditioned court. A gray sweatshirt with the sleeves cut out and a pair of red cotton jersey shorts completed his far from modish outfit. His opponent looked to be a good ten years younger than Cam. He was blond, with a dark tennis tan. Their sneakers squeaked across the wooden floor as they lunged after the hard rubber ball ricocheting from one high wall to the next.

They broke for service and the blond went to the back of the court. Cam moved nearer the front wall. While the blond bounced the ball and took a breather, Cam tugged at the front of his sweatshirt, pulling a few puffs of air in to cool his chest. He ran his forearm across his upper lip, then prepared to receive the serve. He crouched down and bounced lightly from foot to foot, staring at the wall ahead with an unyielding concentration. His posture reminded Malou of that first time she'd watched him through her binoculars.

The blond bounced the ball several unnecessary times to try to break that iron concentration. He failed. Malou remembered that the first thing that had impressed her about Cam was his predatory intensity. He was a hunter, a stalker, one used to either bringing down his prey or going hungry. And it had been a long time since Cameron Landell had gone hungry. She knew that she could forget those facts only at her own peril. Hers and that of the monkeys of Storm Mountain.

The blond served the ball with a cracking sweep. Cam was up and moving practically in synch with the ball blasting forward. The smooth rush of motion thrilled Malou. Everything worked together in that one sprint. The deep gullies of muscle above Cam's knee bunched, then lengthened explosively. His right arm flowed back, bringing muscles into play from his shoulder to his cocked wrist. The ball caromed off the front wall, a perfect, devastatingly low serve. Cam swept down to scoop it up and send it rocketing back.

The blond pounded forward to return the volley, sending it spinning off of a side wall. Then he sagged back for the rest that was sure to come. There was no way Cam could reach the ball on the other side of the court.

Cam worked out the game's impossible geometry quickly enough to position himself precisely where he needed to be to peel the killer shot off the side wall and send it slicing back up into the front right corner.

With a startled grunt, the blond lunged forward, diving

for the corner where Cam had placed his shot. He stretched out his racket, but his arm was about two feet too short. He tottered, then went sprawling out on the court. The ball thunked to a dead halt. Cam had won the serve back. He'd bagged his prey.

Cam rushed up to give the blond a hand getting back onto his feet. Malou saw the bitterness of defeat sour the man's handsome features, pinching them white beneath his tan. Cam had soundly romped him. Malou imagined that Cam was used to sound romps and uncomfortable with anything else.

"Supreme effort," Cam said with a casual ease, his hand still clutching the other man's. "I don't think I would have even tried for that one."

"I shouldn't have given you the chance to make it," the blond replied. "I should have put you away with my last shot."

"And next time you will," Cam said.

The tightness cracked and the man smiled, already savoring a future triumph.

That small exchange ran counter to the direction of Malou's thoughts and stirred up yet another memory. "No losers, no tears." It seemed to be Cam's motto, and she'd just gotten a firsthand demonstration of how he made it work. He'd given the blond man back his dignity and reframed the entire game so that he wasn't a loser; he was a man who was simply still working toward victory.

The collision of perceptions dizzied Malou. Which was the real Cameron Landell? The hunter who must win or go hungry? Or the man who believed there should be no losers?

Cam paced back to the service area, brushing the back of

his hand across his forehead and bouncing the ball off of his racket. He took his position in the service box, leaned over, shook out his arms to loosen his shoulders, bounced the ball, reared back, and swatted it forward. The ball cracked off like a rifle shot, and as Cam followed through, Malou entered the edge of his vision.

"Malou! You're here!"

The blond scrambled for the serve, slamming it off the front wall. The returned ball whizzed by Cam's head as he stared up at his visitor.

Malou basked in his open delight.

Cam's racket dangled forgotten off of his wrist, the ball dribbled unnoticed across his feet, and still he continued to stare.

"Yo, Cam, you want to play that point over?" the blond man asked.

Cam held up his hand, flagging surrender. "No, it's yours. The whole game's yours. I forfeit."

"That doesn't sound like you, Landell. You feeling all . . . ?" The blond man's question went unasked as he followed Cam's gaze up to the balcony above the court where Malou watched. "Oh. Listen, give me a call next time you want a game. You owe me a chance to clean your clock."

"You got it, Jeff," Cam promised the man as he left. Then he turned back to Malou. "My receptionist told me you were on your way. I didn't expect you so soon. You make good time, woman."

"When I have the proper motivation." Malou could barely believe that she'd spoken such flirtatious words. Cam seemed capable of evoking all manner of uncharacteristic responses from her.

A large grin cut across Cam's face at her saucy riposte. "Stay right where you are, Lou-Lou Belle."

Lou-Lou Belle? Malou wondered as Cam disappeared out the court door. A few seconds later, a door opened and he was beside her. His presence was overwhelming. It surrounded and pressed against her, making her feel short of breath and mildly claustrophobic.

"Lou-Lou Belle, indeed," she scolded, trying to hide how flustered she was behind mock ferocity.

"Would you prefer Malou the Monkey Girl?" Cam asked, moving closer. "Or perhaps Mary Louise?"

"Okay, Lou-Lou Belle wins over Mary Louise. But I'm still not wild about either one."

He put a hand, still warm from the exertion of his sport, on her shoulder. "I'm happy to see you." All jocularity was gone. His tone was intimate.

Malou turned from the power of his touch to grip the railing and look down into the now empty racquetball court. Her thoughts were ricocheting just as wildly as any ball ever hit in that court. She fought to steady them, just barely managing to recall the purported reason for her visit.

"Yes, well, I . . . I came because Dr. Darden wants you to call him immediately."

"Dr. Darden, *the* Father of American Primatology?" Cam's hand slid down her arm, then back up, the pads of his fingertips lightly raking a pattern. "Is that the only reason you rushed up here? I certainly hope not. Not after yesterday."

No, yesterday had changed things. Irrevocably. Malou felt that in her bones. But now that she was here, with Cam beside her, the implications of those changes loomed very large. She chased them away and tried to concentrate on her mission. "Dr. Darden sent a telegram to the station. He has a plan he'd like to discuss with you. You were out of the office when I called, so I drove up."

"And now that you've delivered your message you'll simply turn around and rush back home?" Cam teased.

"That's probably not a bad idea," Malou conceded.

"Are you kidding? That's a wretched idea. Why don't you go on into my office and give me ten minutes to shower and call Darden. Then I want to take you out for the best dinner San Antonio can produce. Now, scoot. It's at the far end of the hall. I have magazines, television, and liquor in there. That should be enough to keep you occupied for the two minutes I'm in the shower. After that, I intend to keep you fully occupied for as long as you'll allow."

Malou stood listening to the brisk tattoo of his steps as they faded down the stairwell. Cam's office was a true entrepreneur's lair complete with a couple of computer terminals, several phones, a telex machine, and all the trappings of power, such as a desk large enough to roller-skate on. She'd barely completed a perfunctory inventory when Cam burst in still toweling beads of water from his hair and wearing a casual outfit of slacks and a teal blue polo shirt.

"Did you find the liquor cabinet?" he joked.

"I managed to restrain myself from cleaning it out."

"How about some juice? A club soda? Bloody Mary? You name it," Cam offered, walking to a rosewood cabinet. Malou opted for orange juice, and he fixed himself one as well. He took the drink and sank into a high-backed swivel chair.

The cold juice cut through the dust in Malou's throat from the drive up.

"Do you always play racquetball that way?" she asked.

"And what way might that be?" Cam answered, gulping down a long draught of juice.

"Oh, I don't know. To win, I guess."

"Doesn't everyone?" Cam queried back.

"After their own fashion. I suppose it's just that most people's fashions aren't as openly ferocious as yours."

"You'd better get the ivy out of your eyes," Cam teased. "Ferocity is the name of the game in my business. Although, you're right, most people do put bigger smiles on their games than I do."

Malou put a hand to her hair, wondering how many kinds of a fright she looked.

Cam watched the small gesture, wishing that it were his hand touching those sun-streaked waves, those sun-browned legs, those lips. Before he knew it, his heart was raging again within his chest, stirred by the wanting that had deviled him from the first moment he'd set eyes on this puzzling and provoking woman. They had been so close last night, ready to share all a man and a woman could share. And now, today, she seemed like a timid doe ready to flee if he breathed too loudly. He wasn't used to shyness, to reserve. To someone like Malou, whose world couldn't be summed up in three lines in a society column describing the new gown she'd worn to the latest gala along with the name of the powerful man escorting her.

His money, the position he had scrambled to attain, meant nothing to her. Her work was and always would be foremost. She would never be content to be that woman in the new gown on his arm at the gala. That knowledge acted upon him like the most potent of aphrodisiacs. What there was between them came from a more powerfully primitive place than any attraction he had known before. And there *was* something between them. He felt the chemistry even now, sitting in his office, and, cast as many downward glances as she might, Cam would bet his soul that she was feeling it too.

He drained his glass. There were hurdles, far too many hurdles, to be gotten over—her reluctance, that infernal troop of monkeys, his own financial entanglements. But get over them he would. He put the glass down.

"Shall we find out what the Father of American Primatology's plan is?"

Chapter Seven

Malou watched Cam as he spoke with Edward Darden. He clearly felt none of the awe that afflicted her. She doubted if there were many people in the world who could awe Cameron Landell. Her thoughts kept drifting away from the conversation she should have been paying attention to, fixing instead on details like the way his fingernails wrapped clean and square around the sturdy tips of his fingers. Or the way sandy brown hair tufted at his bottom knuckle. Or how he gripped the phone, not at the middle, but at the bottom near the mouthpiece.

And then she thought of those strong, capable hands on her, doing the wondrous things they had done last night. A flush of heat swept through her, and she looked down as if something fascinating were happening amid the ice cubes in her orange juice. Bits of Cam's responses filtered through her discomfiture, enough so that she caught the drift of the conversation. Darden's plan was an exciting one, so exciting that her eyes were gleaming by the time Cam hung up.

Malou eagerly recapped her understanding of the discussion. "He wants you to turn Los Monos into a tourist park."

"That's about the size of it."

"What a fantastic idea! It works in Japan. They restrict visitors to one area that doesn't interfere with normal troop interaction. We could do the same thing at Los Monos. That way you could generate revenue and we could still keep the troop together."

"A very nifty plan except for one detail: Time. We don't have nearly enough of it. My note is still going to come due at the end of May. The Japanese got their start-up capital in the form of government grants. I don't see Uncle Sam offering to back us on this one, Malou, and there's no way I can currently finance it. So, essentially, we're in the same position we started in—you still need to drum up some grant money."

Malou nodded, her enthusiasm leaking away. She stood stiffly, putting her glass down. "Well, I guess I'd better go find a phone somewhere and start calling again."

Cam came around to her side of the desk. "I guess you'd better not." He twisted his wrist around so that his watch faced Malou. "See, way past five. Wouldn't be anyone in. What you'd better do is come to dinner with me."

Malou smiled at his goofy tactics, her nameless fears subsiding in the wake of Cam's easy joviality. "I can't, Cam. I'm not dressed."

"And you think I am?" he asked, indicating his casual

outfit. "I don't patronize restaurants that don't allow women with beautiful legs to show them off in khaki shorts."

"A wise policy." Malou smiled in spite of herself and took the arm that Cam held out to her. The receptionist and Cam's other employees had already left for the day, and Cam locked up as they stepped out into the balmy spring evening freshened by a light breeze.

The drive into downtown San Antonio was a short one. They parked near a famous landmark that Malou had been meaning to see but had never quite gotten around to—the Alamo. Its curved outline looked like something out of a myth cutting across the dusky Texas sky. The old mission's grandeur was crowded and reduced, though, by the skyscrapers pressing down upon it. Cam led her to an entrance to the Riverwalk that wound through the city's heart. It was a surprisingly peaceful and lovely refuge. Cam took her hand and they walked in silence beneath the sheltering palms and past riotous displays of flowers at the peak of their springtime splendor. The river flowed past beside them with a sinuous elegance. Both looked around them, commenting on the charm of San Antonio's sights, but both really aware of little beyond the rapturous feel of each other's flesh.

The restaurant Cam took her to was right on the water's edge. The maitre d' greeted Cam with a warm familiarity that ignored trifles like a pair of khaki shorts or the absence of a tie. He led them past high-heeled and jacketed diners to a secluded table on the patio with the river lapping only inches away. A mimosa tree spread a cloud of pink blossoms over their heads that drenched the air with an unearthly fragrance.

"This is lovely," Malou said, breathing in the pastel scent.

"I was hoping you'd like it." Cam caught her gaze, and she sank into the drowning warmth of those melting brown eyes.

Cam slid his hand over hers. "So, we're finally together for the first time today."

She didn't have to ask what he meant. She'd been holding herself aloof from him, from the tumult of her feelings all day. She could no longer deny them. "I guess I've just spent too many years around the lower primates," she admitted. "I'm not very good at dealing with all the complications of human involvements. My usual reaction is to run away from them." She gave a dry chuckle, attempting to lighten her confession.

Cam's hand tightened over hers. "Don't do that."

"I don't want to, Cam. It's just that I'm not used to having my emotions in such a snarl."

"Mine are pretty snarled up too, Malou. You're not in this alone. We're not on opposite sides. It's like with the monkey troop. I want you to have what you need."

"But it might not be in your power to give me what I need."

"I don't know what that is, Malou, but I'd like to learn."

Malou felt her hand grow hot beneath Cam's.

A waiter appeared carrying a tray laden with the specialties Cam had ordered. Malou snaked her hand out from under Cam's as the waiter slid artfully arranged plates in front of them.

They both toyed with their meals in silence for a few minutes before Cam spoke again. "I don't want to crowd you, Malou. To frighten you away. Would it help if we took things very slow and easy?''

Malou looked up, the light from the guttering candles catching in her eyes. ''Yes,'' she whispered. ''That would help a lot.''

Cam sighed and let his fork drop onto his plate, abandoning the pretense of eating. ''In that case I'd better see you back to your car while I have a shred of willpower left. If I wait too long, I might not be able to resist trying to convince you to continue where we left off last night.''

Malou nodded, and Cam rose to help her with her chair. ''Damn Alexander Graham Bell,'' he hissed, referring to the phone call that had interrupted them the evening before.

Full darkness cloaked the city by the time they reached Malou's jeep back at Cam's office. For a moment they both sat, staring silently through the windshield of Cam's Mercedes.

''Those things aren't particularly safe, you know,'' Cam finally commented, pointing toward the open jeep.

Malou laughed, evincing a quizzical look from Cam. ''I'm sorry, it's just hard to take highway safety tips from someone who chronically drives as fast as you do.''

''I'll have you know that it's been nearly three months since I've gotten a speeding ticket.''

''Such restraint.''

''Such restraint, indeed,'' Cam echoed, leaning toward Malou. ''It's superhuman.'' His last words puffed softly against Malou's lips before Cam's covered them. His kiss set Malou's blood to singing as his hand reached out to gently stroke her cheek.

''Restraint. Restraint.'' Cam whispered the words, then,

with a great effort, obeyed them. He leaned back into his seat, sucked in a deep breath, then hurled himself out his door and came around to open Malou's.

Malou grabbed the few seconds to steady herself, astounded at how one glancing kiss could so rock her equilibrium. She had to get back to Los Monos. Quickly. Had to get away from Cam, from the uncontrollable power of her attraction to him.

"Your coach, m'lady." Cam took her arm and handed her back into the dusty jeep. She smiled tightly. Fighting the urge to wrap her arms around his strong shoulders, to feel the caress of his hair against her palms, she gripped the jeep's steering wheel. She fished the key out of her purse, jammed it into the ignition, and turned. All her movements felt wooden and awkward beneath Cam's unwavering gaze. A dull grind issued from somewhere under the hood. Cam cocked his head toward the abnormal sound. She clicked the key off and her smile tightened even further.

"The battery's just cold," she explained, something like panic pushing up her pulse. She knew she had to get away from Cameron Landell tonight or surrender to the power he exerted over her.

"Cold battery," he repeated with a sage nod.

She made sure the lights and windshield wipers were off, then tried again. Again the dull grind answered her effort. She pumped the accelerator pedal.

"Bum alternator." Cam pronounced his diagnosis just as the engine sputtered resentfully to life.

Malou smiled with relief.

"You won't make it out the driveway," Cam predicted.

"And just what crystal ball is giving you this great

insight into auto mechanics?'' Malou asked teasingly, relieved now that the jeep was running and her escape was secure.

"No crystal ball. I just know a bit about cars. Another symptom of my misspent youth. As soon as you turn on your headlights, the engine'll die.''

Malou smiled at his jest, flipped the headlight switch, and heard the engine rumble twice, then die. Malou whacked her palm against the steering wheel. "You did that, didn't you?'' she shot at Cam, who was looking impossibly innocent.

"You're so cute when you're irrational. I just diagnosed the disease; I didn't cause it.''

"Well, how do I cure it? Tonight!''

"Tonight you don't. But first thing tomorrow I can have someone out here. In the meantime, fate forces us together. Let's enjoy it.''

"No.'' Her answer was too quick, too anxious. The playfulness drained from Cam's face. "No, I . . . I have to get back to Los Monos. Ernie . . . I've left Ernie by himself too much lately. And Lorre. I have to see if Tulip is taking care of her. I . . .'' She ran out of excuses. "I have to go home.''

Cam saw through her excuses and into the heart of her final, plaintive appeal. He was startled, and a tiny bit wounded, by what he saw—fear. "I'll take you,'' he offered. "Tonight. Right now.''

The cornered panic that had swept over Malou subsided, leaving her feeling foolish and exposed. She laughed feebly, hoping to pass the whole episode off as a weak joke. But the honest concern in Cam's eyes did not disappear with her laughter. He understood. "Thanks," she said simply, getting out of the jeep. "I'd appreciate that."

The lights of San Antonio had given way to an immensity of darkness pricked only by the pinpoint brilliance of stars a galaxy away before Malou fully relaxed against the pewter leather car seats.

"Nice night for a drive."

Malou was touched by Cam's sweetly clichéd effort to break the ice between them. "I'm sure that a drive down to a monkey ranch you never wanted to own is just what you wanted to do tonight."

Cam smiled, happy to see that the tension that had held Malou rigid since the jeep had failed was relaxing. "You're too perceptive," he teased. "But, if it's important to you to get back to the station, it's important to me too. I told you before, we're on the same side in this."

Without thinking, Malou covered Cam's hand on the gearshift with her own in a gesture that she had intended to show gratitude. It turned instantly into something far more. Cam pivoted his hand beneath hers until their palms touched. The gesture had more intimacy than Malou had known through entire affairs with other men. Affairs in which she had always been the one to set the tempo, to initiate and to stop the flow of events. She had always been the one with the control. Now, just the merest touch of Cam's palm against her own reminded her just how far out of her control her feelings for him were. She withdrew her hand.

"So, you never told me if you worked out an agreement with the protesters." Her voice sounded abrupt and artificial, shattering the crystalline moment beginning to enclose them.

Cam sighed and flipped his hand over onto the gearshift, tightening it as he rammed the car into a higher gear. "We reached an agreement," he answered flatly.

"A 'no-losers-no-tears' agreement?" She tried to lighten the pall she had cast.

"It was the agreement I'd planned to propose all along. Once they stopped trying to grab headlines long enough to come in and talk with me about it, they were delighted."

"What are you proposing?"

Almost against his will, enthusiasm for his work caught Cam and his voice took back its customary animation. "To establish a greenbelt area, a long, thick stand of junipers, where the birds they're trying to protect usually nest."

"That's wonderful! What an admirable thing for you to do."

"Hey, before you make me patron saint of the Audubon Society, let me point out that this greenbelt will enhance property values and buy me a lot of goodwill to boot."

"Yeah, but you still didn't have to do it."

"You're right. I will accept canonization," Cam bantered. "I just hope your buddy, Ernie, doesn't have the deciding vote. What does the guy have against me, anyway?"

"He's just upset about the possibility of the troop being broken up, and it's made him suspicious of everything in general and you in particular."

"I picked up on at least one of those suspicions. What else has he accused me of?"

"Nothing. It's silly."

"Tell me, Malou. I want to know if there's a whispering

campaign going on behind my back, particulary if you're the prime target.''

"It's really nothing. He just mentioned that it seemed awfully odd that you didn't know where the main house was.''

They drove in silence past the ghostly outlines of cattle sleeping on their feet and a windmill slicing the night air. Cam's voice was strained when he finally spoke. "And you think it's fairly strange too, don't you?''

"Well . . .''

"The thought did cross your mind.''

Malou could not deny that it had. Outside, the countryside began yielding a few familiar landmarks; they were nearing Los Monos. An unbearable tension had gripped the car. Malou could feel Cam straining to keep a volcano of emotion dammed up within him. They passed the wrought-iron gate that marked the road leading to the main house and drove on. Malou feared that Cam would deposit her at Los Monos without breaking the angry silence. But, at the entrance to the stone house, Cam pulled the Mercedes off the road and came to rest beneath Stallings's age-weathered lazy S. He turned the motor off and turned to Malou.

"What you're implying, then,'' he said, his jaw tight with anger, "is that I deliberately took you down this road with the sole intention of seducing you.''

"No, I . . .'' Malou stammered.

"No is the correct answer, Mary Louise Sanders. Because, had I intended to seduce you, I would have told you so. Just as I'm going to do now. Malou, I want to make love to you. Tonight. More than I've ever wanted any single thing in my life and you're a fool if you put me off because I'll not try again.''

Malou looked at Cam illuminated by the dim glow of the dashboard lights. His face was a mask of intensity, of desire translated into smoldering eyes, a rapacious mouth. She felt herself teetering on the edge. Behind her was a wide, flat plain. A known plateau uninterrupted by any unexpected bumps or turns. A terrain of vast and unlimited boredom that was her emotional past and would be her future if she chose it to be. Ahead was a precipice. A place shrouded by mist, impenetrably dark and, for now, unknowable. Choice lay before her. Malou knew with a bone-deep certainty that this moment would come only once in her life. She swallowed deeply and mentally swatted away the million and one reasons that tugged at her, dragging her back onto the flat plain of reason. She grabbed for the slender vine of passion that twisted through her and swung over the edge.

"Yes." The word formed on her lips, but never passed her tightened throat.

Cam, though, did not need to hear it with his ears, for her acceptance was already inscribed upon his heart.

The stone house seemed to be waiting for them, seemed now to Malou to have been created for them, for their love. It was as Stallings had meant it to be, a place outside the boundary of time. They stepped into it together and shed the nattering cares of modern life. Moonlight more luminous than that which fell anywhere else that night streamed in through the windows. They breathed the wonderfully cool air exhaled by the sturdy stone walls and were caught up again in the otherworldly enchantment of the cottage.

It was as if the last twenty-four hours had been erased. Malou was swamped by the weightless feel of her dream, of the pool last night. It swirled warmly between her legs and lapped over her breasts, leaving them aching for Cam's caress. His hair had gone silver in the moonlight, and patches of platinum splashed across his lower lip, his eyes.

"Is it going to be all right?" He wanted to know if there had been any second thoughts.

"Yes. More than all right. So much more." She had crossed the precipice and was alone with Cam on the other side.

He came toward her, cutting through moonbeams and the still, cool air to reach her. Everything was decided; he felt it from the first touch. With the first kiss she was welded to him. It was as if they had spent the past day teasing and wooing, bringing one another to the highest endurable pitch of arousal.

They clung together in this alien territory ruled only by sensation, unable to taste, to touch enough to make up for the hours of denial. She pushed at his shirt with an unbridled will and it was gone. Her hands sought out the smooth, hard contours of his chest, while his hands trapped her wandering mouth to tilt it upward and receive his. A groan tore from them, from whose throat Malou couldn't say. He clawed at the blouse separating them, sighing at the relief of her breasts naked against his chest.

She moaned his name as his hand slid down between her legs to find the place that waited most ardently for his touch. Her hands found his buckle and unfastened it. Then his zipper.

Cam slid her shorts off, then her underwear. She was as undeniably ready for him as he was for her. The reins of control slipped then entirely from his hands.

Malou felt as if she were floating off the ground, wafted

away on the breeze that was Cam's strong arms crooked about her, lifting her, bringing her to him. Her heart thundered out a message that Cam's answered with a harshly pounding rhythm. Aching for the deliverance of union with him, she parted her legs and twined them about his waist. He filled her and they were one. Their joining came as the completion of the dream of weightlessness that had started the night after she'd first met him.

Great surges of ecstasy pulsed through her. Increasing in power, they drove them both before the unleashed fury of their intensity. They dictated the rhythm of Cam's hands as he pulled Malou closer. She rose and fell against him with a will as mindless and inexorable as the tides. Cam mated the pace of his need to hers so that they soared together to a shattering crescendo. Her lips found his at the moment of fulfillment. She collapsed against his chest, her head wilting against the spasm of pleasure pulsing through her.

Cam's legs began to buckle. He sagged onto the couch still holding Malou tightly. She nestled against his neck, breathing in the wild scent of their abandonment to one another. He stroked her back, running his fingers up and down the slender column of her spine, then stopping to gather her to him in a fierce hug. Gradually, conscious thoughts replaced the pattern of sensation that had occupied their minds.

"Malou, I . . ." Cam struggled to put a voice to the enormity of his emotions, but Malou silenced him with a kiss. Now was not the time to try to corral the wildness they had unloosed. To try to brand it, marking it as something that it might not be. She wanted only what they had now. But she wanted all of it.

She sat up, still straddling his lap, and traced her finger across the sweep of his brow, the hard slash of his cheeks, the arch of his nose. She dragged the finger lazily across the bow of his mouth, and as it passed over the fullness of his lower lip, Cam's tongue flicked across the tip of her finger. He pressed her palm to his lips and licked its lacework of delicate lines. Nerves tingled from Malou's sensitive palm up her arm and across her breasts. He nibbled at the fleshy pad at the base of her thumb.

"You have a very sensuous nature," Cam joked, his mouth still a whisper from her hand. "I know. I can read palms."

"How very insightful of you," she bantered back, a sense of deep, rollicking joy beginning to fill her. "Could you lick along my life line and tell me how long I have to live?"

His tongue flickered tantalizingly along the curve of her palm. "You will live a long and happy life filled with much accomplishment and even more love."

The last word stabbed Malou in the one spot she had momentarily left unprotected. It pained her far more than she wanted to admit to hear Cam speak of love as part of a trifling jest between them. The pain was fleeting though, obliterated by the liquid feel of Cam's tongue inscribing bewitching new demands upon her palm, demands that continued to bring her breasts to ever-fuller, tingling life until they too strained for the velvet massaging of his tongue. As if her desires had become his, Cam took her hand from his lips and, coaxing her forward across the scant inches separating them, brought the yearning tip of her breast to his mouth.

Leisurely he explored it while fondling her other breast, drawing dizzying circles about first one, then the other nipple. Malou's eyelids fluttered shut. As if Cam's tender ministrations were putting her into a deep sleep, she bent her neck and rested her forehead against Cam's, bracing herself against his shoulders. Even as her nipples came to life in his mouth, Malou felt Cam come alive within her once again.

"This time, we'll take as long as we want," he promised in a whisper that renewed desire was already turning to a hoarse rasp.

Malou swallowed at the unimaginable delirium of the promise. He pulled her closer and brought her mouth to his. His hands washed over her with the warmth of a tropical rain. He drew her to him and, guided by instincts she'd never given rein to before, Malou pleasured Cam with an infinity of sinuously fluid motions.

Cam's head rolled back against the couch, his eyes shut against the waves of delight that battered him as her hips rolled against his.

Malou felt herself compelled by rhythms she had never felt before. Following that beat, she led Cam, again and again, to the very limits of his control. But always it guided her back just in time so that the voluptuous rapture could continue.

Together, they both learned the absolute boundaries of their appetite for one another. The enormity of it was frightening. Malou was the first to retreat before it. The teasing, undulating dance of her hips quickened into something more insistent as she pressed toward the climax that neither of them could forestall any longer. In his moment of fulfillment, Cam grabbed for her in an embrace of shuddering intensity, whispering her name over and over like a benediction of what they had created together.

Malou shivered within the grip of his impassioned embrace as the coils of the love they had made together and wound so unbearably tight began to unwind, spiraling out in ever-widening ripples.

"Bedtime, my dozy darling."

Malou jerked awake, the slight crick in her neck alerting her that she had been napping for quite some time against Cam's chest.

"I didn't fall asleep, did I?"

"Afraid so. Even snored the tiniest bit."

"I don't snore," Malou maintained stoutly.

"Probably just the wind." Cam chuckled in the absolute stillness of the night. With his forefinger, he curled one of the ringlets that petaled against Malou's forehead.

"I've never done that before. Never fallen asleep like that. I'm sorry."

"Don't apologize. Only women who are well loved fall asleep. It's one of the infallible indicators."

"And what about men?" Malou asked, raising herself up to look into his face. "You appear inhumanly alert."

"Just been amusing myself watching you sleep, and thinking."

"Thinking? About what?" Malou rolled smoothly off of Cam's lap and snuggled beside him on the couch.

"Oh, about . . ." His eyes searched hers. For the first time, Cam seemed at a loss, uncertain of himself. He retreated from her question. "About why on earth I ever dragged out that trunk of clothes last time we were here and allowed you to wrap yourself up. We're not going to repeat that error when we sleep together tonight.''

''Sounds far from restful,'' Malou jibed back, wondering what Cam had really been thinking about. Could it possibly have been the same question that now deviled her mind?

As they walked to the bedroom, Malou dismissed the possibility. Cameron Landell was not a man to be derailed by love.

Chapter Eight

M alou awoke the next morning to the crystalline notes of the canyon warbler's song, filled with a sense of joy she had not known since childhood. It was the kind of feeling that had percolated through her on the first morning of summer vacation as she lay in bed contemplating the prospect of three months of freedom. Reality had intruded when she entered high school, and all her vacations after that had been diligently filled with the kind of summer work and research that eventually won her grants and awards before her time. Now Cam had come bringing a reprieve from reality.

She watched him sleep, just as he had watched her last night. Swatches of buttery morning sunlight splashed across him. He'd managed to capture most of the sheet they'd slept under, and it lay clumped in a wad between his legs, one corner drawn up togalike over his shoulder; he looked like a fallen Roman. One knee was cocked and his fist was jammed beneath his jaw, so that he seemed to be puzzling out a problem in his sleep. A deep well of tenderness opened up in Malou as she watched him so hard at work at sleeping. For a few minutes she felt she knew exactly what he had looked like as a little boy—spindly arms, and eyes too big and dark and intense for his face.

Then those eyes opened and filled with joy; they were the eyes of the young boy she'd been imagining. He smiled.

"So it wasn't a dream after all," he said, lazily reaching for her. At his touch, all hints of the little boy he might have been vanished. Cam had been a man for a very long time. "You're depraved, do you realize that? You shouldn't go around masquerading as the prim primatologist when you can do the things you can to a man."

"I suppose the high-dollar developer image fits in pretty well with the kinds of things you're able to do to a woman." Malou loved the easy bantering between them, the feeling of comfortable sensuality, the fact that they could tease about their careers.

"Come here, you little minx, you." He grabbed her and pulled her to him. "This high-dollar developer has all kinds of things he wants to do to one very special woman." Then, with a leisurely abandon, he proceeded to make good on his threat.

"Malou," he whispered into her ear much later on as she lay with her back curled against him, drifting in a mindless reverie in the comfort of his arms. "Those 'kinds of things' you were talking about earlier . . ."

"Mmm," she mumbled, barely able to focus on anything but the wonderful glow within her.

"I've never done them with other women. Never been inspired to. There is something very, very special about you. Between us."

The glow turned to a summery radiance at Cam's proclamation.

"I'm really afraid of blowing it. Of going too fast. Of overwhelming you."

Malou snuggled closer to Cam, encouraging him to go on, to say the words that he wouldn't have had the courage to voice if she'd been staring at him.

"I don't know," he continued. "Sometimes I look at you and in my mind I see this image of a doe at a water hole and she's just heard a noise. A twig cracking in the distance. Something. But she has her head up, listening, poised, ready to flee if she hears that noise again."

Malou was astonished to hear Cam speak of such vulnerability. Even more amazed that that was his image of her. She rolled around in his arms to face him.

"I don't want to run, Cam. I like it here with you. I like it a lot."

"I like it a lot too. Ummm," he growled with contentment, rolling over and pulling Malou onto his stomach. "I wish this little idyll could go on just as long as we wanted it to."

"I was thinking along those same lines. I'd like to officially declare this the first day of summer vacation."

"I second the declaration, except that we have none of the props necessary for summer vacation. No TV for watching endless reruns and horrible horror movies. No tenement walls for playing handball against. No empty bottles to collect and turn in for two cents apiece."

"That was *your* summer vacation," Malou chided Cam. "Today I propose that you learn what a *real* summer vacation is all about."

" 'Real' meaning yours, I presume."

"Presumption correct," Malou declared, hopping out of bed, eager now to start the day. She darted over to the trunk where Cam had found the cache of country clothes they had worn their first night in the stone cabin, and pulled out jeans and shirts for both of them. She tossed Cam's outfit at him. "Come on, sleepyhead, we've got to pack three months into this one day."

The morning air was heavy with the scent of wildflowers and with the blossoming of promises. Malou breathed in both as she stepped out into the day with Cam. They wandered through a large meadow behind the cabin, which was overgrown with bluebonnets and Indian paintbrush. As if cued by the stage directions in a script, Cam picked a bouquet for Malou. Following the creek that meandered among the century-old live oaks, they ended up at a cool, grassy knoll. The creek widened into a small pool that Malou insisted they wade in. Next came berry gathering when Malou found a patch of dewberries trailing vines heavy with the dark fruit.

With a hatful of berries for snacking resting on Cam's stomach, they lay on their backs and picked faces, animals, and airy castles out of the clouds puffing across the endless blue sky.

"Look, there's Pegasus." Cam brought a finger up to paint the outline of the winged horse of myth he saw flying across the sky.

Malou tilted her head against the thick grass cushioning it

to follow the shape he traced. "Oh yeah, I see it. Sort of. Do you see Mr. Magoo?"

"I give you Pegasus and you give me Mr. Magoo? Don't forget, I'm supposed to be the one who spent his summer in front of the tube."

"But you didn't, did you? Somewhere in the misspent youth, you put in a lot of time with your nose buried in a book."

"That's our secret. Think what it would do for my high-dollar developer image if it got out that I grew up reading *Bullfinch's Mythology* instead of *Conan the Barbarian* comics."

"Oh, devastating," Malou teased. "Your secret will go with me to the grave. But don't you see Mr. Magoo there? The bulbous nose. The squinty eyes."

"You Ph.D. types are hopeless," Cam snorted, and they settled into a companionable silence, lying next to one another and following the shifting patterns in the sky. It was Cam who, sometime later, spoke next. He plucked a berry from the hat, then put the hat aside as he rolled over and propped himself up on his elbow above Malou.

"A berry for your thoughts," he said, holding the fruit above the lips that curled into a smile.

"I suppose then they should be berry important thoughts."

Cam groaned. "Primatologists who make ghastly puns like that should be drawn and quartered."

"You're right. I don't know what came over me." But Malou did know what was coming over her, though she didn't want to stop and analyze it now. To tear apart the marvelous, giddy feeling effervescing through her that made her want to laugh out loud and utter ghastly, silly puns. "It will never happen again."

"If that's a solemn promise, then you may have your berry now."

"On my honor as a prim primatologist," Malou swore with mock solemnity. "There will be no further puns."

"Good girl. Eat your berry." Cam lowered the fruit and she parted her lips. But he didn't let go of the stem. Wrapping her tongue around the plump berry, Malou pulled it away from his fingers. Wine-colored juice flowed over her lips. "Oh, what a wicked mess we seem to have made," Cam said. "Let me clean that up for you."

His head, as he bent over her, blocked the sun from Malou's eyes. In the shade he cast, Cam teased the burgundy juice from around the corners of her mouth. When the last drop of juice had been scoured away by the velvety roughness of his tongue, he parted her lips and made slow dipping forays into the hollow beyond.

Malou was stunned to again feel the forces she was sure had been thoroughly dissipated. They gathered within her just as if she and Cam had never come together, and she hungered for him as desperately as she had before their long night of discovery.

Loving Cam beneath the broad canopy of the open sky seemed so right and perfectly natural that the earth might have been created solely as a bed for them, the grass as a thick, soft coverlet. The sun kissed and tantalized the few bare inches that Cam's lips did not adore.

For a long time after the final spasms of fulfillment had rippled through them, Cam lay within her, his weight on his elbows, and stared into her face, unwilling, unable to break away.

"How did you get that tiny scar?" His forearm curled around her head as he traced a finger across a silvery scratch above her right eyebrow.

Malou touched the scar as if the memory were stored there. "Oh, that. Fell out of my crib not too long after I learned how to stand up." Malou felt Cam's warm chuckle in the pit of his belly.

"So even then you were bent on running away."

"Running away?" Malou asked. Did he, could he, already know her that well? It didn't matter. That person, the girl who had fled from human complications, was gone. She had no intention of running from Cameron Landell.

"You know, you never did tell me your thoughts. You snatched that berry away, but you never told me your thoughts."

Malou stared up into the face above hers, searching it the way she had searched the clouds earlier for hidden patterns. She looked into his eyes, and for a second she almost spoke, so sure was she that she saw in his eyes what was in her heart. She almost answered Cam's question truthfully. She almost told him that she was falling in love. But, with the words already forming on her lips, she remembered that the fanciful animals they'd seen in the sky were little more than the projections of their own fantasies. She dared not project the love growing within her onto Cam and assume that it could ever be his.

"I was just thinking that it's been a long time since dinner and wondering how long dewberries can sustain human life."

Something flickered across Cam's face. Malou thought for a moment that it might have been disappointment, but then she reminded herself again sternly about projecting fantasies.

"You're right, of course," he agreed briskly. "We've played hooky from the real world long enough. It's time to start thinking about things like food and bank notes."

Malou regretted having such mundane things intrude upon their interlude, but she was the one who had allowed them to bull their way in. She had only herself to blame. Cam turned to collect the clothes they had strewn about like patches of wildflowers. They dressed quickly, and Cam bounded to his feet with what struck Malou as an excess of energy, then helped her up.

"I guess school's back in session again," Malou said, as Cam brushed a few wisps of dried grass from her hair.

"I guess so. I was starting to forget there for a moment just how close we are to my deadline at the bank. Only two weeks left. It's a date that neither of us can afford to forget."

Cam flashed a smile that died away too quickly. Already his thoughts were back on the tangle of details tying Landell Acres together and binding it to El Rancho de los Monos. And to her. She could see his preoccupation in his walk. Gone was the lazy lope that had carried them out into the sunny fields. He was again the tightly coiled mass of inexhaustible energy, his aggressive stride eating up the grassy acres as if they were teeming city blocks he had to negotiate his way through at the greatest speed possible.

The idyll has ended, Malou thought as they stripped off the borrowed clothes and folded them back into the trunk like actors laying aside the costumes and personas they had worn during a play. Something tore inside Malou as the trunk lid banged shut. It couldn't end. Not yet. She wasn't ready for it to end.

"My parents are celebrating their thirtieth anniversary next Saturday in Austin," she blurted out, grabbing at the first link she could use to forge a bond between them again. "Want to come? You can see the scene of *my* misspent youth."

Cam cocked his head, puzzling for a minute over the mercurial woman before him. Before, in the field, when she had abruptly changed the subject and mood to remind him that they hadn't eaten, he could have sworn that she wanted nothing more than a way to end gracefully what had suddenly looked like merely an episode. And now, inviting him to meet her parents?

"You baffle me," he mused.

"I baffle you. Because I invited you to my parents' anniversary party?"

"Because of a number of confusing and contradictory things."

"So that means you don't want to come? I can't blame you. It'll probably be pretty stuffy. A lot of university people . . ."

"No, it means I'd like to come. I can't resist enigmas."

And with that simple acceptance, Malou's heart soared again.

Outside the station, Cam switched off the ignition. "I'll have someone put a new alternator in the jeep and have them deliver it this afternoon."

"Oh, no," Malou protested. "That's too much trouble. I'll take the bus in from Laredo and pick it up myself."

Cam shook his head. "And how will you get into Laredo? By thumb? Nothing doing. For once, will you stop being so capable and independent? What would be a major ordeal for you, would be a matter of a phone call for me. Let me do it, Malou."

"You win," Malou surrendered happily.

"Now, how shall we get together this Saturday?"

"Why don't I drive up and meet you in San Antonio," Malou volunteered, "and we can go on into Austin together."

"So, you'd take your chances on the jeep again, eh? No, even with a new alternator, I don't trust that pile of junk. I'll come down here and pick you up."

"But it's so far out of your way."

"That's all relative. Perception of distance is a function of one's desire to make the trip. In your case, it is a very short trip."

"Cam, I . . ." Malou started to say more than she could allow herself to say. He stopped her words with a kiss.

"A very short trip," Cam repeated, his lips still nearly touching hers. "But one that won't come soon enough."

With a start, Malou caught herself doing it again. She caught herself searching his face for the feeling that was in her heart. She pulled away from his embrace.

"Gads, it's high noon," she said in a rush. "Ernie's probably inside peeking at me right now."

"Heaven forbid that Ernie should see you in my arms."

Malou hopped out of the car. "Saturday then."

Cam sighed and struggled for patience. "Saturday." With a tight smile of forbearance, he turned the ignition key and circled back to the highway.

Once under way, Cam switched on the radio and a

heavy-metal group blared a shrieking song of prepubescent love at him. He twisted the dial into silence. He punched in the cigarette lighter and reached into his pocket for a smoke. His hand was patting the flat pocket before he remembered he'd given up the habit over ten years ago.

Cam shook his head in exasperated amusement. Ten years. It had been far, far longer since any woman had so thoroughly bewildered him. Quite possibly never, for Malou was unlike any other woman he had ever known. That was the double-edged sword that sliced at him. It both attracted him with a compelling force he was nearly powerless before, and it also absolutely perplexed him. Perplexed and irritated him mightily. He jerked the un-needed cigarette lighter free and stamped his foot against the accelerator. He had an appointment with his landscape architect that, if he sped, he would only be half an hour late for.

Malou walked into the station already haunted by memories of the last twenty-four hours and by that unreadable smile that had tightened Cam's features just before he'd driven off.

"Ernie!" she called. "I'm back!" She tried to make her tone light and casual, wondering why that should require such an effort. Things hadn't been light and casual with Ernie for some time now. Not since the morning that Cameron Landell had driven up. In the same instant the realization hit Malou: Ernie was jealous. It was all so clear now, that she wondered how she could have missed seeing it for so long. Ernie's sullenness for the past two weeks. His immediate antipathy toward Cam, which had grown even stronger as they spent more time together. Ernie's continuing attacks and accusations. They all fit together now. They were all the hallmarks of a jealous man.

"Ernie?" Her call was a bit softer this time. There was still no answer. She walked back toward the lab. The door was locked. Malou rapped gently. "Ernie?" There was a scuffling sound within. "Ernie, you in there?" A bit louder.

The door opened a crack and Ernie pressed his bearded face into it. "So, you're home. Long trip to San Antonio."

"Yeah, well, the jeep broke down and . . ." And what? Malou asked herself. What could she tell Ernie that wouldn't exacerbate his jealousy?

"And that's why you stayed out all night again?"

Why had she tried? Malou knew she was the world's worst liar. "Oh, that. Cam and I had some things we needed to discuss about the disposition of the troop." Well, at least she was edging back into the vicinity of the truth.

Ernie's mouth bunched up skeptically at one corner. "Well, I hope you two had a productive 'discussion.' Now, if you will excuse me, I've got work to do."

"You're hitting it awfully hard, Ern. I thought you might want to come out of hibernation and I could fix us something for lunch. It's been a while since we sat down together."

"Thanks. No. I'm really involved here. I'm surprised you've got so much free time, what with neither of us certain that Tulip is going to adopt Lorre as hers."

As the door shut again in her face, the lock clicking back into place, Malou joined in the berating Ernie had just given her. He was right. How could she have so completely forgotten about the orphaned baby?

Malou threw a quick sandwich together and took it with her out to the compound, munching as she walked. She gobbled down the last bite of her sandwich and opened the latch at the compound gate. Pulling out her field notebook, she put the binoculars to her eyes and began checking off the long list of monkeys on her census sheet, trying to work as quickly as she could down to Tulip. Far off, Sumo was standing upright in a rare bipedal stance to check her out. He looked like a wizened little old man in a shaggy overcoat as he stood there, his hands resting on his bent knees.

"It's only me!" she called across the distance. At the sound of her familiar voice, Sumo slumped back down into his normal four-legged crouch and continued picking tender shoots out of the grass to eat.

Malou noted the females honored to be allowed into his immediate presence. Tulip was not among them. She should have been. She was one of the highest-ranking females. Malou measured out the implications of her absence. Had Tulip accepted Lorre and been rejected by the inner circle for clinging to an outcast's child? Or had Tulip rejected Lorre and was she even now off searching for her own lost baby? Malou chided herself for not being there, not being near to Lorre. She pictured the big-eyed baby abandoned in some remote corner of the compound, hungry, alone, and confused.

And it was her fault.

She followed the path of two juveniles in a never-ending game of tag, chasing each other across the prairie. The pursued escaped his pursuer by scrambling up an old deer-hunting tower and diving off of it into the pool below. He landed with a splash. A crotchety adult bending over to drink at the pool's edge cuffed the splasher, sending him yelping away. Then the drinker crept forward, sliding into the cool water.

Odd, Malou thought, wondering why the adult had been so testy about being splashed. She zoomed the focus of her binoculars in on the swimmer and found her answer as a tiny, big-eyed head sprouted on top of the one gliding through the water. It was Lorre clinging to Tulip as she took the baby for her first swim. Malou rejoiced. The cuffing had been the natural overprotectiveness of the macaque mother. Tulip had accepted Lorre.

The cloud that had settled so suddenly and so darkly over Malou lifted. She watched the baby hang on to Tulip's ears and ride her head like a tiny jockey. Gradually the terror left Lorre's oversized eyes as the cool water lapped up around her. She even turned loose of one ear long enough to splash a paw into the water and bring a glistening drop up to her nose to sniff. Identifying it as nothing more than water, Lorre licked the drop away and beat her hand against the pond. Though she splashed directly into Tulip's face, the older monkey didn't react. She just continued on her way, gliding through the pond with her baby perched up high and safe.

Malou went back to her census list, happily working her way through it, noting who was attacking whom and who was coming to whose defense. She checked to see if any of the young males now reaching four and five years of age had been banished to the periphery, and which ones had been allowed to remain with the females, Sumo, and a few other top-ranking males at the troop's center. She watched to see which mothers came to the defense of their children, knowing that such defense would have a large bearing on the child's ultimate rank in the troop.

And always she watched for her old friend Kojiwa. The day was warm, so Malou assumed that he was relaxing in the shade of a cactus somewhere, probably being groomed by one of the aging females who had remained loyal to him even after he'd lost the leadership of the troop to Sumo. But when Malou came to the end of her list and had still not spotted Kojiwa, she began to worry. The old-timer was tough as a juniper root, but he was also getting on. He'd already outlived every other monkey his age. But, Malou reminded herself, that didn't mean that the old fellow was indestructible.

She picked up her binoculars and searched. On her third pass of the area she focused in on what she had at first taken to be a clump of brush. But no, the color was more a tawny gray than a brown. She zoomed the lenses in and came to the inescapable conclusion—that was the time-bleached coat of a venerable oldster.

She knew it was Kojiwa long before she reached the clump of fur, but it wasn't until she saw sunlight glinting off the blinking eyes that she began to run toward him. Her pulse accelerated wildly when she saw that a limb torn from a coyotillo bush lay beside him. He still clutched a few berries in his hand. Malou gathered him into her arms. He was too far gone to protest. Running as best she could with her burden, Malou rushed back to the station. She nestled him in a blanket and went to pound on the locked lab door.

"Ernie, open up. I need you. It's an emergency!" Her colleague was much better versed in macaque physiology than she was. She knew about macaque society, but Ernie knew about the animal's anatomy.

He burst out of the door and slammed it behind himself. "What in God's name is it?" he asked harshly, alarmed by Malou's urgency.

"Kojiwa." The name came out in a gasp, expelled on the

last bit of air left in Malou's overtaxed lungs. "Coyotillo berries." She telegraphed the situation.

Ernie understood immediately. "He's dead." It was more of a statement than an inquiry.

Malou shook her head.

"Where is he?" Ernie asked brusquely.

Malou pointed to the front of the station, and Ernie brushed her aside as he followed her finger to the sick monkey.

"You carried him in?" Ernie asked as he bent over and lifted Kojiwa's lid to peer into the amber eye. The pupil had shrunk to a pinprick of darkness. Ernie took a small flashlight out of his pocket and flicked it on, directing the beam into Kojiwa's eye.

"He's not going to make it." Ernie pronounced the verdict with a flat finality.

Malou was stunned as she watched him turn to go back to the lab. "No!" she screamed. "He *is* going to make it."

Ernie stopped and looked at her as if she were a raving madwoman. Malou didn't care at that moment what he thought of her mental condition. She started barking orders at him. "We can't waste any more time. There's no telling how long ago he ate the berries. We've got to improvise some kind of stomach pump. You know more about macaque physiology than I do. We could take one of the tubes we use for worming and . . ."

Ernie returned to her side and looked again into Kojiwa's eye. "Won't work," he declared flatly, clicking the light off and repocketing it. "He's too far gone. There's almost no pupil response."

"But we can't just let him . . ." Malou couldn't finish the sentence. "We've got to at least *try* to save him."

"Why? He's lived longer than he had any right to."

Malou accepted Ernie's refusal, but she wasn't about to let it dictate her response—or take up any more of the valuable minutes that were ticking away as more of the poison circulated through Kojiwa's faltering system.

"Stand aside, please," she asked, making her way to the tubes she would need to rig up some semblance of a stomach pump. Ernie stepped aside grudgingly. Hurriedly she prepared an injection of a sedative that would immobilize Kojiwa and slow down his circulation. Next, she selected a length of sterile tubing and, propping Kojiwa's powerful jaws open, began to slide it down his throat.

"Here, let me do that," Ernie said, taking the tube from her shaking hands. "You don't know the esophageal contours." He fed the tube in expertly and proceeded to attach a syringe.

"Make a mild saline solution," he ordered her. "We'll need it to flush out the stomach."

Only when they'd finished and were washing up was there time for Malou to tell Ernie how much his help had meant. "I couldn't have done it on my own," she admitted. "We would have lost him for sure."

"There are no guarantees that you haven't," Ernie said, squirting orange Betadine soap on his hands.

"I know, but at least we tried." Unable to resist the impulse, she stood up on tiptoes to plant a kiss on Ernie's fuzzy cheek. He reddened beneath his beard. As they dried off their hands, Malou went to check on Kojiwa. He had finally stopped resisting the sedative and was sleeping. As he relaxed into unconsciousness, his tightly gripped fist finally unclenched. Some of the berries that had brought him to such grief were still there.

"You know," Malou said, "the old guy must be getting a little senile to start eating coyotillo at his age. He's known for years to avoid them."

Ernie merely grunted in reply and continued toweling off his hands.

Malou bent over the sleeping monkey and plucked the poisonous berries off of his callused palm. They were sticky. She held them to her nose. Unable to believe what she smelled, she licked lightly.

"Hey, no wonder he ate these berries. They're coated in honey!"

Ernie dropped the towel and went to her side, taking the berries from her to sniff and then taste. "God, they are," he concluded. "With the macaque sweet tooth, they'd eat pebbles if they had enough honey on them."

Malou's mind whirred into high gear. "Not only that, but there was a torn coyotillo branch lying beside Kojiwa when I found him."

Ernie tossed the berries into the trash. "I don't guess we need Sherlock Holmes to crack this mystery."

"Someone's deliberately trying to kill the monkeys."

"That's what I've been saying all along," Ernie said with strained patience. It was obvious from the look of distaste that spread across his features that Ernie's chief suspect hadn't changed.

"And you think Cam's responsible?"

"The motivation and opportunity are both there."

"You must be joking," Malou said, knowing full well that he wasn't. "You want me to believe that Cameron Landell, multimillion-dollar developer, drives down here late at night in his Mercedes 380SL to toss honey-coated coyotillo branches to a bunch of monkeys.'' The image was so ludicrous that Malou was able to dismiss it along with Ernie's cockamamie suspicions.

''No, Landell's too smart and too rich to do it himself. That's what hired hands are for.''

Hired hands like Jorge Maldonado. The ranch hand's face came to Malou's mind, as well as the evidences of the Mexican's almost feudal loyalty to *el patrón*. There was no question that he would do his master's bidding, and even relish the doing if it meant a few less of the monkeys that threatened his *vaquero* image of what should be raised on a true ranch. No, there was no love lost between Jorge and the monkeys that infested his domain. She thought of the last time she'd seen the hired hand—on the porch of the stone cabin.

She remembered how abruptly Cam had whisked the man out of the house and onto the porch where they would be beyond Malou's earshot. She thought of Cam's denying that he spoke Spanish, then being quite able to make all his wishes known to the Maldonados.

Ernie watched almost as if he could see the tumblers within her brain falling into place to unlock the mystery of the monkey killings.

Malou could not believe that she was thinking what she was. She rejected the whole idea. ''No, it's impossible. Why on earth would Cam want to kill off monkeys that he could sell for fifteen hundred apiece?''

''Listen, he's made it abundantly clear that whatever he could get for the monkeys would be peanuts compared to what the land under them is worth.''

''Well, killing them off one by one would be an awful

slow way of clearing the land,'' Malou countered, but already an unsettling image was taking shape in her mind. Ernie put a name and a focus to that image.

"Public relations.''

"What are you talking about?'' she snapped.

"I'm talking about sacrificing a few animals so that when he decides to sell off the whole troop he can use them as a way of justifying that decision. He can point to the monkeys who are dying out here in the open and claim that they'd be better off in a lab somewhere.''

"Cam doesn't care that much about public opinion to go to all that trouble,'' Malou said, but her tone had lost some of its starch; she was remembering Cam's reaction to the phone call informing him that protesters had gathered outside Landell Acres. Just the possibility of negative media attention had been enough to send him flying into the night. She knew he was at the mercy of the bank holding his note and that banks did not take kindly to projects that generated that kind of attention.

"Oh, doesn't he?'' Ernie countered. "You told me how enraged he became when you threatened to call in the press if he disbanded the troop. What's happened in the meantime to change his feelings? Or, more to the point, what's happened to change yours?''

Against her will, Malou felt a guilty, scarlet flush stain her cheeks. "My feelings for this troop have never changed; you know that, Ernie. I'm trying to ward off the threats to it just like you are.''

"Maybe it's your feelings about those threats that have changed, then.''

Malou started to lash out at Ernie, to tell him how wrongheaded and unfair he was. But she stopped. He was right. Her feelings about the greatest threat her troop had to face had changed, for Cam was that threat.

Ernie stared, waiting for her response. When none came he merely nodded with a sad understanding, then walked back to the lab. From down the long hall, the sound of the lab door locking behind him echoed up to Malou.

Before she was aware of doing so, Malou had caught her bottom lip between her teeth and was worrying it. Silently she tried to rebut each of Ernie's charges. She fought to scour herself of all that she'd come to feel for Cam, to dispassionately analyze him, his motives and actions.

The effort was a failure. All it succeeded in doing was to stir up a roil of conflicting emotions. She struggled to point the finger of guilt in another direction, but like a compass returning unerringly to true north, it always swung back to Cam. And always her heart rebelled at the notion. She could not believe that the lover who, only a few hours ago, had initiated her into the sweetest secrets that a man and a woman can share could be capable of such treachery, such cruelty. No, it simply could not be true.

From his bed in the makeshift recovery room they had fashioned for him, Kojiwa snuffled in his sleep. Malou went to the old-timer. His breathing was shallow, his pulse still weak and thready. Malou patted his dark paw, so much like a human hand. He was the kindest and the bravest of the troop. He had witnessed more than his aged amber eyes had ever been intended to see. He deserved a gentler, more dignified death than this.

Anger at a faceless poisoner revitalized Malou. She could listen no longer to the siren song her heart was singing to her. As it had for some time now, the survival of all the monkeys that old Kojiwa had led into this new land depended on the clarity of her vision. She'd let love cloud her perceptions for a dangerous interval and even now knew that she couldn't completely wipe away the seductive mist that clung to her. But she could see where the path of her duty lay, and if love twined across that path, trying to trip her up, she would have to cut it away.

She had no other choice.

Chapter Nine

"Why the glum expression?" Cam asked.

They'd made polite chitchat for a few miles as they headed northeast toward Austin and the anniversary party for Malou's parents. But for the last twenty miles a heavy silence had fallen between Cam and Malou. She sat beside him, lovely in an emerald green sundress that plunged to a provocative V in the front, a bow-tied package resting primly on her knees, but her thoughts were miles away.

Malou glanced over, wishing that she could trust what she saw with her own eyes, for the sight was innocence personified. Cam looked and smelled fresh from a shower. His unruly hair was still shiny wet and combed over his forehead like a choir boy's. His firm jaw gleamed from the smooth scrape of a razor. The tie knotted at his neck was a touching concession to the occasion. All in all, he might have been a boy dressed by his mother for a birthday party.

Except that everything boyishly appealing about Cameron Landell was counterweighted by his undeniable maleness, by the aura of raw masculinity that pervaded his every look and gesture.

Why the glum expression? Malou repeated his words, testing them. Did he already know the answer to that question? Had he, in fact, been the cause of the unhappiness that was writ so large across her face? She watched him closely as she answered his question.

"One of the monkeys, Kojiwa, was poisoned. He's still very sick." Cam's features took on a look of worried concern. Malou watched and wondered. Had the expression been waiting there all the time, rehearsed and ready to be hauled out the instant she told him her "news"? Perhaps Cam had even specially selected the old monkey and marked him for death as a particularly insidious way of demoralizing her, of making her want to abandon her fight to keep the troop together. Together on Cam's valuable land. No, she protested, she was letting Ernie's paranoia get the best of her. Even if he'd had such a foul intent, Cam couldn't have told one monkey from another if his life depended on it.

"Kojiwa. I've heard you mention that name before. Isn't he one of your favorites? The original leader of the troop or something like that?"

"Yes." So he did remember Kojiwa and the special place he held in her heart. And even if Cam couldn't pick the old-timer out of the troop, Jorge probably could.

Cam's hand, warm and comforting, covered Malou's. "I know how much these guys mean to you, sweetheart. If you don't feel up to being around a mass of people, we could call your parents and cancel. Have a quiet dinner some-where.''

After the unrelieved stress of the last few days, the long nights spent nursing Kojiwa, the strained days of feeling like an enemy collaborator before Ernie's silent scorn, Malou was almost undone by Cam's gentle concern. Tears leaped spontaneously to her eyes and pooled there as she looked up at him. She wanted nothing more at that moment than to do exactly what he'd suggested, to escape to some tranquil little restaurant. To share a few glasses of wine and a simple meal with the man beside her, then to let him take her to bed and exorcise all the suspicion that was festering within her. Looking at him, and feeling the powerful pull of a thousand conflicting emotions, her misery only increased.

"No," she finally answered, drawing herself up and forcing back the tears. "My parents will be expecting us."

Cam patted her hand, then turned back to the road.

In Austin, they pulled off the interstate to wind their way through the campus of the University of Texas. Malou's spirits rose slightly as they passed through the narrow streets shaded by giant magnolias, with their waxy green leaves and huge white blossoms. She pointed out the anthropology department, where she'd spent the most important years of her life. Cam slowed down as Malou translated the Latin inscription chiseled into the limestone above the entryway.

"Know the truth and the truth shall set you free." She spoke from memory, her eyes not on the chiseled words but on Cam. What *was* the truth? Would she ever find it if she kept losing herself every time he came near her? And, even if she did finally identify it, could the truth ever set her free from the desire for the man beside her that even now, even as she considered his possible guilt, coiled within her, aching to be unloosed?

Cam drove on following her directions. They led to a prestigious neighborhood in West Austin. He found a spot on her parents' street, and he took her arm as they strolled up to the house she'd lived in from the age of ten on. Azaleas were in full bloom, crowding in on either side of the curving walkway leading up to the stately, Greek-columned house.

"Not too shabby," Cam whispered in her ear, breaking the tension that had built within Malou.

She smiled up at him, grateful that this house and its owners didn't exercise the same kind of power over him that they did over her.

A swirl of guests had clotted near the main entryway. She recognized a number of her father's colleagues from the university, most of them in studiously casual Mexican shirts and beards. The women wore styles a couple of years out-of-date that proclaimed how little interest they had in things as frivolous as fashion. Spotted among them were the Nobel Prize winners her father honored in public and envied in private. She'd grown up sharing his belief that while his work was every bit as good as any Nobelist's, it simply wasn't as "showy," which is why he would never make that trip to Stockholm.

White-gloved and jacketed waiters circulated among the guests, passing trays of champagne in tall flutes. "Waiters," Malou whispered in amazement to Cam. "Looks like they're pulling out all the stops for this little do." Her parents rarely went in for such ostentatious displays.

To one side of the crowd was a chamber music group playing the kind of refined, ethereal music that set the tone for a gathering such as this. Through the crush, Malou caught a glimpse of her father. He was studying her and Cam with a cool, detached eye. A scientist's eye, she'd always told herself when, even when she was a young girl he'd turned that analytical gaze on her. She'd never been able to escape feeling as if she were just another one of her father's experiments. And not a terribly successful one at that. Her father made no effort to break away from the guests surrounding him. He let his daughter come to him. Malou's hand tightened on Cam's.

"That's my father watching us," she whispered to him. He covered her clenched hand with his.

"I thought I felt the hot glare of the paternal eye. Quite a distinguished-looking gent."

And he was. Arthur Sanders had, even as a young man, looked precisely like what he now was, a university professor with a world-class reputation as a physicist. His hair, which had gone prematurely silver, contributed to the impression he gave of a man with his mind on matters far too abstract for the ordinary mortal.

Professor Sanders held out a hand as Malou approached him. She presented hers and he clasped it with a practiced warmth.

"Father, I'd like you to meet a friend of mine, Cameron Landell. Cam, my father, Professor Arthur Sanders."

Professor Sanders pressed Cam's hand with the same precise degree of warmth. "Cameron, I'm pleased to meet you."

"And I you, Arthur." Malou was sure she'd only

imagined it, but conversation seemed to suddenly die around them and the chamber group to falter. Malou had never heard another living soul except her mother call her father anything other than Professor, and usually Doctor, Sanders. He never invited anyone to call him Arthur, and there were few, none within Malou's hearing, who had ever presumed to take the liberty. No one who didn't know her father as well as she did would ever have guessed that Cam's presumption had offended him. But Malou saw the slight quirk in his eyebrow that signaled his slow-burning ire, and she knew that Cam had incited it.

"Malou's told me a great deal about you," Cam continued .cordially, oblivious to his violation of university protocol. In his world no man was his superior, and when someone used his first name, Cam took it as an open invitation for him to use that man's first name in return.

"Odd," the professor commented with his trademark abstraction, "Malou hasn't mentioned you to us."

"You remember, Daddy," Malou cut in, trying to head her father off before he got started. "The station phone has been broken. I haven't spoken to you at all for some time."

"Ah, that's right," Sanders said, having already gotten his dig in at the upstart. "Last I heard from you, your whole project was going on the block. Some developer had bilked Stallings out of the title to his ranch and was planning to auction off the monkeys to the highest bidder."

"That's not exactly what I told you, Daddy," Malou said coolly, knowing full well that her father remembered precisely what she'd told him about the situation at Los Monos *and* that Cam was the bilking developer.

"What's your line, Landell?" her father asked. Watching

him jockey for position as blatantly as any macaque, trying to dominate Cam now by using his last name with no title, would have amused Malou if the scene had involved any other two men.

"Development." Cam cut his answer off short.

"You're not *that* Cameron Landell, are you?" Her father feigned ignorance. "The San Antonio developer who's paving over one of the few breeding grounds left to the beleaguered golden-cheeked warbler, cutting down all those junipers they use to nest in?"

"Guilty as charged," Cam answered, *his* eyebrow beginning now to quirk just the slightest bit. With an offhanded glance, he looked about and asked casually, "I wonder how many junipers had to be cut down when this neighborhood was built."

Malou didn't give her father the chance to answer, and since Cam showed no inclination to come to his own defense, she did it for him. "Hadn't you heard, Daddy? Cam's going to leave a big greenbelt running through the project in the prime nesting area."

"Yes," Cam put in. "That should help with my PR profile and maybe even increase property values."

Malou winced. Cam was taking a perverse delight in placing himself in the worst light possible.

"I suppose that, in your business," her father pontificated, "PR and property values are paramount concerns."

"The only concerns, Arthur," Cam said with a needling grin. Before Professor Sanders could begin lecturing on the topic, Malou's mother drifted over to them.

"Mary Louise, darling," she called out, as if she were greeting an acquaintance at the faculty club. "I'm so pleased you could make it.'' She kissed the air around Malou's ears, her fingers lightly grazing her daughter's forearms.

"Happy anniversary, Mother,'' Malou said to her mother, who seemed only to grow more handsome as the years passed. She was as stately and as refined as everything around her. But what Malou had always admired was that her mother had never let her looks or her house be her world. She'd achieved a position for herself nearly as prominent as the one her husband occupied so proudly.

"Thank you, dear,'' she said automatically, animation sparking her voice only when she moved on to the next topic. "Has your father told you my good news?''

"We really hadn't had time,'' Malou replied awkwardly, not daring to glance at either Cam or her father.

"My study has been funded. The Arthritis Foundation is going to pay for me to study that new non-steroidal anti-inflammatory I was telling you about a few months back.''

"Oh, Mother, that's wonderful!'' Malou looked now at Cam to see if he was as impressed as she with her mother's achievement, but his expression was unreadable. Her father's wasn't, though; he was beaming with pride. Malou was grateful for the happy note that had been introduced. Her parents were never better than when they were working together like this, both excited about the other's work.

"I just had an idea,'' her father blurted out. "I'll have my secretary run off some flyers tomorrow asking for volunteers for the study and have her post them around the campus.''

"That would be most helpful,'' Malou's mother said to

her husband as he took a small notebook out of his vest pocket and penciled in a reminder to himself. Though it didn't diminish Malou's pride in her parents, she noticed a strange formality between them. She couldn't imagine them ever taking a ''school vacation'' day, as she and Cam had, to feed each other dewberries and make love in a sun-warmed field.

''Mother,'' Malou said to capture her mother's attention, which had already wandered to the other guests milling about. ''I'd like you to meet a . . .'' She stumbled for the right word. ''Friend of mine, Cameron Landell.''

''Happy thirtieth, Mrs. Sanders,'' Cam said, taking her hand in his.

''Yes, thank you, Cameron.''

Had that touch of condescension always been there in her mother's voice, Malou wondered, or were both her parents just now bringing it out especially for Cam?

''Do you work with Malou at the station?'' her mother asked.

''No, I . . .''

But her mother had already turned from Cam and was asking Malou, ''How is Ernie coming on his myopia study? He was explaining his research design to me last time we were out, and it sounded fascinating. I'd think he'd collect some very interesting data.''

''Uh, I really don't know, Mother. We haven't spoken about it lately.''

''Haven't spoken about his research?'' Mrs. Sanders echoed incredulously, trying to imagine the circumstances under which such a silence could occur. She returned her attention to Cam. ''What did you do your graduate work in?'' The question was as natural to her as asking where someone worked.

"Creative financing," Cam quipped.

The joke was lost on Mrs. Sanders. "Oh," she replied blankly. "And where did you get your undergraduate degree?"

Malou's mind whirred frantically as she searched for a way to head off this impossible conversation.

"School of hard knocks." Cam grinned.

At last, the horrible fact that their daughter's escort held *no* university degree dawned on Mrs. Sanders and she looked to her husband, who with that eloquent quirk of his eyebrow confirmed her fear and her sliding opinion of the man before her.

They stood in awkward silence for a moment before Professor Sanders asked, "How about that Carlo Rubbie discovering the T-quark? What do you make of that, Landell?"

"The T-quark?" Cam asked. "Sounds like a duck with the giggles to me."

Malou could not restrain an impish smile at Cam's jibe or her father's dour lack of amusement. Professor Sanders turned to her.

"I don't see what's so funny, Mary Louise. This discovery confirms some of the theories I've devoted my life to proving."

The smile faded from Malou's lips. She felt frivolous and disrespectful.

Assuming the tone he used to lecture particularly dull students, Professor Sanders turned back to Cam. "The T-quark is one of several subatomic particles that may very well be the ultimate component of matter. Their discovery is the most important event in physics since the invention of the solid-state transistor twenty-five years ago.''

"I don't doubt the significance of the T-quark in the least," Cam stated, his voice cool and even. "And if there were time enough in this life, I would love to learn everything I could about it. But there's not. So, like you, I am forced to tend to the business I've chosen. Perhaps you'd like to tell me now what you think of the adjustable-rate mortgage?''

"The what?" Professor Sanders asked querulously, unused to being challenged. "Just a bunch of financial machinations, I'd say.''

"And you may very well be right, but they represent the most significant departure from the way Americans typically buy houses to come along in the last fifty years.''

"Hmmff." Professor Sanders folded his arms in front of him.

"How very interesting," Mrs. Sanders said mechanically. She put an arm around her husband and began herding him away. "We've been neglecting our other guests." She turned back to Malou. "Now, don't be standoffish the way you usually are. Mingle," she commanded, waving a finger in the direction of a young man who reminded her of Ernie, with his beard and wire-rim glasses. "There's Lawrence Steward over there. Go on over and talk with him. He just got back from Botswana, where he was doing a Fulbright on native linguistics. It really is fascinating." She waved her fingers vaguely at Cam. "So nice to meet you, Mr. Landell.''

Cam waggled his fingers at the couple's departing backs. "Toodle-oo," he called after them in a tone edged with a blade of sarcasm. Malou looked up at his cocky grin and tried to gauge his reaction to the exchange. She thought her parents had been rude, snobbish, and insulting. But it was impossible to tell if Cam had been hurt.

"They can really be pretty high-handed sometimes," she ventured. "I hope you weren't offended by anything they said. Or implied."

"What? Me? Offended? Why? Simply because they treated me like a drooling idiot because I didn't flash thirteen degrees and a Fulbright at them?" The edge of sarcasm in his tone sharpened to a degree that frightened Malou. "And speaking of Fulbrights," he continued, "that enchanting Larry Steward is over there just dying to tell you all the fascinating details about linguistics in Botswana. So, why don't you run and mingle with him and some of these other escapees from a Mensa meeting and let a cretin like myself just slither on out the door." As he looked deeply into her eyes, his features momentarily softened. He caught both of her hands in his and brought them to his lips. "I'm truly, truly sorry, Malou. But if I ever doubted before how far apart our worlds are, I've had my doubts erased today." He turned abruptly and left. His sharp, thrusting stride revealed how deeply angered he was.

Malou watched him pass the butler and charge on toward his car. She looked back at her parents. The president of the university was kissing her mother on the cheek. Her parents would never understand if she were to simply leave without so much as the formal goodbye that usually terminated their meetings. Particularly if she were to leave chasing after an undegreed despoiler of the land. Cam was sliding into his car. The president of the university was shaking her father's hand and patting his back.

She started walking. Past a Nobel Prize winner, past a

white-jacketed waiter, past the chamber music group. By the time she passed the azaleas, Malou was running. She dropped the bow-tied package she'd forgotten to give her parents, and broke into a sprint. She reached the passenger side of the Mercedes just as Cam was starting to pull out, and she threw herself in the door.

"You really don't want to be around me right now," was Cam's greeting.

"Oh, but I really do," Malou countered.

"I'm in as foul a mood as I've probably ever been in in my life, and am planning to spend the rest of the afternoon at my club in San Antonio getting quietly smashed."

"Sounds like an inspired idea to me."

Cam turned to her, an icy distance frosting his gaze. "Malou, I can't, or rather won't, bodily eject you from this vehicle, but it really would be a better idea if you stayed here where you belong."

Malou's answer was somber. "I don't especially feel like I belong here anymore."

"And you *do* feel like you might belong with me where I'm going?" His question was harsh.

Malou's heart pounded at the enormity of the response she gave. "Yes."

He stared at her. "Maybe it is time for both of us to find out the answer to that question." He seemed galvanized into action by that decision. An odd purposefulness filled the car as Cam swiveled to look behind him. He accelerated past the Greek-columned house a bit too fast. A snatch of chamber music lilted into the car before it was grabbed away by Cam's burst of speed. The last thing Malou saw was her mother's puzzled expression as she bent over and picked a brightly wrapped package out of her azalea bed.

As Malou settled back against the leather seat, she felt that a tiny bit of her fate had been sealed. For good or ill? she wondered, glancing over at Cam. His expression was grim, his gaze locked onto the highway spooling out in front of them. She doubted whether knowing the answer to her question would have made any difference. Good *or* ill, she would have gone with Cameron Landell.

Cam's club was private and sat on the top of San Antonio's tallest bank building.

"Why, Mr. Landell," a hostess in a silk dress and pearls purred as they walked off the elevator into the reception area, "what a pleasant surprise. It's been far too long since we've seen you. Sam Stevens and Lou Chesler are in the bar. Or would you like a private table?"

"No," Cam answered with a quick look at Malou. "The bar will be fine. We're on a sort of tour here. A tour of Cameron Landell's world, so we'd better see all the animals in the zoo."

The hostess smiled as if Cam were making a joke that she understood perfectly and pointed a gracious hand in the direction of the bar.

It was crowded, and at every table they passed, someone stood up to grip Cam's hand or pull him aside to meet someone or to extract his promise to talk with them in private later on. It took nearly half an hour for them to make their way to the center table where two men, like twins with their identical tans, blow-dried silver hair, two-thousand-dollar watches, and female companions one-third their ages, were holding court. Chesler and Stevens. Even Malou knew the names. Anyone who read a newspaper in Texas did. Chesler had been a U.S. senator for years, ending his political career with an unsuccessful run for the presidency. Stevens was reputedly even bigger in politics than his partner ever had been. But Stevens was a back-room maneuverer, a kingmaker who wielded more power than those who held the offices whose doors he opened.

Both men rose as Cam and Malou approached the table. Chesler spoke first, in a booming voice trained to be heard across the floor of the Senate and bars crowded with powerful men.

"Durn your hide, Landell, it worries me when I don't see your face for a couple of months. What city have you snuck out and bought up while our backs were turned?" Hearty guffaws rose from an appreciative audience.

"It's states now, Chesler," Cam answered, shaking the hands extended to him. "I don't deal in anything smaller than a state these days."

Chesler whooped at Cam's comeback and pulled up two empty chairs. Cam introduced Malou.

"You may not know a damn thing about development, Landell, but you know a fine-looking woman when you see one, don't you, you old barn owl!" With a smarmy grin he turned to Malou. "I hope I didn't offend you, Miss Sanders."

Malou had no choice but to smile sweetly and take the chair Chesler held out for her. After that, she was ignored entirely as the talk turned to development deals and who was speculating on what land and what the inside word from the capital was about what property the state was planning to buy. Occasionally one of the women sitting beside one of the half dozen men around the table would make a comment. The man she had spoken to would nod without looking at her and continue his conversation as if she hadn't spoken. From time to time, Chesler would circle his finger over the table and the waitress would bring fresh drinks.

Malou listened for an hour, though she had gotten the message in the first five minutes: Cam's was a world where money and power were synonymous. A world where university degrees were worthless. It was a world in which Cam had succeeded handsomely at an exceedingly early age. She was totally out of her depth with all the talk about flipping land and grandfather clauses and municipal utility districts. Finally their eyes met, and in one glance she told him that she was more than ready to leave. Cam gulped down the drink in front of him and put the empty glass down with the small collection he'd already assembled.

"Cam," she said as the elevator doors slid shut, closing them off together, "you didn't have to drag me all the way up here to make your point."

"I didn't?" he asked, his voice giving nothing away.

"No. I know that it's no fun feeling out-of-it and unaware. I probably like the feeling even less than you do. I'm sorry about what happened at my parents'. But those are my parents, not me. I love and respect them, but I recognize that they're snobs. Intellectual snobs. Just because they don't respect your world and what you've accomplished doesn't mean that I don't."

"Don't you?" Cam asked thoughtfully. "I wonder." The elevator doors slid open. Though evening was crowding in fast, it was still light outside. "I think that before we come to any final decisions, we need a bit more data. We need one more stop on the tour. Landell Acres."

"But Cam," Malou enthused, "I'd love to see your development."

"And so you shall," he announced, sweeping her into the car. As he slammed the door shut, Cam looked off into a distance that encompassed more time than space, and he repeated solemnly to himself, "And so you shall."

Malou saw signs reading "Landell Acres, Affordable Housing" for several miles before they pulled off the highway. Within minutes they were winding down the roads of the half-completed subdivision. The expectant smile on Malou's face froze as she studied the frames for the houses that were Cam's dream. She couldn't believe what she was seeing. Couldn't believe that *these* were what he was willing to sacrifice her troop for. Nor could she stop the words that tumbled out, unloosed by her shock.

"The houses . . .," she muttered, oblivious to what she was saying, "they're so . . ."

"So what?" Cam prompted, though he had no need to hear the words. He'd known what they would be for a long time. Though his heart had for a time tried to make him forget that sure knowledge, he'd known precisely how Malou Sanders would react to the materialization of his dream. She looked over at him with startled guilt, and he asked again. "So what?"

"So . . . so small," she finished.

"So small and what? Tacky?" Cam probed.

Malou heard him badgering the words from her and felt she no longer knew Cam. Maybe she never had. Her father's face, eyebrow cocked in disapproval, superimposed itself on his handsome features. Then came Ernie's face, his round glasses two circles of light as he told Malou his worst suspicions about Cam. Behind Cam were the boxlike houses, crammed one against the other, that meant everything to him. Certainly far more than she could ever mean. She remembered him as he'd been on the racquetball court, a relentless predator who played to win or didn't play at all.

"Yes," she agreed, "tacky."

"I had a terrible feeling that you'd see the houses that way." Regret was the dominant emotion in Cam's voice. He turned away from her to stare out at the row upon row of identical house frames cramped together. When he spoke, his voice had the flat monotony of his project. "I had a chance to see where you grew up today. Would you like to see where *I* grew up?"

Cam didn't pause at her puzzled expression. "Well, just go to any movie that takes place in a big city slum. Watch any TV show where kids play in the street and their big brothers shoot heroin in abandoned buildings and their parents never have enough time or money or love for them. That's *my* neighborhood, Malou. That's where *I* grew up. There wasn't chamber music playing in the background; there was the sound of the guy next door beating up his wife, and ambulance sirens and bottles breaking on concrete. That was where *I* grew up."

"Cam, I . . ." Malou didn't know what to say, how to answer the pain that was still raw and fresh on Cam's face. She knew he'd grown up in the city and come a long way from his beginnings, but she'd never really stopped and thought about just how far he had come.

He was still staring out at the shell of one of the houses when he went on, oblivious to her. "You know something?" he asked, not caring if she answered. "I would have cut my little finger off when I was a kid to be able to live in a house like that one there is going to be. I didn't know how I was going to do it back then, but I knew I would be one of the few that escaped. That I'd live in a real house someday with a real yard.

"Well, I did it. I got out, and these 'tacky' houses that you scorn are going to make it possible for a lot of others to get out too. That 'affordable housing' we advertise is not just a gimmick. The lots are small and the houses are small so that we can keep the prices small. People who could never dream of owning their own home before will be able to buy into a little plot of Landell Acres."

He took in a deep lungful of air and turned to face Malou again. "And besides all that, I stand to make a lot of money. Not nearly as much as Chesler would make on one of his subdivisions filled with million-dollar houses, but a lot of money. That's my goal, to make enough to go on to the next bunch of 'tacky' houses. No doubt you and your father would regard that as a fairly despicable goal. I'm sure the good professor would have been much more impressed if his daughter had brought home someone who was devoting his life to studying Botswana linguistics or something equally obscure rather than providing decent housing at decent prices. And you, Malou, you say you're not like them, not a snob. But you are. In your own rarefied way, you're a snob too."

Malou, wounded by the judgment, leaned forward ready to defend herself. But Cam didn't give her the chance. He had more to say and he said it.

"I imagine that you would have been much more impressed if Landell Acres had consisted of a lot of tasteful houses with ecological designs set on sprawling lots. And even more impressed if I'd cancel the whole project and let Los Monos go on draining my cash flow." Cam's features hardened against the prospect.

The truth Cam spoke did not set Malou free. It trapped her with a net she didn't have the strength to struggle against. She could not deny what Cam had said, what he seemed to have known about her all along. She *was* her parents' child and carried their particular variety of snobbism within her like a mutant gene.

Cam took her silence for the assent it was and started up the Mercedes. The drive back to Los Monos was filled with words that echoed in each of their heads but that they did not speak. Malou stared off into the darkness outside the car, and Cam trained his gaze on the narrow trail of brightness cut by his headlights. At the research station, he turned off the motor, and took up the conversation they had abandoned as if the intervening miles had never happened.

"Well, I'm not going to do that, Malou. I'm not going to give up the project. I *am* going to build my tacky little houses. I haven't let anything stop me before, and I've already jeopardized the project by slowing down now. I have barely more than a week left to pay off my note. There's no more time to search for alternate solutions. I'm putting Los Monos on the market Monday and contacting the labs that have expressed interest to tell them that the monkeys are available."

Malou felt as though an invisible fist had knocked the wind out of her. "But what about Dr. Darden's proposal? You said you were considering it."

"I was until I remembered my place in my world. Dr. Darden's proposal is to turn the ranch into a tourist attraction and charge to let people view the monkeys. I would eventually bring in some money, but not nearly enough and not nearly soon enough. There are no other choices left, Malou. The monkeys will have to be sold."

"You never intended to do anything else," Malou blurted out, anger now her only defense against crumpling into tears of despair. "You always planned to sell the troop. You were just leading me on, holding out false hopes."

"Believe what you will," Cam told her coolly. "You would anyway."

In that instant one image stuck in Malou's mind: Cam on the racquetball court, a relentless predator for whom winning was survival. Suddenly Ernie's suspicions seemed neither wild nor paranoid. Ridding himself of the nuisance of the monkeys without soiling his image would be so easy for Cam, just as Ernie had said it would be. A phone call to Jorge and the job would be done.

"You *would* do anything to get that damned subdivision built, wouldn't you?" she asked, a chilling certainty already building in her. "You *have* to win, don't you, Cam? At any cost. Even if the price is the lives of some innocent animals."

"What are you talking about?"

What else had she expected? That he would admit poisoning the monkeys? She reached for the door handle. "No losers, no tears. That's a fine motto for you." She bit off the words, her outrage and anger growing with each one. "Because you never lose, do you? You're never the one to shed the tears."

Malou was inside the station, the door locked behind her, before she heard the motor start up again. She listened until it was a distant hum that blurred into the incessant buzz of the cicadas. But she would not allow herself to go to the window. There would be no last, lingering looks for Cameron Landell.

Chapter Ten

The sound of the lock on the lab door clicking open brought Malou back to present reality. She took several deep breaths to steady herself as she both heard and felt Ernie's tread approaching from the back. What she desperately wanted to do was to bolt for her room and lick her wounds in private. But she could not afford such histrionics. Not in front of a colleague. She remembered all the refined academicians at her parents' party. Cam had illustrated to her in graphic detail that she was one of them. For a dangerous interval, she'd forgotten that. She'd forgotten and allowed herself to act like a love-struck teenager, running off and leaving Ernie with the full responsibility for the station. That must all stop. Beginning with this very moment, she vowed, she would start acting like a scientist again.

That vow was the reason that, when Ernie asked how the day had gone, Malou answered cheerily, "Fine."

"Fine?" Ernie echoed. "Isn't Landell's time running out on his note? Seems like he would have come to a final decision about the troop."

Malou knew that if she discussed anything about Cam or the troop, the tears would start, and she was determined not to cry in front of Ernie. He already had enough evidence to think she was a complete ninny. No need adding tears to the list.

"It does seem that way, doesn't it?" she commented noncommittally. Tomorrow would be plenty of time to give him the bad news. Tomorrow, when she had a grip on herself. At the moment there was something even more important to tend to. "How's Kojiwa doing?" she asked, bracing herself for the answer.

"Not much change." Ernie shrugged. "Is it that late?" he asked, glancing at his wristwatch. "Time for a little shut-eye. See you in the morning."

As he clumped heavily down the hall and into his room, Malou went to the cage holding the old-timer. Kojiwa was lying on his side, his eyes open, staring dully ahead. She despised Cam for doing this to the innocent monkey. Like warring rams, another thought rose in her mind to collide with the first—she ached for him with an intensity that nothing and no one had ever fired in her before. She raged internally for the loss, not only of Cam, but of the dream she'd tended of who Cam was and what they might be together. It was only then, in the extremity of her grief, that Malou was forced to acknowledge that what she was truly mourning was the loss of a love. What a cruel irony that it was to be a love she would only fully recognize at its death.

Grateful for the small tasks that demanded her concentration, Malou cleaned and filled Kojiwa's water bowl, then diced up some carrots, apples, and cactus pads for the old-timer. She placed them next to him, but he showed no interest in the treat. Malou found the bottle she'd used to nurse Lorre with and filled it with formula. Cautiously approaching Kojiwa, she held the bottle to his lips and dribbled some of the fluid in. A tiny thump of happiness beat through her when he managed to swallow a mouthful. Malou continued dribbling until he turned his face away from the bottle to stare at the wall beyond his cage.

There was nothing else for her to do. Malou went heavily to her room and lay on her bed. Pain congealed around her, swaddling her with once-ecstatic memories that were now turning bitter. She brought them out one by one: the honey-wine taste of the sun-warmed dewberry Cam had pressed to her lips; the patter of rain on the tin roof at the stone cabin; the feel of Cam as he lay within her. Then quickly, before the hurt stabbed too deeply, she put the memories away, storing them up for another night, years away, when she would be able to bring them out again and remember without being lacerated by pain. But they wouldn't stay stored away. Unbidden, the memories rose of their own accord to devil her.

Abruptly, she whirled off the bed. It was too easy for the memories to trap her there in the small room. She needed escape. She needed solace. She dressed quickly, grabbed her sleeping bag, and tiptoed out of her room, shutting the door behind her quietly so as not to wake Ernie. She would find that solace where she always had—with the animals that she understood better than treacherous, hurtful humans.

Kojiwa was still staring listlessly at the wall when she went to check on him. And he still hadn't touched his food bowl. Malou slung the sleeping bag over her shoulder, lifted the cage, and left the research station. The cool night air seemed to revive Kojiwa. He lifted his head and sniffed at it. Malou was glad of her decision to bring him with her. If he was not meant to last out the night, surely he would want to spend it close to his fellow creatures.

The moon was full and shining silver on the field where the troop was huddled in sleep. No alarm was sounded by the peripheral males roosting in the trees at the outskirts of the compound. Instead a few soft hoots greeted her familiar presence. Malou felt welcomed. Kojiwa strained to right himself in the cage, to see the faces he had missed. They headed for the core of the troop, where Sumo slept surrounded by his court. The monkeys were all awake by the time they reached the center. The juveniles immediately began playing. Sumo stood on his hind legs to check out the intruders, saw that it was just the shiny-haired human female, then grumpily went back to sleep.

Malou settled the cage in Kojiwa's usual spot a bit removed from the center. When she opened the door, the old-timer looked up at her, moonlight sparkling in his eyes, and he weakly crawled out. Malou left his food and water bowls beside him, then backed off a ways and unrolled her sleeping bag.

After a few minutes, some of the older females who had always remained loyal to their original leader cautiously approached. Hesitantly they sniffed at the ailing oldster; then, completely reassured that it really was the patriarch they'd known for so long, they began to gently groom him. The look of resigned apathy left Kojiwa's face and was replaced by serene contentment, his customary expression when he was being groomed. Malou couldn't have hoped for a better reception. For the first time she thought there might be a possibility of recovery.

Then one of the females stopped her grooming to pick a chunk of apple out of the food bowl. Malou's heart sank. Unable to defend his food, the other monkeys would scavenge what she'd brought for Kojiwa, which meant that she'd have to take him back to the station. But the female didn't gobble down the rare bit of apple. She sniffed it thoroughly, then took it to Kojiwa and pressed the chunk into his mouth. In the moonlight, Malou watched him begin to slowly chew.

One of the females grooming Kojiwa was Tulip. Lorre scampered about at her side. The baby looked plump and happy running about deviling her elders in an unexpected midnight romp. She even had the audacity to run up to the old monkey lying on his side who was the object of all this unusual attention. Whether he was too weak or whether he recognized the little one as his adopted daughter's baby, Malou couldn't make out. All she knew was that Kojiwa did not swat Lorre away when she crawled on him, tugging at his chest and neck fur until she had found a secure perch on Kojiwa's grizzled head. He even allowed the little upstart to snatch away a piece of the fruit that was being fed to him.

Though an enormous hole still gaped in her life, Malou suddenly felt there were ways of building bridges over it and paths around it. There were ways of going on with life despite the emptiness she felt. She rolled out her sleeping bag, and, lulled by the comforting rhythms of the animals she knew so well and exhausted by the day's turmoil, she slept.

She jerked awake at the first cry of alarm sounded by a peripheral male in a distant tree. She didn't know how long she'd slept but guessed it had been hours rather than minutes, for the moon had set and the compound was lost in an inky darkness. She felt the troop's alert wakefulness and heard them stirring about her. The cry of alarm was taken up by more shrill voices. Malou wondered what could be exciting such an urgent reaction. Perhaps a javelina was sniffing at the fence or had even found a hole somewhere and gotten in. Or a bobcat.

Dimly, she saw Sumo's vague silhouette as he stood up to survey the menace. She heard several dozen macaque noses sniffing at the air, trying to identify the danger that was approaching. Even Kojiwa, reacting to instincts buried deep within him, struggled to right himself so that he too might confront the intruder and protect his little band. Malou was thinking what a rare research opportunity she'd stumbled upon when she heard the steps. The crunch of dry vegetation grew louder as the source of the sound came closer. She strained to hear it, to make out a pattern of four quick crunches. But there weren't four light crunches. There were only two. And they were heavy.

The sounds were footsteps.

Malou's heart lurched within her chest. Cam had sent Jorge on one final mission. For revenge? So that he could claim one last monkey death before he sold them all off? She imagined the hulking Jorge and felt for her flashlight in the darkness. She tested its heft. It was precious little protection, but it was all she had to defend the troop. And herself. The metal flashlight grew slick with sweat in her hand.

Which monkey had Cam instructed his hireling to eliminate tonight? To which one would he offer the lethal honeyed berries?

A beam of light leaped out of the darkness. Its circle snared the wizened old face of Kojiwa.

No! Malou screamed to herself. Cam couldn't be so cruel as to send Jorge back to finish off the old-timer. But the orb of light traveled on, searching out another victim. It danced over several more startled faces and stopped this time on a tiny monkey picking a chunk of apple out of Kojiwa's dish. Two enormous amber eyes reflected back the beam of light.

Lorre.

Malou's mind whirred frantically as the circle of light trapping the little one grew larger with each footstep crunching through the darkness. What would the feudally loyal Jorge do to her if she tried to interfere with *el patrón*'s orders? Could she risk letting him give the poison berries to Lorre? She could snatch them away as soon as Jorge left. But even if Lorre had time to ingest even one or two berries, that might be too much for her tiny system.

But it wasn't any calculated thought that drove Malou when the footsteps finally halted only a few yards away from where she was hidden in the darkness. No, as she heard the dry rattle of the coyotillo branch being held out to the baby, and saw the honey-slicked berries glistening so temptingly before the widened amber eyes, it was anger that finally moved Malou out of fear and into action.

A vision of Jorge's menacing face loomed in her mind's eye as she switched on her flashlight and turned it toward the hand holding out the lethal offering. But it wasn't

Jorge's face that her beam illuminated. Her light danced wickedly over two round lenses, then was lost in a dark growth of beard.

"Ernie!"

The tableau frozen in the narrow shaft of light had a nightmarish quality that belonged to the dark illogic of the unconscious. She could make no sense of the sight of her fellow researcher squatting down on his haunches and extending the branch of death to a tiny member of the species he'd dedicated his life to studying. But this was not the slip of a half-sleeping mind. The evidence before Malou was irrefutable. Once she accepted the testimony of her eyes, Malou's reaction was one of terrible sadness. She let the beam of the flashlight drop to her side, where it cut a precise circle on the ground beside her.

"Ernie. Why?" It was all she could bring herself to ask. Why? She could think of no possible explanation.

In the darkness, her colleague's knees creaked as he slowly got to his feet. The dried branch rustled as it brushed against the ground. After several moments of silence during which Malou prayed that Ernie wouldn't have the gall to deny what he was doing, he heaved a sigh of resignation.

"Why?" The word was a hollow echo of her question. "You have to ask why, don't you? You couldn't possibly fathom the reasons. It's always been so easy for you, hasn't it? Primatology's little princess. I heard Darden himself call you that. The little princess who could do no wrong. Getting grants, fellowships right and left. Even before you were out of grad school they started pouring in. And the awards." Ernie gave a sharp snort of mirthless laughter. "Oh God, the awards. And the publications. Let us not forget the publications. Every journal in the field."

"Ernie, answer my question." A new kind of shock was replacing what she'd felt when she first discovered Ernie. This was a completely different person from the one she'd thought she'd been working beside all these months. The rancor and introverted bitterness that soured Ernie's words stunned Malou.

"No, you answer a question, little princess. How old do you think I am?"

She'd never really considered it before. She'd just assumed he was near her own age. "Twenty-seven, twenty-eight," she guessed.

"Make that *thirty*-seven. Thirty-seven and still a field researcher at a station run by someone ten years younger than me. No awards. A few crummy, insignificant publications. Do you know how that feels?"

A surge of pity went through Malou, but it was not strong enough to obliterate the knowledge of the suffering Ernie had inflicted. "Why did you do it?"

"I needed those monkeys. Those and a lot more like them. I needed subjects with a complete genealogical history. There aren't any other monkeys like them in the world. I needed them for my myopia study to find out if the predisposition to myopia is passed down or if it's a function of living in an enclosed environment. All I was trying to do was collect some preliminary data; then, jeez, can you imagine the funding I could get for a study that might save mankind from nearsightedness?"

A manic excitement drove up the pitch of Ernie's voice, and an awful realization shivered its way into Malou's brain.

"You've been working on Jezebel back there in the lab,

haven't you? You have to dissect monkeys for your study. That's why you've kept the door locked.''

"She was an outcast. In life she was worthless, but as a research subject she's contributed a significant amount of raw data. Data that I'll be able to build on.''

"No you won't, Ernie." She spoke calmly, stating an unassailable fact. "You'll never work in primatology again.''

"What are you talking about? Sure my methods were a bit unorthodox, but I'm getting the results. That's what's important," he insisted. "The results." He trailed off into a weak whine. "It's Landell. None of this would have happened if he hadn't shown up.''

"Don't keep trying to pass off the blame for this on Cam. I can't believe I ever let you twist my mind against him in the first place. Cam was your opportunity to take the subjects you'd wanted all along. He was just the scapegoat you'd been waiting for. With my unintentional help, you made him into the perfect villain with the perfect motive for poisoning the monkeys.''

"So now he's the white knight and *I'm* the villain of the piece," Ernie said, oozing self-pity. "Even though he's the one who wants to break up the troop, and all I ever wanted to do was cure mankind of an affliction. Surely you can't fault me, Malou, for what I was trying to do.''

"I can and do, Ernie," Malou answered evenly. The barest sliver of pearly pink was just starting to crack along the eastern horizon. "The sun's coming up. I don't want to see you in the light of day, Ernie. No matter how noble your aims were, you killed two monkeys and inflicted needless suffering on a third. If you leave, now, with no further discussion, I won't report you. But if I ever hear of you working anywhere near monkeys again, I'll tell this whole sad story to every authority I can think of."

"Malou—"

"Not another word. Leave. Now. Before I change my mind."

Ernie hesitated for a moment; then, in the thin predawn light, Malou saw him start to lunge forward. Her hand tightened around the flashlight, and she became acutely aware that there was not another living soul for miles in any direction. Ernie could easily overpower her, knock her down, and claim she'd met with some nasty accident. She braced herself. But the attack never came. The glass in Ernie's flashlight shattered as he let it fall to the ground. The light jerked upward in a crazy arc, strafing across his face before it blinked off forever. From that momentary glimpse of his expression, Malou knew that the danger had passed. Defeat was written on his face.

There was nothing more to say. Ernie turned, his shoulders slumped, and plodded back to the research station. Shafts of dawn light were spoking out from the east when Ernie came back out of the station, a duffel bag thrown over his shoulder. Malou watched him walk all the way out to the highway. A pickup truck pulled over for him as soon as he stuck his thumb out. And then Ernie was gone.

Malou slumped onto a boulder. There could be no justification for what he had done, but still Malou was saddened as she sat pondering the motives that propel lives, the secret gears that keep us all spinning. How often, she wondered, did people really only come to know one another at the very last moment? Just as she'd finally come to know Ernie. To know Cam.

But with Cam she had misjudged him far worse at the very end than she ever had in the beginning. How could she have been so blind? Like Ernie, she had erred, and erred tragically.

In the gathering light she saw Kojiwa stir, prop himself up, and begin eating from the bowl. The return to his troop had worked its miracle; he was rallying. Malou felt little cause for celebration. Kojiwa would live for only one more week of freedom before he had to end his days in a cage in a lab somewhere.

Sure now that the venerable macaque would pull through, Malou felt relieved of the last of her immediate responsibilities. She headed for the compound gate, pushed it open, and kept on walking. She had to keep moving. If she stopped or even slowed down, the regrets would pile themselves upon her in a suffocating heap. But none weighed so heavy as the terrible knowledge of how she had wronged Cam and exiled herself from his love.

She let her feet take her where they would. She wanted nothing but to be an unthinking passenger for a few hours. Sunlight poured in around her with a glaring brightness that taunted her sorrow. She cut into the woods that lay beyond the cleared fields where cattle and monkeys were fenced. She rushed into the shadowy gloom, grateful for the respite from the mocking sunlight. She walked on, oblivious for once in her life to the symphony of birds and insects calling to one another. To the fawn poking its nose out of a thicket to watch her passing. To the jackrabbit scampering for cover at her approach.

She walked on without seeing or hearing or thinking, but none of these were needed to bring her to the destination her heart had chosen. It was the song of the canyon wren, the crystal notes tumbling through the air, that first penetrated the numb fog of her misery. Next she noticed the creek whose serpentine trail she had been following as it wended its way beneath rocky bluffs and through grassy meadows alive with wildflowers and finally back to this dark, enchanted spot. Malou felt the presence of the stone cabin before she actually saw it, and knew instantly that she had instinctively sought it out as the sanctuary it was. A place beyond time, beyond the sadness that pounded at her.

She stood still and listened to the chattering of the creek running clear and sweet. It was cool in the shade of the great spreading oaks. As cool and as serene as she'd always imagined it had been for the monkeys on Storm Mountain hundreds of years ago when the samurai had brought their mistresses to the piney retreat. Malou stood listening for many minutes more before the connection was made. When it finally was, she wondered whatever had taken her so long.

This place could be a sanctuary not just for her but for the monkeys as well!

The instant the idea occurred to her, Malou started working out the details. As Cam himself had pointed out, the whole area around the stone cabin had been left as a shrine to Stallings's love, with no improvements made in half a century. They could move the troop down here, sell off the more valuable, fenced-in pastureland, and Cam would probably have enough to pay off his note. Excitement beat through her. Then Cam would be happy, the monkeys would most certainly be happy, and she . . .

She. She was the stumbling block. Cam wouldn't speak to her much less go along with a scheme she'd devised. Her excitement abruptly switched off. In its place came a weariness unlike any she'd ever known. She stumbled to the stone cabin absolutely drained, physically, mentally, and emotionally.

She pushed open the back door and stepped back in time fifty years. Fifty years to a night that had passed just slightly more than a week before. The night Cam had loved her. Brushing aside the ghosts of love that populated the small dwelling, she made her way to the bed where she had awakened on that one, most perfect morning of her life in Cam's arms. Only utter exhaustion saved her from regret's now-familiar sting, and she collapsed into sleep.

The sun climbed high in the sky to beat down on the tin roof over Malou's head, then sank back into the western distance, and still Malou slept. The canyon wrens awoke singing, fanned out over the open fields to seek food, and returned back to the rocky bluffs above the twining creek, and still Malou slept. She slept until the phantoms of regret she had temporarily exhausted regained their strength. Then they all joined forces to swirl images of loss and horror across her troubled mind.

In her sleep Malou battled the phantoms, striking out at bed sheets that were ropes binding her to a boulder sinking beneath black waves as she screamed at the malevolent creatures forcing her down.

"Calm down, Malou, darling. It's a nightmare. You're only dreaming."

She had banished the nightmare and was dreaming the dream of her choice: to be there in the stone cabin, with Cam's arms sheltering her, wrapping her in love. She snuggled into this exquisite moment of wish fulfillment she had created for herself, this delirious intermission between nightmares. She sighed contentedly, breathing in a fragrance that was like no other on earth, the smell of Cam's body. In a distant corner of her sleep-fuzzed mind she asked herself if dreams had smells. The answer was no. The deep chest and strong arms cradling her were gloriously real. She sat up with a start.

"Cam, what are you doing here?"

Chapter Eleven

$\mathcal{I}$ happen to own the place, Goldilocks. A more appropriate question might be what are *you* doing here?''

They looked at one another from opposite sides of the bed they'd shared so joyously such a short while ago. Malou didn't answer. There was too much to say, to apologize for. Cam watched her, waiting for an explanation. None came. The gap between them seemed so wide. When had it grown to such an immense size? he wondered sadly. How had she slipped so far from him? But it had taken this damnable, unbridgeable gulf to make him see how close they had been. Memories of that closeness clouded his vision, so that instead of seeing an unruly crown of sunny curls, he recalled the feel of them against the palm of his hands, the scent of them when she had lain beneath him, their bodies tangled in love.

"Cam, I . . ."

It was the catch in her voice that undid him completely. That, and the haunted, tortured look in her eyes that hadn't disappeared even after he'd pulled her from whatever nightmare she had been flailing and screaming against when he walked in. He abandoned his tough-guy pose.

Malou saw the change in his eyes, saw the wall he had built against her melt away, leaving nothing but a bed between them. Her gaze as it traveled from those now-tender eyes to his full, demanding lips was a tongue of flame that licked heat into Cam.

It was a heat that sought release as it built within him, stoked ever higher by a bellows of desire that blew through him each time he looked at Malou, making him remember. The feel of her breasts, full and yearning beneath his fingers, of her arms wrapped around his neck, of her legs about his waist. All other thoughts, all other doubts were immolated in the heat of the blaze burning through him. He reached a hand out across the whiteness of the sheet and Malou met it with her own. Their fingers twined together. It hadn't been so difficult to bridge the gap between them after all.

Gently Cam pulled Malou to him by their locked hands. She slid across the sheet, stopping inches from his out-stretched body. Cam devoured her with his eyes. They were no longer creatures from different worlds. He saw in her face, uptilted to his, that together they created a separate world that only they inhabited. It was the world of their desire for one another. That desire had been overpoweringly physical from the very beginning, but it had grown even stronger as he came to know more about the strong-willed woman quivering next to him. Perhaps that was the secret, that, knowing her strength, her intelligence, it excited him all the more to realize that she wanted him as mightily as he desired her. Passion throbbed through him as he saw it reflected in her eyes.

I love this woman. It was Cam's last thought before he surrendered to instinct's primitive power.

Malou quailed before the urgency of her need. The heat between them seared her the length of her body as she lay stretched before him. Though nothing but their hands touched, she was left gasping at this barest of touches and aching for so very much more. It was an ache that their physical joining would momentarily slake but never fully satisfy. She wanted Cameron Landell in every way one person can experience another, physically and spiritually, but at that very moment she wanted him physically with a hunger that left her reeling.

She reached out a trembling hand and slid it along the whipcord sinews of Cam's arm all the way to the swell of his shoulder, then over to rest against the curve of his neck, where she could feel the tidal surge of blood pulsing beneath her hand. They lay that way for a long moment, sharing the same breath, holding passion at bay, letting it build to a sweet and maddening power.

Malou could never say who broke first. Had her hand tightened on Cam's neck, pulling him forward that fraction of an inch? Or had his lips already begun their decisive descent? It never really mattered. All that mattered was his mouth on hers, devouring what she offered and returning an even greater sensuous bounty of his own. He rose to cradle her head in his two strong hands, trapping her lips and slowing the frenzy that was shivering through her at this first release. With an agonizing slowness, he began making teasing forays, easing his tongue in and out between her lips until Malou had relaxed into a narcotizing languor. Then Cam's hand stroked her neck, her back, until she went slack with sensuous abandonment, until her straining body was convinced that Cam's would be there for a good long time. She pressed softly against him and he held her, whispering into her hair.

"I want this to be long and sweet and then, maybe, there will be nothing left for us to talk about when we're through."

"Oh, Cam, darling. I was so stupid. So wrong . . ."

Lightly he pressed a forefinger to her lips to silence her. "Hush. 'Darling' is all that I want to hear right now, for you are that to me, Malou. You are my heart's darling and there can be no way around it."

"Cam, I've dreamed of you. I dreamed of you the first night after we met, but I'd been dreaming of you for years before that. You are the one I've been waiting for."

"And you, Mary Louise, always you."

When their lips met again there was a new richness, an indescribable sweetness that neither of them could savor long enough or deeply enough.

"I can't believe you still have all this on," Cam said with a lightness that was betrayed by his ragged breathing as he began fiddling with buttons and zippers.

Malou couldn't believe it either. She already felt loved to the depth of her soul. Cam made swift work of her clothes, then began to tear away at his own. This time it was Malou's turn to slow and steady him. Kneeling beside him, she captured his hand with hers and removed it from the buckle he was jerking open. Instead, with the same mad-dening slowness he'd used to tantalize her, she toyed languidly with the fastener. After she'd finally unbuckled it, she tugged gently at the zipper. Cam's eyes slid shut, and a groan rattled in his throat. She unbuttoned his shirt and caressed it away from Cam's chest and over his shoulders, trailing the teasing tips of her nails along every inch of the firm flesh she left exposed.

As she knelt above him, her breasts came to tautened life beneath the stimulation of his ardent gaze. But when Cam, still only half-undressed, reached out toward Malou, she backed away, moving back to the trousers that still needed to be removed. She slid them out from beneath him. When Cam rose up on one elbow, his muscles bunching above it, Malou pressed him back to the pillow with a debilitating kiss. Her lips still pinioning him to the bed, she drifted her hand across his chest, pausing to circle his nipples until they hardened. Then down to where his wide rib cage sloped into the hard, flat plane of his stomach. Her hand went lower but skirted along the outer edge of his pelvis, across the powerful band of muscle that joined his thigh to the pelvis there, then down. The springy hair of his upper leg tickled Malou's palm as she brought her hand back up, and as she reached the juncture between Cam's thighs, a sharp intake of breath met her touch. He was alive beneath her hand. Alive and ready for loving her.

Nothing Malou could have done would have restrained Cam when he rose again. She dissolved into his kiss, sinking beneath it back onto the bed. Their tongues warred in a duel where the victor was the one who could inflict the most pleasure. Cam won by claiming new territory; his mouth brushed down along her neck and fastened on her breast, sucking surges of pleasure through her that pulsed out of her deepest core. Then Cam was seeking that very core, probing for it with a tongue that washed shivers of ecstasy through Malou. And still it probed with a rhythm and constancy that pounded delirium into Malou's blood. It probed until the ecstatic shivers gathered together and centered on that one bliss-lavished spot, crowding together, denser and denser, until there was no more room for any more pleasure. Until all the delicious feelings exploded together, all at once.

Only then, feeling Malou tense and arch toward him, then twist away, only then did Cam stop to move back up and hold Malou in his arms as the quakes of release swept through her. Her quick, short breaths battered against his chest. When they had evened, her eyelids fluttered open and, still dazzled with love, she looked up at him.

That gaze ripped something loose deep inside of Cam. He squeezed a warm rain of kisses on Malou's face, her eyes, cheeks, brows. And Malou returned every one of them. But there remained an even better way of showing Cam all that her heart held. She slid close until she felt him, still ready to love her. She swung her leg on top of his and, facing each other, side by side, their kisses never stopping, he sought entrance.

Cam's hand moved along the length of her leg, over her hip, her waist, and came to rest on her breast, where it massaged wondrous patterns. He bent forward until his lips replaced the hand. He teased the nipple with his lips and teeth, intensifying desire. As desire stirred within Malou, his nuzzling grew slightly rougher as he tugged the nipple to tautened, pulsing life. Feeling Malou's building response, he clasped her buttocks and pressed her more tightly to him.

Malou felt all of him driving more deeply into her, reigniting a profound need. She clung to him, unable to resist the primal rhythms that moved them, undulating to the tempo dictated by Cam's hands on her hips.

His mouth closed over hers, his kiss a frenzied taking of all she could give. His breathing matched the staccato hammer of his heart pounding against hers. His face was transfixed. He was as much a captive to the pleasure she gave as she was to the ecstasy that held her in thrall.

"Oh, darling, I'm close, very close," he whispered fiercely, as she moved against him.

"Yes, Cam. Oh, yes," she mumbled, her response an insensate affirmation of what they were reaching together.

Knowing that he need restrain himself no longer, Cam's motions grew more frantic. With each wild thrust the heavenly feeling built. Malou clung to Cam now, answering his raw need with her own. And still the pulsing rhythm increased to an almost unbearable pitch. It catapulted her higher and higher until she floated into a realm of oblivion and exquisite pleasure heightened by the feel of Cam's fulfillment pulsing deep within her.

She came languidly back to reality to find her hands grasping Cam's tight buttocks. She stroked his hard, muscled torso, then curved her arms about his broad shoulders to cradle him against her tenderly. To hold this bold, powerful man who had quivered in her arms just as she had in his. He lay so still, so obviously wrapped in a cocoon of contentment, that Malou was sure he'd fallen asleep until he spoke.

"Are you an angel or an enchantress or both?" he asked, a warm, soundless chuckle rumbling against her in his chest. "I can't make up my mind which."

"I'm just the prim primatologist, don't you remember?"

"Who on earth ever said that? Someone severely lacking in taste and perception, obviously."

"Obviously," Malou agreed happily.

Reluctantly, Cam shook off the marvelous, blanketing layers of contentment and propped himself up on an elbow above Malou. He traced a finger across her cheek and over her lips, sighed, and asked, "Mary Louise Sanders, what *am* I going to do with you?"

"I rather liked the things you've come up with so far," she answered impishly. But Cam's thoughtful expression told her that the time had arrived for the serious discussion their lovemaking had only postponed.

He sighed again and let his hand drop. "I don't want to get into this, do you? It was a miracle that you happened to be here. What happens between us in bed together is a miracle. And it's a miracle that our worlds ever intersected long enough for us to meet. Should we question miracles?" he asked, a smile lightening his intense features.

"I've always maintained a strict policy against the practice myself," Malou quipped, joyous relief flooding into her smile.

"But what *were* you doing here?"

"I needed sanctuary," Malou said simply, "and this is mine."

Cam nodded in solemn agreement, for she had spoken his heart and the reason why he too had been drawn to the stone cabin secluded from time.

"And speaking of sanctuary," Malou said, sucking in a

deep breath for courage, "I've come up with a great idea for a monkey sanctuary."

Cam groaned. "If someone had told me a few months ago that I'd be in bed with a gorgeous woman talking about monkeys, I'd have advised that person to seek professional help. Now, maybe I'm the one who should see a shrink," he said with mock disgust, but a grin was flirting at the corners of his mouth.

"No, really, it's the perfect plan." Now that Malou was actually putting her idea into words, they burbled excitedly from her. "Move the monkeys down here," she blurted out.

"Down here? Perhaps you'd like to get them all in bed with us?"

"No, silly," Malou laughed, buoyant with relief and exuberant in the glow of Cam's love. "Move the monkeys onto this land around the cabin."

Cam cocked a doubtful eyebrow at her.

"No, listen," she insisted, not allowing Cam an opportunity to object. "You've said yourself that this property isn't worth much. It's wild, overgrown, hilly, rocky, remote. There's not a decent road out here, and it's on the flood plain. All qualities that make this land worthless for cattle or crops but ideal for monkeys."

Cam continued to look doubtful. Malou ignored him.

"It has a natural water supply running through it, and since it's hilly, the troop wouldn't need such a large compound so it wouldn't be too terribly expensive to fence it in."

"One thought . . . ," Cam attempted to interject, holding up a finger, but Malou didn't even slow down.

"Sell the land they're on right now, and you'd make

enough from that to pay off your note on time and have plenty left over to fence in the sanctuary. That's what we'll call it, the Landell Monkey Sanctuary."

"Malou, if I may just interrupt to . . ." But Malou wouldn't let him. She had to convince him. Had to make him share her enthusiasm.

"But that's not the best part of the idea. The best part is this: With the monkeys in a smaller area, it would be more feasible to turn the sanctuary into a tourist attraction. We could just build some viewing platforms with telescopes on the edge of the sanctuary, and tourists could watch without disturbing the troop. The troop could be self-supporting with that and the grants. And I'd keep writing the grant proposals so you . . ."

"Sounds good," Cam finally put in.

"Okay," Malou replied, still charging ahead too rapidly to stop and really listen, "maybe you don't like having a monkey sanctuary named after you. We could call it the South Texas Sanctuary or . . . What did you say?"

"I said it sounds good to me."

"You like the idea?"

"Wasn't I supposed to?"

"Well, yes, of course, but I thought you'd be more, well, resistant."

"Why? It's a good solution. Obvious once it's been presented. But then, most of the best solutions do seem obvious once someone's thought of them."

"You like the idea," Malou muttered, stunned with happiness.

"Don't act so surprised," Cam chuckled. "Although you seem not to believe me, I always work for deals where there are no losers and no tears."

Malou winced at the reminder of the cruelly misguided charges she had hurled at Cam the day before. He saw the cloud gathering over her sunny joy, and he tapped the end of her nose. "Hey, just one thing."

She looked up at him.

"Don't think I'm developing any late-blooming affection for those furry nuisances. It's just that, when it floods, monkeys are so much better at climbing trees than cows are. With that in mind, you've got yourself a deal. Now kiss me, or every one of the sorry beasts goes on the block."

Malou was preparing to do just that when, her relief clouding her judgment, she made one final remark. "I just knew you couldn't have done it."

Cam halted. "Done what, my lovely?"

"Oh, it doesn't matter anymore. None of it matters. Everything is solved and you're beside me and nothing else matters."

"But what is it that doesn't matter? That I couldn't have done?"

He'd stopped bending toward her and was leaning back now, set on finding out what it was that Malou suddenly seemed so nervous about.

"Oh, Cam, just forget I ever said anything."

"Malou, if you'll recall, there are already quite a few things I've made myself forget you ever said. I don't feel like adding another one to a list that's already too long, so tell me what it is you think I couldn't have done."

Surely he must have already guessed at her suspicions, Malou told herself. Though she was loath to bring up the subject again, perhaps now was the time to have done with it once and for all. Her voice was small and tentative when she spoke. "Poisoned the monkeys. I knew in my heart that you never would have ordered that. It was Ernie who kept badgering me about it; then it turned out he was the scoundrel all along.''

Cam's look of disbelief told Malou a tale that she did not want to know. "You thought *I* poisoned those monkeys?''

"Not really,'' Malou protested. "Not deep down inside. Anyway, it was Jorge who Ernie kept saying had done it.''

"And you believed him?'' His voice was scoured clean of all emotion except astonishment.

"Well, there were certain things that had me wondering. Like you knowing what coyotillo was. And our first morning here when Jorge came and told you, 'Everything is done as you ordered,' and then you hurried him outside so quickly that it seemed like you had things to say to him that you didn't want me to overhear.''

Cam's mouth dropped in amazement. "What I didn't want was for Jorge to see you bedded down here with his *patrón*. In his culture the judgments are harsh for a woman who spends the night with a man she's not married to. I wanted to shield you from that. And the 'everything' I'd ordered done were some repairs that he'd told me about over the phone. What other things had you wondering?'' A new harshness was entering his voice as the shock wore off.

A sick feeling was welling up in Malou's stomach, but there was no way out of the trap she'd laid for herself except to keep going straight ahead.

"Just you, and my misunderstanding of who you are. To me you seemed like a man who would do anything to get what he wanted. You even said as much to me.''

"Malou, did you and dear old Ernie ever stop to consider that if what I'd wanted was no monkeys, I could have cleared them off my land with a phone call and made money in the process? Why on earth would I have to send Jorge in the dark of night to poison the creatures?''

''I told you it was stupid,'' Malou admitted. ''But you reacted so violently when I threatened to call in the press, and then Ernie had a theory that you wanted to neutralize any bad press you might get from selling off the troop, so you tried to show that they were dying off in the wild.''

Cam looked at Malou as if she'd turned into a stranger before his eyes. He sat up, backed away from her, and swung his legs over the side of the bed. The gulf between them had opened again. When he spoke, his eyes were fixed on the wall in front of him. ''Believing what you did about me, Malou, how could you have let me touch you? Love you? How?''

A thousand protests sprang up in Malou's heart, but they were all stopped dead by the lump in her throat caused by the grim finality of Cam's question. He had asked it like a man for whom no answer would suffice.

''What kind of man do you really think I am? Yes, I like to win. But what is a victory worth if it has to be won with the kind of sleaze you suspected me of?'' Now anger began to seep into his tone. ''You ivory-tower types,'' he lashed out, standing to hurriedly pull on his pants. ''You think you've cornered the market on ethics and that anyone who sullies himself by actually working in the real world of business would stoop to anything to get ahead.'' He jerked on his shirt. ''Wrong, Malou. Fundamentally incorrect assumption.'' He drove his feet into his shoes without bothering with socks and started for the door.

Pausing there, he pounded his fist against the frame and said, without looking back, ''You'll still have your sanctuary, and I'd like you to stay on at least long enough to supervise the transfer. After that, what you do is up to you. Just one thing—all communication between us will be through my receptionist. Call her and leave messages if you need to get in touch with me and I'll have her convey all my instructions to you.''

''Cam, no, don't . . .'' But he was gone before Malou's tear-blurred words could reach him.

The tears dried shortly after that when the numb fog set back in just as if it had never lifted. Only now it was worse. Now Malou had this short, sharp memory of ecstasy waiting to lance her whenever she stumbled across it in the fog.

Chapter Twelve

$\mathcal{T}$he day of the transfer dawned with white heat already shimmering across the land. Everything had worked out just as Malou had predicted it would. The land had sold quickly and Cam had met his financial deadlines with enough left over to get the sanctuary under way. Or that, at any rate, was what his receptionist had reported to Malou. The woman had also conveyed Mr. Landell's wishes that Malou supervise the relocation and that she handle it in whatever way she deemed most expedient.

"In other words, don't bother him with the details," Malou had translated the instructions.

"I think that's about what it comes down to," the secretary had agreed.

Those instructions had taken a month to translate further into reality. Working with Jorge and a crew of laborers, she'd first fenced in the sanctuary and dug out a wide spot in the creek for a swimming pond for the monkeys. Small sparks of something as close to excitement as she was able to muster glowed in Malou as she surveyed the new compound. The troop would be so much happier in this new home with its tall, sturdy trees for them to scramble up and down and the cool creek meandering through it.

Back at the old compound she oversaw the building of several large, wire-screened enclosures. When they were finished, she baited each one with a cache of peanuts and apples. Then the wait began.

For the first few days the apples merely withered in the heat and the peanuts went untouched. Then, as Malou knew they would, the adventurous juveniles were the first to venture into the foreign structures, darting in to snatch a peanut or a chunk of apple, then scurrying back outside with it. But gradually, as they learned that nothing terrible waited for them inside the structures, they began to linger, squatting on their haunches to finish off a few peanuts before making off with an apple chunk.

The higher-ranking males, with Sumo at the lead, were the next to dare entry. After a cautious entrance, they grew bold and claimed the privileges of their rank, swatting the youngsters away from the apple chunks and appropriating all the choice bits for themselves. Once they were comfortably ensconced, even the females with babies took to frequenting the strange new places to grab off the windfall snacks. But always, for those first few weeks, the door was left wide open for the timid to race in and out of. After a while, even the most wary became accustomed to the new buildings and took to staying inside beneath their shade for longer and longer periods.

But it was Kojiwa that Malou watched, just as she'd been watching him since that first night when she'd returned him to the troop. Concern for him was what had finally given her the strength to drag herself from the bed in the stone cottage, where Cam had left her, and to stumble back to Los Monos. The old monkey had been in better shape that night than she had, and over the weeks that followed, he had managed to gain strength and energy until he now seemed fitter than he had in years.

But the wily patriarch had not survived these many years without learning some hard lessons about caution. Lessons that had recently been vividly refreshed by the disguised bitterness of those bright, honeyed berries. Of all the troop, Kojiwa was the last to succumb to the temptation of the piles of treats within the walls of wire. On the day that Malou saw him amble into an enclosure, she knew that the transfer would be a success. Quickly she arranged for her mentor at the university, Professor Everitt, to bring a dozen of his best primatology students down to Los Monos to help on the day of the relocation.

And now that day was here. From across the field, she saw Jorge riding up on his chestnut bay. He tethered the horse beside a water tank and came up to the station, where Malou was standing at the door.

"*Buenos días*," he called to her.

"*Hola*," she answered back.

Malou wondered how she could ever have thought Jorge menacing. Over the past few weeks, as they'd worked side by side stringing fence lines and hammering chicken wire into place, she'd seen what a warm, good-hearted man he was beneath a thin layer of peasant reserve and natural shyness. He'd even managed to develop some late-blooming affection for the monkeys and to teach her some Spanish, like the word for "smile," which he felt she didn't do nearly enough of late.

And so, this morning, she tacked one on her face as she answered his greeting. As it had been for the past month, however, the act of turning up the corners of her mouth seemed to require an inordinate amount of energy.

Together they hauled out baskets of apples and peanuts and dumped them in the wire enclosures. Monkeys habituated now to the morning snacks scrambled in from all across the field. Kojiwa was the last. When he'd finally entered, Malou did what she had not done in all the long weeks of waiting: She shut the door and the enclosure became a cage. The monkeys continued munching away on the day's extraordinary largess. Once Malou was sure that the monkeys were contentedly feeding, she and Jorge moved on to bait and then close up two other enclosures set up to lure the peripheral males from the outskirts.

They were just finishing and the confined monkeys were just beginning to grow restless when Professor Everitt pulled up leading a convoy of pickup trucks. The students piled out, eager for the experience that lay ahead. Malou led them to the enclosures and pointed out the feature she and Jorge had built onto each one: a small section off to one side that monkeys could be admitted to one at a time.

Trained by Professor Everitt, the students skillfully let the first monkey, a scrappy juvenile, into the little room. After a chase made short and harmless by the limited space, the little fellow was tranquilized, weighed, measured, and gently set in the back of a pickup. The trucks filled quickly with dozing monkeys, who were then shuttled over and set free in their new home. Malou went with the first truck of drugged monkeys to oversee their release.

She was glad that Sumo had been among the first group transferred. With their leader to guide them, she was sure that the other monkeys would adapt swiftly to this new paradise she had carved out for them. As she waited for Sumo and the dozen monkeys with him to come around, a tiny thought of the variety she was always on her guard against assailed her. She wished that Cam could see her. Could see how competently she was handling everything. Could see the wonderful new home she'd created for the monkeys here, just beyond the stone cabin. Could . . . But then the wishes took an even more dangerous turn toward thoughts of sheltering arms wrapped around her, pulling her from the awful loneliness that she had only come to know for the first time in the last month. A loneliness that her work alone could no longer fill.

She drove her straying thoughts back to the macaques. Sumo and a couple of the others were groggily trying to get to their feet. They had been put down near the creek on a spot that was thickly carpeted with grass and shaded by a spreading oak. A tiny thrum of excitement went through Malou as she imagined their happy frolics once they awoke fully in this wonderland.

Sumo finally sat up and the other monkeys crawled to their leader, waiting for his reaction to the dumbfounding chain of events. They watched closely as he blinked his amber eyes, looking first in one direction then the other. Hesitantly he put out a long black finger and touched the velvety green stuff he sat on, then drew it quickly back. He'd known grass before. But only the scrawny, brown stuff that could survive in their parched field, not this suspiciously luxuriant green stuff. He looked up at the immensity of the thing he sat beneath. It was so monstrously different from the few wispy mesquites back in the compound.

And that sound. Sumo whirled around to confront the brook babbling behind him. He knew nothing of this creature of water except that it chattered belligerently and slithered across the green stuff, infinitely huge and longer than any enemy he'd ever before battled.

And so Sumo did the only thing a monkey faced with such fearsome foes could do. He surrendered. In abject, quivering terror he ceded the monster's ground and scampered away to the farthest edge of the sanctuary to escape it. The other monkeys, infected by the terrible fear of this alien place that had gripped their leader, ran after him. Only the fence prevented them all from running back to their old parched home.

"*Los monos* no like this new place." Jorge, who had come with the second load of monkeys, had slipped up next to her as she watched the trembling monkeys.

"I can't understand it," Malou answered, disappointment weighting her words.

"Is hard in new place," Jorge offered. "Even if new place most pretty in the world, still hard. *El corazón*"—he put his callused brown fist over his heart—"still in old place. I know."

Malou attempted a smile for him, but the sight of the new arrivals joining the others to quake at the fence sank her spirits even lower.

The day passed swiftly with load after load of transplanted monkeys taking one look at their new home then immediately rushing to the safety of the troop, where they were all infected with fear of a place that should have been paradise to them.

Professor Everitt rode over with the last batch. As Malou might have guessed, Kojiwa, one of the last to venture into the tranquilizing room, was with that group. She personally carried him off the truck and set him down in the cool grass. She knew that the move had been a strain on his old heart, still recovering from the last trauma.

"Not taking too well to the new place, are they?" Professor Everitt observed with his usual understatement.

"They hate it."

"Well, they hated the open field when we brought them there ten years ago."

"Yes, but this is so much like their native home in Japan. I was sure they'd love it."

"Don't forget," Professor Everitt cautioned, his eyes lively beneath beetling brows of sandy brown, "most of them weren't even born then, and those that were have long forgotten the ancestral home. I've never heard of any long-term memory studies being done with macaques, but that's probably because there's no such memory to test. So this place is just as foreign to them as Los Monos was at the beginning, and they'll have to adjust to it just as they did to Los Monos."

"I know it was hard at the beginning," Malou said hesitantly, "but tell me, just exactly how hard was it?"

Professor Everitt's eyes squinted as he tried to see back to that time ten years ago. "Pretty bad, Malou, I'll be honest with you. We lost probably a fifth of the monkeys we brought over. Some of them just weren't strong enough to make the adjustment. I guess that, like you, I was hoping the adjustment wouldn't have to be quite so difficult."

"We were both wrong, then, weren't we?" Malou said as she stared at her answer—the terror-stricken monkeys clumped together along the fence.

"Don't be too hard on yourself. They'll make it. Most of them."

Most of them, Malou thought as she drifted away from the professor toward the cowering group. Kojiwa was still dozing. It was taking him longer than the others to shake off the effects of the sedative. Would he be one of those who didn't make it? After all he'd been through? She squatted down next to him.

"I'm sorry," she whispered to the sleeping monkey. "I thought you'd all be happier here. I'm sorry you've had to go through all this."

She straightened up when Señora Maldonado stepped onto the porch of the stone cabin to clang out a call to dinner on a triangle of steel. The students pushed into the cabin where the feast the señora had prepared on the cabin's wood stove awaited them. Malou was the last one in, and though Señora Maldonado's *carne quisada* was superb, Malou had no appetite and was the first back out.

The sun was lowering on what had been a very long and, ultimately, very disappointing day. The first hint of an evening breeze cooled Malou as she walked back toward the sanctuary hoping that the drop in temperature might have caused an increase in courage among the monkeys.

Such was not the case. She let out a long, wilting sigh when she caught sight of the entire troop still clumped together in fright along the fence, then began calculating what the cost of their fear would be. The most immediate one was monetary. With the monkeys too frightened to forage for food themselves in their new home, they would have to be fed. Which would mean going to Cam for additional funds. The prospect depressed Malou. She had wanted so badly to report unadulterated triumph.

But that wasn't the worst of her problems. She walked along the chain link fence ringing the sanctuary. For yards in either direction the fence bulged with the weight of monkeys pressed against it. She walked along until she spotted Lorre clinging to Tulip's chest; then she bent down to greet the tiny, wide-eyed monkey baby. As she did so a shriek of alarm rippled through the troop and the agitated monkeys began milling about, bumping into one another as they tried to flee.

Malou straightened back up, even more dispirited than ever at this latest demonstration of how badly unhinged the troop was. Never, since her earliest days, had her presence caused them the least concern. She knew the certain outcome if they didn't adjust quickly and fan out over their new territory. With all the troop jammed together, the number of confrontations between the leader males and the peripheral males would skyrocket. The losers of the fights, too scared to flee into the unknown, would face an awful fate at the hands of the leader males.

A stab of pain made Malou aware that she was gnawing fiercely on her lower lip, trying to think of a solution to an insoluble problem. She was crushed by the weight of her helplessness in the face of the certain doom of so many of the troop she had labored so long to save. A stew of frustration boiled within her, heated by the searing flame of the loss of Cam's love. Tears stung at her eyes. She was ready to admit defeat. She'd done all she knew how to do, and it hadn't been enough. She was tired now. Tired of trying, tired of fighting back pain. Malou, too, wanted to surrender.

Maybe she should. Malou thought for the first time about leaving Los Monos and all the memories that it now held. The researcher within her rebelled at the idea: Los Monos was where she wanted to do her life's work. No other subject interested her as much as the monkeys' adaptation to this harsh land, and now, with a second move, the data she could collect would really be fascinating.

But emotionally she was ready to throw in the towel, to retreat to safe ground that wasn't already mined with wounding memories set to explode in her face whenever she wasn't on her guard. She could go to Professor Everitt tonight and talk to him about leaving. He could find someone to take over for her. Now that the monkeys no longer regarded her even as a familiar and comforting presence, there was no further point in her staying on. She'd been offered a research fellowship in Kenya working with the baboon troops there; she could find out if the offer still stood. Kenya should be far enough, Malou guessed. Far enough that she might have a chance of beginning to forget Cameron Landell.

Night was fast approaching, the canyon wrens winging back to the high bluffs on the other side of the creek to roost, when Malou saw old Kojiwa finally begin to stir. He was having a harder time than the others shaking off the dose of tranquilizer, and she worried about the old-timer's being so groggy with night coming on.

He sat up slowly, stretching his muscles, which had grown stiff during his long nap. As soon as he was upright, he took a long slow look around at the tall trees spreading over him, at the creek sparkling in the last, slanting rays of the sun, at his troopmates huddled along the fence. Then he held out a long finger and touched the grass.

Malou waited, expecting him to recoil in terror as Sumo had done, then flee to the safety of the troop. But Kojiwa didn't do that. Instead he held out the rest of his fingers and drew them along the velvety grass, stroking it. Stiffly, he rolled over and crawled through the soft stuff, stopping at a bush trailing vines. Without hesitation, he poked his hand in and plucked something off that he sniffed then popped into his mouth. It was a dewberry.

Malou tried to fight back her excitement. She reminded herself of what Professor Everitt had said about the probability that macaques had no long-term memory. Surely Kojiwa couldn't remember the sweet berries he had plucked on Storm Mountain, or the thick grass he had tumbled upon as a youngster more than three decades ago. No, Malou decided; as soon as he recovered fully from the tranquilizer, he would shrink in terror from the "paradise" she had consigned him to and join his fellows quailing by the fence.

But each minute that passed took Malou farther from that unhappy hypothesis for Kojiwa continued to revel in his new surroundings. The grizzled fur around his lips was stained purple by the time he'd eaten his fill of berries. Once sated, he plucked a few from the vines and tossed them over his shoulders. They landed in the grass trampled down by the troop. Every amber eye had been trained on Kojiwa since he'd first sat up. They were all waiting, watching. One adventurous juvenile reached out for the nubby purple thing that the old-timer had tossed his way, but Sumo barked out a warning and the young monkey froze.

Kojiwa glanced back at his timid troopmates, and for just the second before Malou could censor such anthropomorphic thoughts, she was certain that the old monkey grinned, gloating at the evidence of his successor's cowardice. Then he was off, forcing his creaky old bones to climb one of the irresistibly tall trees that grew nearly as thick and straight as they had back on Storm Mountain. He made it halfway up a towering live oak, then perched on a branch and crowed down at his bedazzled troopmates. From that height something even more appealing than a real, honest-to-goodness tree instead of a mesquite caught his attention, and Kojiwa clambered back down.

Swallows were skimming along the surface of the creek in the place where it bulged into a small pond. As Kojiwa approached the chattering monster, Sumo stepped out in front of his troop, ready to do battle if the befuddled old-timer stirred the slithering enemy to attack. The troop watched, silent and wide-eyed, as the old gray one boldly stepped forward and took a daring swat at the silver snake. They jerked back in terrified wonder when the beast exploded into glittering shards that sprayed across the setting sun. Then Kojiwa jumped onto the creature and it engulfed him in one gulp.

The baby Lorre toddled away from her new mother toward the old one who had been so nice to her and who had suddenly disappeared. Tulip snapped Lorre back to her side and all the monkeys huddled a bit more closely together. Sumo's lieutenants stepped forward, ready for the combat, and death, that was surely to follow. Some of the young females began to shriek uncontrollably, letting off the tension that had built so unbearably high. They were silenced with rough cuffs, and the whole troop settled down to await the inevitable. For surely now the chattering monster would rear up and obliterate them.

At just that moment of darkest dread, Kojiwa burst to the surface, scattering the swallows, which had returned to feed, and sending a rooster tail of water droplets spraying across the sky. He gave a jubilant cry of celebration. In that instant, the young males knew that the silver thing was no enemy; it was just a stretched-out version of their pond back home. Once they'd deduced that, even Sumo's warning cries could not hold them back. They scrambled forward, bursting with the energy of fear now transformed into exuberance. Their rollicking bodies became furry projectiles as they launched themselves from the bank to sail splashing into the water around Kojiwa.

When Kojiwa relinquished the creek to the splashers and settled himself in the waning light of the far western sun, the older females who had always remained loyal to Kojiwa left Sumo's side and went to his. Some of the younger ones approached as well, and they groomed the old monkey who had shown them all the way in this scary new place that wasn't so scary after all.

Soon Sumo was holding back only a few of his lieutenants, and even they were eyeing the creek with growing longing.

"Hah. That'll be the last time you chase Kojiwa away from the center of the group."

Sumo furrowed his brow in response to Malou's outburst. She laughed, a full-throated, releasing laugh that was more rejoicing than amusement. She'd done it. They'd done it. Kojiwa had done it.

"Bless your grizzled old hide," Malou shouted out to the patriarch in the center of the attentive group of females. He looked over at her with a lordly disdain as if to ask what all the fuss was about. Lorre marred his haughty nonchalance, however, by scrambling up his back and clinging to his head like a dark, furry hat that had gone askew, sliding forward over one eye.

In the waning light, Malou stood back, at last relaxing her grip on the chain link fence, and took in the scene before her. It was one of those rare, perfect images that she liked to store away to bring out and linger over later on like a favorite snapshot in an album.

But no photograph could ever capture all this. The grass sinfully lush in the fading light, the monkeys light and tawny against it, gleefully discovering the wonders of dewberries and tall trees. The troop spread across the sanctuary, just waiting for an eighteenth-century landscape painter to happen by and include them in a bucolic masterpiece.

Malou lingered, savoring the monkeys' newfound happiness, until the last drop of sunlight had been squeezed thin over the darkness that finally absorbed it totally. Even in the darkness, she carried the scene in her mind. It was a scene that was perfection itself until that one inescapable thought wormed its way in to ruin everything: If only Cam could be here.

Cam. Just three letters, one syllable, but they defeated Malou. They stole her zest in what she was doing and left her with a blanketing weariness and too many regrets. There was no point in staying on. As she turned back to face the cabin, a mocking jack-o'-lantern of windows bright in the night, she made up her mind to speak to Professor Everitt about finding someone to take over for her at Lo

Monos. Then she would write to Kenya and tell them that she would be taking that fellowship after all.

The one-year fellowship wouldn't be nearly long enough. Maybe she could get them to extend it another year. Time. That was what she needed. Time to heal. To forget. Malou knew she couldn't depend on distance to do the job. Kenya wouldn't be far enough. No place on earth would be far enough since she would be taking her heart with her wherever she went. A heart that belonged to Cameron Landell.

Chapter Thirteen

"Yes, but I still don't understand precisely why you bolted off from the party like that."

Malou's mother's eyes, as steady and as piercing as a hawk's, probed her for an answer. In the week since Malou had fled the station and come to her parents' house to stay, it was as close as her mother had come to asking why she was there and why she was behaving as if her world had come to an end.

Malou, sprawled across her bed with her mother seated in a white wicker chair next to her, searched the eyes probing hers, looking for an opening into which she could pour her burdened and breaking heart. She yearned to do just that. To tell someone how bad it hurt and to be held and comforted and told that, someday, it would all be better. That someday she would stop hurting. Was this the moment? Was her mother, for the first time, inviting her daughter's confidence? Her mother answered that question.

"I mean, Malou, what was I supposed to think when I found your present lying there in a heap amid the azaleas? And a lovely present it was, too. I've been wanting that particular piece of Steuben glass for some time now. I meant to write you a note, but my study has just completely preoccupied me. Anyway, about your running off from the party. Helmut asked where you'd gone to and I had no answer."

Helmut. The Nobel Prize winner. So that was what it had taken to ruffle her mother's concern.

"I hope it didn't have anything to do with that young man."

She looked again into her mother's eyes and saw for the first time that they weren't piercing at all. They were blind. Utterly, totally blind. How could she not see that it had everything to do with "that young man"?

"Well, if you're in one of your noncommunicative moods, I'll just leave you to stew in your own juices. Your father recruited two hundred subjects for me, and now I have to go break them down into my study groups." Mrs. Sanders stood to leave.

"Mother, wait. I have a question for you."

Mrs. Sanders cocked her head toward her daughter. "Yes, Malou, what is it?"

The expression on her mother's face and her tone of voice, even the question, were all so familiar. They had ruled Malou's early life with a kind of gentle tyranny. She remembered herself as a young girl coming to her mother after she'd fallen out of one of the tall pecans in their backyard. She'd bravely staunched her tears and gone to tug at her mother's skirt. And she had been greeted by, "Yes, Malou, what is it?" and by that expression. Even more than the brisk question, the expression had communicated her mother's air of strained patience. It told Malou that she would be willing to listen to her complaint only if she would state it clearly and succinctly and not make any more demands than were absolutely necessary on her time.

And so, Malou had learned that whether it was a bump from falling out of a tree, or a girlfriend who had stopped asking her to come and play, or boys who didn't like girls who were so much smarter than they, her mother had very little time and no comfort to offer her. Now the expression of strained patience was just about to put her off again. But the question that had popped into Malou's mind, formed in just the past few seconds, seemed too important to stifle. Malou knew that if she didn't ask it now she never would, and that, somehow, she needed badly to know the answer.

"Yes, Malou," her mother prompted.

"Why did you marry Father?"

Mrs. Sanders's lovely, patrician brow crinkled with peeved bewilderment. "What an odd question. Are you feeling all right?"

"Yes. Perfectly," Malou lied. "Tell me, why? Was he handsome? Did he make your heart sing? Could you not live without him?"

"Malou, you sound like some song off of a jukebox."

"Just answer me, Mother. Please."

The note of pleading in her daughter's voice coaxed Mrs. Sanders into answering. "Well," she began, flustered now by memories nearly three decades old. "Handsome? Yes, I suppose I'd have to say that your father has always been a good-looking man, though I've never been one to be particularly impressed by looks. Did he make my heart sing? I think, more to the point, we were in tune." Mrs. Sanders smiled, pleased with her response and feeling more sure of herself.

"We shared the same aspirations. Yes, that was it. Neither one of us had his head all stuffed full of this 'moon in June' nonsense. We both knew that we wanted to do something important with our lives. And your last question, could I have lived without your father?"

Malou nodded, and her mother's gaze turned inward. She'd been trained as a scientist and always prided herself on looking at the facts straight on and reporting them as accurately as she could. She did so now.

"Yes, of course I could have lived without him. But my life would have been poorer for it."

For the first time since her mother had begun, Malou felt a surge of emotion. It died away quickly when she continued.

"Your father has been of immeasurable help to me in my work. He's always been supportive, always ready with new ideas and approaches. Does that answer your question?"

Malou met her mother's clear-eyed gaze. She still did, and would always, admire her tremendously. Her answer had been honest and had described a marriage that had been happy and successful for close to three decades. Still, Malou couldn't help thinking that they would have been just as happy and successful being research associates as they were as husband and wife.

"Yes, Mother," she answered gently.

Mrs. Sanders smiled distractedly at her only child. "We'll have to chat like this more often." She strode to the door, then paused and looked back. "Oh, have you heard anything yet about Kenya?"

"Not yet," Malou said, struggling to inject some animation into her voice. "Professor Everitt said he'd call as soon as word came from the sponsoring foundation."

"Well, I wouldn't worry too much if I were you. With your reputation, you're a shoo-in. I was talking about this with your father last night, and he agrees that you've made the right decision. You've gotten everything you can out of Los Monos. If you're really going to distinguish yourself, you need some field experience out of the country now. I mean, Africa *is* where Goodall and Fossey established themselves, isn't it?"

"It is." Malou gave a wan confirmation to her mother's statement.

"Good. Listen, you will be able to fend for yourself for lunch, won't you? Your father's invited me out. He has some ideas about setting up my control groups."

"Sure, I'll be fine." Malou flagged a limp wave to her mother and Mrs. Sanders was gone.

Malou turned her face to the wall. She didn't want to think. Not now. Not for a very long time.

Malou let the phone ring a half dozen times before she remembered that her parents were out. She struggled to her feet and answered the call. It was Professor Everitt.

"Well, kid, you got it," he announced.

Malou made an effort to sound jubilant and came close enough to fool someone over the phone.

"You know, I thought it was kind of rash of you to leave Los Monos the way you did," Professor Everitt confided. "But it worked out, and good thing it did, too, or you wouldn't have had a field placement anywhere. I'm sure that by now Landell has replaced you with one of the candidates I suggested, so you couldn't have gone back to Los Monos if Kenya hadn't come through.''

"But it did," Malou repeated.

"It sure did. The spot is open and waiting, so the quicker you can get yourself over to the other side of the world, the better. Congratulations, Malou. I'll be looking forward to reading about your work in the journals, and probably *National Geographic* as well.''

Malou faked a tepid laugh and they hung up. She stared around her room. Her collection of bird eggs was still propped up on top of the bookshelf crammed with volumes about animal behavior. The pictures on the wall showed her at various stages through her teens, holding up the ribbons she'd won at science fairs and grinning into her father's camera. Her first microscope, a present on her ninth birthday, occupied a place of honor inside a glass case.

She could still remember how excited she'd been when her father had pressed a droplet of water between two slides for her to look at. She was astonished to see the teeming, wriggling life that could exist in that one tiny wet globe. That simple sense of joy and discovery seemed now to have occurred in someone else's life. Perhaps one of those dedicated young pioneers of science she'd read about as a girl.

She turned her gaze up at the wall and snorted a dry laugh. With no changes, her room could be preserved as a shrine to the Great Scientist that her parents had raised her to be. All she had to do now was to fulfill her destiny in Kenya. Do some ground-breaking fieldwork, making sure to take enough good color photos that *National Geographic*

would be able to do a nice spread on her and her research.
Then marry someone "supportive." Perhaps a linguist
working on a Fulbright in Botswana. And then what?
Malou asked herself. And then the linguist and I have
ourselves an appropriately brilliant offspring that we can
thoroughly train in the scientific method.

"But just one," Malou whispered to the ceiling. "Any
more than one would take too much time from our research."

She saw, in that moment, with stunning clarity, that this
was her parents' vision of her future. It was the vision that
had brought and kept them together. It was a vision that
Malou realized now had guided her through most of her
conscious years. It was one she would even have been
happy living out had it not been for one devastating
event—meeting Cameron Landell.

But she had met him. She had loved him. She loved him
still. And those very significant details had changed everything. Now the vision she and her parents had once shared
seemed dry as a corporate merger. A life with all the grants
and fellowships and awards any scientist could ever win
seemed nothing without that one secret ingredient that Cam
had introduced her to—passion. Without it all the rest
seemed hollow.

Hollow though it may be, Malou reminded herself, it
would have to be enough, for Cam had left her, and with
him he'd taken all the passion that would ever be in her life.

It was meager indeed, but self-pity was the only comfort
that offered itself to Malou. She was just giving in to the
tears that had been puddling every time she thought of life
without Cam, when it finally struck her—she was the only

responsible for her destiny, for where she was right now, and where she would be going. Her parents may have given her the native intelligence, the microscope, and the desire to succeed, but, she reminded herself, she'd been the one to fulfill the promise. She'd been the one who'd stayed home studying when other kids were out playing. She'd been the one who'd put in the long nights in the lab and the long days in the field. She'd written the papers that had won the awards. Her parents may have set her in a certain direction, but she'd been the one to walk the rocky path in following it.

And now, I want to change directions. She sat up in bed. Energy she hadn't known for weeks coursed through her from the hidden power of these revelations. Kenya and awards and a collegial relationship with a linguist who helped her work out experimental designs wasn't what she wanted anymore. She wanted Cameron Landell.

But he doesn't want you, a cautionary voice pointed out. Malou felt like sticking out her tongue at the voice that spoke for the emotional coward dwelling within her. It was this coward who had caused her to run from anything in her short life that looked remotely like an entanglement that would tie up her timid heart. Well, for the first time she was seeing quite clearly what listening to a timid heart would get her—one linguist and all the journal articles she could type.

So Cam was going to be hard to get! What in her life had ever come easy? she wanted to know. She'd chased after everything she'd ever gotten; why should Mister Cameron Landell be exempt?

Malou was giddy with the bubbles of new courage percolating through her as she jumped out of bed and

flipped through her closet. For the first time she regretted
how heavily her wardrobe ran toward khaki. Fortunately
she did have a few numbers suitable to her purpose today.
She whipped out a wonderfully skimpy jersey creation and
held it up against herself. It was a new-wavish dress of
bright white and blue stripes that stopped quite a fair
distance short of her knees. She'd purchased it in a fit of
disgust with her usual khaki drabness, then had never been
able to work up the daring to wear it.

Well, she had the daring today. Besides, since Cam had
expressed so much admiration for her legs, shouldn't he be
entitled to see them? She hung the dress on the back of the
bathroom door while she took a quick shower. Once bathed,
powdered, and perfumed, Malou slid into the bold dress
and went to view herself.

Yes, the legs, long and tanned, showed up to spectacular
advantage. She ran her fingers through her hair and let the
wet strands settle into curls to air-dry. Cam seemed to like it
that way. She fumbled a bit with her eyeliner and mascara
but was finally satisfied with the result. Now, she laughed to
herself, remembering Cam's joke, if I only had a monkey to
perch on my shoulder.

It was only on the drive to San Antonio that Malou's
newfound courage began to desert her a bit. But she parried
the doubts and second thoughts that assailed her as she
zoomed down I-35 headed for San Antonio and Cameron
Landell.

She couldn't hold them off entirely, though, once she
was standing in front of Cam's receptionist asking if she
might have a moment with him.

"He's in a conference right now," the woman informed

her, "and he's asked me to hold all calls and visitors. Would you care to wait?"

Malou nodded, wondering if the woman knew why she was there. She took a seat on a dove gray sectional. Her skirt hiked up to the middle of her thigh when she sat down. Malou tried to tug it down, but there wasn't enough fabric to stretch. After the hot drive, the air conditioning chilled her, raising goose bumps all along the expanses of exposed flesh. Malou suddenly yearned for a nice, concealing pair of khaki slacks. What had possessed her to wear this *scrap?*

With each moment, Malou's goose bumps and anxieties rose until she finally stood, ready to retreat. She went to the receptionist, who glanced up at her and kept on typing.

"Could you tell Mr. Landell . . ."

The receptionist kept staring.

"Never mind. Don't tell him anything. I can't wait any longer."

The receptionist's eyes shifted from Malou's face. Malou followed them.

"Are you here to see me, Malou?"

Cam. He'd never looked better. For a moment his attention was diverted by the formalities of bidding farewell to the half dozen men who filed out of his office, their smiles indicating the completion of a successful meeting. How on earth, she wondered, could one man be so meltingly attractive while pumping a banker's hand? At last they were gone and he was staring at her again.

"Come in." He stood back from his office door.

Malou straightened, swallowed hard, and went in. The door shut behind her.

"I understand from Professor Everitt that you're planning to go to Kenya," Cam said as he sank into the high-backed swivel chair behind the vast barricade of his desk.

Malou's heart sank as she took the chair he indicated. They might have been nothing more than distant acquaintances that business had thrown together for a time. He seemed supremely unconcerned whether she went to Kenya or the moon.

"Well, I did get a grant to do some research there," she equivocated, hoping to wring a shred of emotion out of him.

"Congratulations," he replied stiffly. "What was it you wanted to discuss with me?"

Was there absolutely no emotion to wring? Could he be as totally unaffected as he appeared to be? Malou found it staggering that a relationship that had completely unhinged her life and left it swinging open and empty could have meant nothing to him. But apparently it had. She scoured her mind for an excuse for why she'd come to see him.

"I wanted to . . . ," she stumbled. He leaned forward ever so slightly. Did he seem to be listening a bit more intently? Had the chill in his eyes warmed the barest bit? But then he leaned away again. "I wanted to ask you about my replacement at Los Monos," she finally blurted out.

"And that's why you drove all the way over here?" he asked skeptically, continuing to stare at her. To be exact, he was staring at her mouth.

With a jolt Malou realized that she was gnawing away at her lower lip. Oh, what the hell! She had one chance at a life with passion and this was it. So the odds were a hundred to one that all she'd succeed in doing would be to make a complete fool of herself. She'd take them.

"No," she stammered, "that's not why I came here at all."

Cam's left eyebrow cocked slightly to indicate interest. Moderate, casual interest.

"I came to tell you that I'd made a mistake. I misjudged you. I'm sorry. I'll probably make a lot of other mistakes before I'm through, but I think the worst one I could make is to leave without telling you one thing." Malou felt as if the floor were dropping away beneath her.

"What is that one thing?" Cam asked, not urgently but with a little more warmth—like the interest one friend takes in another.

Malou now openly chewed at her lower lip; she needed strength and would take it from any source available. She had never in her life felt so vulnerable. What was worse was that, if she answered Cam's question, she would increase that vulnerability a thousand times. She would strip herself bare in front of him. Malou felt herself perched on a thin wall. On one side was a potential abyss of humiliation. On the other was Kenya and the linguist. She drew in a deep breath, then turned loose of her lip.

"I love you."

She'd said it. She wanted medals for bravery, bouquets, fireworks, and champagne toasts, but most of all she wanted Cam's arms around her. But none of that happened. Cam sat, unmoved and unmoving. Malou drew herself up and repeated one word over and over in her mind: dignity. She would not cry. Would not say another word. She had said all she possibly could and it hadn't been enough. She'd tried for that one chance in a hundred and had lost. She was thankful now that she hadn't done anything so rash as to turn Kenya down. She longed to be there at that very moment. Longed to be miles and years away from the humiliation starting to burn along her spine and up into her cheeks. She stood stiffly, pivoted, and walked on wooden legs toward the door.

Her hand was on the doorknob when Cam caught her covering her hand with his to stop it. To keep her from opening the door. He whirled her around in his arms. Tears leaked from Malou's downcast eyes, and her face from hairline to neck flamed with embarrassment.

"You love me?" he asked haltingly.

His hands were warm and gentle on her bare arms, but Malou could not look up. "You probably already knew that," Malou mumbled.

"How would I have known that?" Cam demanded, his hands tightening on her. "What were my clues? That you thought I was a monkey murderer? That you're planning to run off to Kenya? These things are supposed to tell me that you love me? God, Malou, I'd hate to be around when you were trying to tell someone you didn't like him."

"Well, I'm not," Malou shot back, prickled now at having to endure his scrutiny. "I'm trying to tell someone that I love him, but if he doesn't care to hear it, I'll take my leave and the first boat to Kenya." With that, Malou whirled back around to open the door.

"If you really, really feel that way," Cam said, grabbing her again, "you're not going anywhere."

Then Malou felt her feet being whisked away from under her as Cam scooped her into his arms and carried her from the door. He sat them both down in an overstuffed chair with Malou firmly trapped on his lap.

"I've wanted to hear that for a long time," he said

quietly. Malou stopped squirming, trying to get away, when she saw the truth of what he said written in his face. For beneath the veneer of cool formality lay a pool of misery. Malou knew it as the very same one she had been drowning in for the past weeks. She held up a hand as tentative as any the young monkeys had ever held up to her and touched his face. He captured her seeking hand and, closing his eyes, nestled a kiss against her palm.

"Oh, Malou, I love you. I've loved you from that first moment you came over to the gate and tried to one-up me in your little khaki shorts with your hair shining in the sun."

"Cam."

It was all Malou could say before they found other, more gratifying ways to occupy their lips. Their kiss echoed and confirmed all they had each said, finally convincing them both that it was real. Cam leaned back and laughed. It was a joyous, exultant cry of jubilation and release.

"So what do we do now, Mary Louise? I love you. You love me. And one of us is packing off to the other side of the world."

Malou cut a saucy glance Cam's way. "Maybe we could work out a deal here."

"A deal?" Cam echoed. "And just what sort of proposition might you have in mind, Ms. Sanders?"

"Possibly something along the lines of an assistant to whomever you've found to replace me at Los Monos."

"You mean the Landell Monkey Sanctuary? Well now, there might be the possibility of an opening there, Ms. Sanders. Particularly since I haven't as yet come up with a suitable replacement."

"You haven't? Why?" Malou asked, astounded. "Didn't

anyone want it? I can't believe that there's a single person over in the anthro department who would turn the job down."

"There may be; I don't know," Cam admitted. "I never asked. I couldn't bring myself to think of Los Monos without you, so I kept putting off finding another manager. Jorge's been pinch-hitting so far, but his complaints about being a monkeyboy instead of a cowboy keep getting louder, so I suppose I'll have to find someone who's a bit fonder of the beasts. Any candidates?" Cam teased with a smile.

"When do I start?"

"You mean you'd turn down Kenya for south Texas?"

"In an instant. Provided you're part of the trade."

"What's the Landell Monkey Sanctuary without Landell, I'd like to know!" Cam asked. "I'm yours, Malou, for just as long as you'll have me."

An unearthly sense of happiness wafted over Malou as she cuddled up against Cam's chest and lay there for several utterly contented moments listening to his heart beat strong and steady against her ear.

"You know, I never really wanted to go to Kenya," she murmured. "Besides wanting to be with you, the research at Los Monos would be more interesting. There's still so much work that needs to be done on the troop's adaptation. I mean, I've only just begun to scratch the surface. There's still years, decades, more research to be done."

"That makes me happy, Malou," Cam said softly. "I always want you to have whatever it is that your heart desires most." A gentle chuckle rumbled against Malou's ear. "And, naturally, I want the same for myself. Just like I have right now with you in my arms."

Malou snuggled a bit closer. "You know, I could get to like making these deals."

"I should hope you could. After all, you learned from the master."

Then Cam stretched a long arm across his desk to buzz the receptionist. He told her to hold all his calls for a long time. A *very* long time.

Silhouette Special Edition. Romances for the woman who expects a little more out of love.

If you enjoyed this book, and you're ready for more great romance

...get 4 romance novels FREE when you become a Silhouette Special Edition home subscriber.

Act now and we'll send you four exciting Silhouette Special Edition romance novels. They're our gift to introduce you to our convenient home subscription service. Every month, we'll send you six new passion-filled Special Edition books. Look them over for 15 days. If you keep them, pay just $11.70 for all six. Or return them at no charge.

We'll mail your books to you two full months *before they are available anywhere else.* Plus, with every shipment, you'll receive the Silhouette Books Newsletter absolutely free. *And with Silhouette Special Edition there are never any shipping or handling charges.*

Mail the coupon today to get your four free books—and more romance than you ever bargained for.

Silhouette Special Edition is a service mark and a registered trademark.

An epic novel of exotic rituals
and the lure of the Upper Amazon

THE
TAKERS
RIVER
OF GOLD

JERRY AND S.A. AHERN

THE TAKERS are the intrepid Josh Culhane and the seductive Mary Mulrooney. These two adventurers launch an incredible journey into the Brazilian rain forest. Far upriver, the jungle yields its deepest secret—the lost city of the Amazon warrior women!

THE TAKERS series is making publishing history. Awarded *The Romantic Times* first prize for High Adventure in 1984, the opening book in the series was hailed by *The Romantic Times* as "the next trend in romance writing and reading. Highly recommended!"

Jerry and S.A. Ahern have never been better!

TAK-3

A Gold Eagle book from Worldwide, available now wherever
Harlequin and Silhouette paperbacks are sold

READERS' COMMENTS ON SILHOUETTE SPECIAL EDITIONS:

"I just finished reading the first six Silhouette Special Edition Books and I had to take the opportunity to write you and tell you how much I enjoyed them. I enjoyed all the authors in this series. Best wishes on your Silhouette Special Editions line and many thanks."

—B.H.*, Jackson, OH

"The Special Editions are really special and I enjoyed them very much! I am looking forward to next month's books."

—R.M.W.*, Melbourne, FL

"I've just finished reading four of your first six Special Editions and I enjoyed them very much. I like the more sensual detail and longer stories. I will look forward each month to your new Special Editions."

—L.S.*, Visalia, CA

"Silhouette Special Editions are — 1.) Superb! 2.) Great! 3.) Delicious! 4.) Fantastic! . . . Did I leave anything out? These are books that an adult woman can read . . . I love them!"

—H.C.*, Monterey Park, CA

*names available on request